SOMEBODY OUT THERE

KEVIN LYNCH

INKUBATOR
BOOKS

PROLOGUE

It wasn't your fault what happened, yet she blamed you. Your own mother, rocking in her chair, and how you adored her. You would do anything for her. You were the most devoted son any mother could have, but that thing happened. It came between you and her, and now she is gone. This is your chance to make amends, to put what was seen as wrong back right again. Remember, she is watching you. Her devotion to Saint Brigid—she must surely have her place in heaven, or is she in another place, waiting? Maybe she is waiting for you to release her, to let her know that you can make things better again, that she can rest now, that her memory is safe. You know how to do that. The strangers are coming now. Your mother is uneasy. What will they do to her memory? You don't want those thoughts coming back, those horrible, haunting thoughts. And they will if you don't stop the strangers. Remember, it is her house. She still lives there in spirit. She is watching your every move. You must preserve her memory, show her the devoted son you can be. The strangers will change everything if you don't stop them. You know what to do.

1

They drove in silence for a few minutes. Ben had noticed the gradually changing landscape as they passed through the midlands and began to hit the West proper. A line of grey-blue hills stretched across the skyline, like a group of giant sentinels watching for intruders. Farmhouses had become more frequent, with their outsize barns, herds of cattle, and farmers on dull red tractors pitching themselves against the enormity of the landscape.

The road had narrowed steadily as they progressed west, so now there was just enough room for two vehicles to pass close together so that he felt the backdraft of each car as it passed. Driving required concentration, and he could feel the tension in his fingers as they gripped the steering wheel. Brambles from hedgerows at the side of the road reached out to scrape the windscreen. He saw his wife, Deborah, draw back in her seat if a big bramble suddenly made contact.

Still, they were finally getting out of the city with all the troubles it had thrown at them in the last while. They had been living on edge, and now, with the promise of a new horizon beckoning from the west, he hoped they were leaving all that behind. Setting up a health food shop in a small country town seemed like the perfect antidote to the tensions of urban life, and particularly to the imminent threats that Deborah's crime reporting job had presented.

'I'm glad to be out of the world of crime reporting and into the sleepy pace of rural life,' she had said as they started out.

'Oh, and haven't you seen the movie *The Hills Have Eyes*?' Ben had teased. 'They'll be up at our house with pitchforks and burning torches. You'll see. Just kidding, but that guy Jeremiah should be over at some stage. He used to live there, and he's going to help us out for a while. Local knowledge and all that.'

Ben flicked a glance in the rear-view mirror to see Jack and Molly glued to their screens. Jack at age twelve was just into playing games, his brow furrowed with concentration. Molly, at age fourteen, was up to her neck in social media. Any time Ben caught a glimpse of her screen, there were multiple little dialogue bubbles open with emojis dancing all over the place. He wondered what the hell they said to each other all the time, but he certainly didn't ask. The response would be sharp, acerbic, and world-weary.

At the start of the journey, Ben had implored them to at least make a token effort to take the scenery in, but he had long since given up. Molly had responded by taking her earphones out and looking pointedly out the window. 'Wow, a field,' she had said sarcastically. 'Oh, and another field. The excitement is just too much. I can't handle it.' With that, she had plugged her earphones back in. Ben hoped she'd get into the rhythm of country life, but he felt it was going to take something dramatic to grab her attention on the drive.

That something appeared sooner than he would have liked. As the road had narrowed, the speed of the traffic had to slow proportionately, so Ben found himself at the front of a snaking caravan of cars moving in unison around sharp bends and accelerating into short straight stretches before hitting sharp bends again. He felt like one of those Formula One drivers leading a restless, agitated pack of snarling vehicles. One small mistake and they could end up in a smoking pile of mangled steel.

To his horror, about a hundred yards up the road, Ben saw a rickety, old tractor pull shakily out of a field and start driving at an achingly slow speed right in front of him. He had to hit the brakes and slow right down. The tractor was pulling a large round slurry tank behind it. The tank pitched and bobbed only yards away from the front of their car. Ben could see the cars behind him slow to a snail's pace, and he instantly felt anger and impatience begin to build.

Pretty soon the sweet, rich smell of compacted manure was drifting into the car. They rolled up the windows, but the smell fully inhabited all the air around them, so it seeped in through every vent and sat like a nauseous fug in the pristine confines of their hybrid SUV.

'Jesus, Dad. I'm going to, like, retch. Overtake, for Christ's sake,' Molly said, holding her hand over her mouth.

Ben sneaked a look out past the tractor, but the road stayed narrow, and there were bends every hundred yards or so. 'I can't at the moment. It's too dangerous.' There was very little traffic coming the other way, but the odd car that did come flew past at what seemed to Ben to be reckless speed.

'For Christ's sake, do something,' Molly shouted. 'It's disgusting.'

Ben could see the snaking line of cars behind him moving at the same funereal pace. He could feel the agitation of the other drivers as they pulled out to check if the road ahead was clear. He made a sudden lurch as if to overtake, but at the same time saw a flash of blue metal hurtle towards him from the other side, so he had to wrench the car back in again. The car on the other side gave a loud beep as it flew past.

The car directly behind Ben started flashing its lights, pressing him to make a move.

'Stupid country drivers,' Ben hissed.

'It's all right. Take your time,' Deborah said nervously.

'Don't take your time, Dad. I'm going to puke. For real,' Molly said. She looked pale to Ben and had her head in her hands.

He lurched out again, this time pressing his foot right down on the accelerator so the car engine roared and spurted forward. There was a bend right up ahead, but Ben kept his foot pressed on the pedal while the grasping branches of the hedgerows whipped the windscreen.

'Jesus, Ben, watch out,' Deborah screamed as they rounded the bend and saw a white delivery van hurtling towards them. Ben could see the driver of the van was on his phone, laughing at something, when he saw their SUV powering toward him. His mouth flipped open, and he dropped the phone, grabbing the wheel with both hands and steering it as far to the left as he could.

'*Dad!*' came a single unified scream from Jack and Molly. Ben whipped the steering wheel to the left, praying that they were far enough past the tractor. He saw a blur of red in his wing mirror, then a blur of white to the right as the van careened past, but there was no contact on either side, so with a frantic pulling of the steering wheel back to the right, he managed to straighten the car. The road in front of him was clear.

Ben dropped his head and said, 'Shit, that was close.'

'You nearly killed us, Dad,' from Molly at the back, but Ben was suddenly too drained to respond. His heart beat in rapid fluttering movements for the next few minutes as they drove in a solid, three-dimensional silence.

Once the feeling of panic had dissipated, Deborah reached over to put a comforting hand on his leg. 'Don't worry about it, love,' she said. 'You'll be flashing your lights and beeping the horn with the best of them once you go native.'

Ben laughed quietly, a sense of relief flooding through him. Deborah was always the one to defuse a situation, and he admired how she could still do it, even after all they had been through.

2

The house was at the top of a long, gravel-strewn driveway that wound up a gentle slope. Ben could see its outline against the puffy white clouds of an early summer evening. It was a rangy, bungalow-style affair with a brown-tiled roof and a double chimney that pointed like a finger towards the sky. The house stood still against the drifting clouds, yet something about it yielded the sense of individual character in contrast to the shifting backdrop. Ben and Deborah had been down to view it a couple of times and had decided that its timeless features gave the sense of strength and independence, qualities they felt were badly needed after the recent events in Dublin.

Ben was fully aware that the kids were seeing it for the first time and, looking through their eyes, he could see something old-fashioned and a little forbidding.

Harry, the springer spaniel, was the first to jump from the car when they arrived. He'd been perched on top of various items of luggage for most of the journey. When Ben opened the boot, he leapt onto the gravelly drive that led to their new house. He ran, then stopped, sniffed around the ground, then ran to a wooden picnic table to the left of the front door, where he cocked his leg and peed generously while turning his head this way and that to take in the new surroundings.

Molly slouched from the car, dragging a trail of wires from her devices behind her. Ben heard something metallic thunk on the gravel as she extracted herself, but he knew better than to look or to ask if something had got damaged.

'So, here we are,' Ben said with an exaggerated, majestic sweep of his arms. He put an arm around Deborah, and the two of them took in the view of rolling green hills that swooped and dipped all the way to the horizon. Ben found something profoundly peaceful, almost spiritual, in the wide fields that were divided by chunky stone walls with little clusters of trees or hedgerows dotted here and there. Cattle and sheep grazed in some fields, while others were given over to pasture, and only occasionally could a tilled lot with arable crops be seen. It was rough-hewn, taciturn West of Ireland land, where he felt that he and Deborah could grow their own veg, plant a few fruit trees, keep chickens and maybe a few goats.

'It's lovely,' Deborah said quietly, as if afraid of disturbing the peace.

'And it's ours. A fresh start. C'mon, let's see what the kids make of it.'

Ben fished in his pocket for keys and led Deborah, arm still around her shoulder, over to the front door. It was situated in the middle of the house and faced west. The sellers had left it untouched, as the family home it had been for so many years. It was a thick-walled bungalow that stretched out on either side from the front door. The door itself was wood framed with frosted glass panels on top of a central wooden divide.

Ben had a refracted, shadowy view of the hallway as he turned the key in the door.

Stepping in, he got the smell of damp that proximity to the sea and the wet West Of Ireland weather gives. There were blank spaces on the walls where religious ornaments or pictures had probably hung. Inside there was a short hallway with lino floor that gave way to a longer hallway running perpendicular, leading to the main living-room/kitchen on the left and the bedrooms to the right.

Ben and Molly traipsed in after them. Molly stopped and stared in disbelief. 'Jesus, are you guys for real? What the hell is this place?'

'It smells of grannies,' Jack said cheerfully as he walked the stretch of hall down to the living-room/kitchen. Ben and Deborah walked in after him to see the large yellow-coloured stove, long wooden table, a couple of comfy armchairs, and then a little rocking chair that sat between the stove and a large window.

'That's where Granny obviously sat, enjoying the heat of the stove and looking out the window. Nice way to pass your old age,' Ben said.

'Looks creepy to me,' Molly said sullenly. 'And look at that super-creepy straw cross beside the rocking chair.'

'That's a Saint Brigid's cross,' Deborah said. 'My granny used to have one of them, funnily enough, speaking of grannies.'

'Nothing funny about that,' Molly replied. 'Can we get rid of this crap and put in something that comes from, like, at least the twentieth century?'

Harry seemed pretty happy with the new venue, sniffing every last item of furniture and giving the space under the sink an extra-long sniff that made Ben think he should definitely check for mouse droppings once the women were out of sight.

'We'll see about the furnishings,' Ben said. 'They just left everything as it was and said we could make our own minds up about what we're keeping.'

'That's a no-brainer,' Molly said. 'Let's dump the lot of it.'

'Our Dublin stuff's coming down tomorrow,' Deborah said, 'so we can get rid of anything that people find deeply offensive.'

'Like this whole house,' Molly replied.

They brought their luggage in and ignored the rolling sighs and dissatisfied utterances from Molly.

'Want to take a walk on the land?' Ben asked Deborah.

'I believe it's a tradition,' Deborah said with a smile.

'Not to mention the fact it gets us out of earshot of our disgruntled teens,' Ben whispered as they wheeled right at the front door.

'Disgruntled teen, singular,' Deborah said. 'Jack seems happy enough.'

'And he will be, I'd say. Fishing is good around here, apparently. We're just half a mile from the beach and some big piles of rocks that are supposed to be good.'

'And for our darling daughter?'

'More disgruntlement but with healthy country air.'

They walked through a green space to the left and behind the house with a couple of apple trees and behind them some tall, thin birch trees that swayed gently in the light wind. Behind the birches, there was a stone wall with a big rusted gate leading to an empty field now overgrown with grass and thistles.

'That's where we'll plant our veg, I suppose,' Ben said, nodding towards the empty field.

'You're the expert,' Deborah said, knotting her fingers into his.

He turned to kiss her, and they both felt the light, warm air like a cocoon around them. The moment didn't last. There was a piercing scream from the direction of the house.

'That sounds like Molly,' Ben said, breaking into a run. He tore across the grass, Deborah hard on his heels. A million thoughts rushed through his head. What the hell could have happened so soon? He had visions of her with her foot caught in a drain or sliced open by some rusty farmyard implement.

He rounded the front of the house at pace but saw nothing, then dashed in the open front door and saw Molly standing just inside. Her hands were covering her mouth, and she looked pale.

'What happened?' Ben asked.

She said nothing but kept her hands over her mouth. 'What happened?' he asked again, moving closer to her.

Molly moved her hands slowly away from her mouth and pointed behind him. Ben turned to see a figure standing in the doorway. With the light behind him, it was hard to make any features out, but Ben could see enough of the stocky frame and the glint from the thick glasses to know it was Jeremiah.

'He was at the window looking in,' Molly whispered.

'It's Jeremiah,' Ben said. 'The guy I was talking about in the car. He's going to help us settle in.'

Molly's expression didn't change. She still looked pale and shocked until finally she turned away and went back down the hall.

'Sorry about that,' Ben said to Jeremiah. Deborah had arrived and was standing just behind Jeremiah, who stood and stared dourly at Ben. He was broad enough to fill the narrow hallway, and Ben felt momentarily trapped until Jeremiah turned slowly to take Deborah in.

'Hi, I'm Deborah,' she said with a hand outstretched. Jeremiah didn't move to shake her hand. He just nodded in her direction. 'We're delighted to have someone show us the ropes,' Deborah continued, not letting an awkward silence gain any foothold.

'I was jest looking in, see if ye were home,' Jeremiah finally said. 'I seen the dog but no people.' Harry was looking quizzically up at Jeremiah. He was usually a dog to jump in first with exuberant greetings, but not with this man.

'We were out having a look at the land,' Ben said cheerily, 'and you know kids these days. They were just in looking at their screens. I'm sure that's why Molly got a fright. It's nothing. No bother at all. Now, do you want to show me the fiddly bits in the house, like showers and hot water, before we get down to the nitty-gritty tomorrow?'

Jeremiah looked up at him from under a raised eyebrow like he was trying to figure out what he'd said.

'You lead the way,' Ben said, gesturing with his hand towards the inside of the house.

Jeremiah squeezed in, his thick jacket scraping off the sides of the narrow entrance hall. Ben had noticed when he'd met Jeremiah before that he seemed to wear layers of jackets and outdoor gear. It was a look he'd seen before in small country towns, but usually on much older men. It made Jeremiah look strangely timeless. *It also explains why Molly would scream when she saw him*, he thought. She'd never come that close to someone as raw and rural as Jeremiah before. *It'll be the first part of what's going to be a long learning curve for her.*

'That's your immersion tank there,' Jeremiah said,

opening an airing cupboard at the end of the hall. 'Put it on to sink for the dishes an' that.'

'We'll probably get a boiler installed. They're handier, but sure we'll see as we go along,' Ben said in as breezy a manner as he could muster.

Jeremiah responded with a darting glance from under the eyebrow. He shuffled off into the kitchen.

'You have your fuse box up here,' he said, opening a small cupboard-like door over the main kitchen door. 'Anthin' goes, you just hit the trips.'

Jack had started following Ben and Jeremiah. He watched with boyish fascination the gruff tour guide who smelled of earth and petrol.

'Cooker is gas, and there you have your bottle beside it.'

'We'll probably look at getting mains in at some stage,' Ben said.

'It'll cost ye. And the hoors will keep ye waiting long as they like.' Jeremiah made solid but brief eye contact when he imparted this as if he was holding a grievance against the utilities. Ben nodded vigorously for lack of any better response.

'The stove is solid fuel.' Jeremiah opened one of the yellow stove doors to give Ben a look inside. 'Bit of turf out the back, but ye'll need to order some in if ye're using it regular.'

'Well, hopefully the weather will hold up, but it's nice to get the old turf smell in the house.' Ben looked at the chair and the Saint Brigid's cross beside the stove. 'We might think of replacing these when our own stuff comes down tomorrow.'

Jeremiah stiffened. 'That's the chair the mother sat in to end her days, looking out the window. The postman was very good to her, and it made her day to see him come up that drive. I was here with her to the end. I never thought the day would come.' Jeremiah looked up at the straw cross. 'She had great devotion to Saint Brigid, God be good to her.' He reached over to touch the arm of the rocking chair, setting it gently in motion. He watched it rock for a few long seconds. 'I hope you'll be good to her memory, show her the respect she deserves.' He looked solemnly at Ben before turning to walk up the hall. Ben hesitated, momentarily thrown by Jeremiah's sudden gravity.

'I think it's cool,' Jack said. 'I like the old-fashioned stuff.'

Jeremiah looked at him and nodded but said nothing.

Jack's room was the first room after the bathroom, and Jeremiah lumbered into it. 'D'ye see the wall here? It's agin the shower, so you need to watch for any damp come through. Tiled on the other side it is, but I think the tiler had two left hands.' Jeremiah was deathly serious as he imparted that information, but Ben still let out a short guffaw.

'You have to keep an eye on them all right. I'm sure we'll be doing a few bits and pieces, so we might look at retiling.'

Jeremiah turned and looked at the far bedroom wall, where Jack had already stuck a Captain America poster. 'That's the best of them,' he said to no one in particular.

'Yeah, it's class, isn't it?' Jack agreed.

'I like the superheroes I do. Superman's the strongest though. He can get out of any situation.' He clenched his fist and raised his arm straight out in front. 'To infinity and beyond,' he shouted, and Ben started back with the sudden noise.

Jack smiled nervously. He looked first at Jeremiah, then at Ben. 'That's Buzz Lightyear,' he said quietly.

Jeremiah dropped his arm and walked quickly to the

front door. He stood outside and looked sharply left and right as if he were expecting someone. 'We'd have a fair share of foxes around here,' he said. 'I've the job for them if ye want to see it.'

Without waiting for an answer, he headed to the back of a scruffy Jeep that he had parked at an angle to the house. Ben immediately felt uneasy as he watched him pull out a large rusty steel object and lay it on the ground. Molly had wandered out to see what was going on. Jack was there too. Jeremiah pulled the steel object apart so they could clearly see jagged jaws on either side.

'It's a trap,' Jack said excitedly. Molly scrunched her face up in disapproval. Ben's feeling of uneasiness magnified. The thing looked like a bear trap with its two menacing jaws prised open like deadly rows of sharp *T. rex* teeth.

Jeremiah pulled it right back so it locked, and grabbed a small stick that was lying around. 'Now, this'll do for any fox that comes wandering in.' Just as he prodded the centre of the trap, Ben saw Harry come dashing over to see what was going on. He stopped just short of the trap.

'Watch out,' Molly roared as Jeremiah prodded the stick in, and the steel jaws sliced the air and crashed together with a deathly thud. Molly grabbed Harry's collar to pull him away.

'Jesus, that was close,' Ben said, looking from Jeremiah to Harry.

'I'm after saying it would do for any foxes ye might have.'

'We don't want your traps,' Molly hissed as she led Harry off to safety.

3

'C'mon, we need to show you kids the town,' Ben shouted as crows circled towards the trees behind the house. It was evening, and he was trying to lift the mood, which had been sullen since Jeremiah's visit.

'He absolutely creeps me out,' Molly had said after he had left.

'Part of country life,' Ben said. 'You're going to get plenty of eccentrics like him. The trick is to ignore them.'

'So what the hell are we doing here if we have to ignore people?' Molly asked.

'I meant just the ones like him. Country towns are small communities, so it's a question of finding your place. Anyway, c'mon, let's have a look at the town.'

Their house was about a half mile from the town. Ben parked up outside a big supermarket at the top. There was one long main street, which sloped down to the centre. Ben saw it as a typical Irish market town with some small streets like veins slipping off the main artery that dissected the town. He had thought it quaint at the centre, where there was a small, open square with a big stone drinking trough. He'd figured that was for animals that had been sold at the market in times past. One Sunday a month they still had stalls that sold fresh fruit and veg, eggs, and general farmyard produce.

The family walked on the narrow pavements, peering in shop windows, seeing here a fishing tackle shop, there a small drapery with coloured, knitted pullovers and cardigans in the window, a few pubs, one with open doors and the steady rise and fall of chatter and a loud TV coming from inside.

To Ben it had the feel of somewhere timeless. He had sensed that the very first day they'd come down to scope it out. Its pavements were narrow, the main street wide, paint and plaster peeling on many buildings. It had reminded him of the small town near where his grandparents had lived. He'd spent summers there with his mother when he was a kid. The main event for him had been a sweet shop at the top of the town where an old woman in a blue shop coat used to laboriously drop loose sweets into a paper bag with a steel scoop. The anticipation of the sweets dropping in and filling the bag was nearly as good as the actual eating.

The shop they were leasing was quite like that old place in many ways. There was a big display window with a thick wooden frame running around it, and the main door was wood-framed with a long glass panel running down its length.

Ben stopped outside it and gestured with open arms towards the window. The kids looked nonplussed.

'And look what I have,' Ben said, jangling a set of keys. He twisted the thick Chubb key in the lock, pushed the door open and went in, followed by the others.

Inside the light was murky, as the shop faced away

from the sun, but they could see enough to figure that in its previous life it had been a butchers, as the cutting slabs were still visible behind the counter. Some even had traces of blood on them.

'Oooohhh,' Molly said, looking at the scene that was in direct contrast to the cute exterior.

'It used to be a butchers,' Ben said.

'You don't say,' Molly replied acidly. 'I'd never have guessed.'

'It's a cute little space. We can do something really nice with it.'

Ben had ventured in behind the counter to where there were some old freezers. He peeked into one, and as he did, an overwhelming stench of rotting meat soared up to fill the air.

'Oooh, Jesus, that's nasty,' Deborah said.

Molly stuck a hand over her mouth and ran from the shop. Jack winced and covered his mouth but stayed where he was.

Ben slammed the cover shut and reeled back from the smell. 'Jesus, that's bad all right. They should have done a better job cleaning the place.'

'Oh, should they?' came a deep voice from the doorway. 'Well, maybe they were too busy trying to earn a living.'

Ben turned quickly to see a thickset, middle-aged man with a mop of curly hair crowning a ruddy face. He walked into the shop and ran a hand along the counter with a proprietorial air.

'This used to be mine before the supermarkets sucked the lifeblood out of it.'

'Ben Higgins,' Ben said with an outstretched hand.

'Pat Doyle,' the butcher said, taking Ben's hand in an iron grip and holding it. Ben felt enormous strength as

Doyle squeezed, and had to shake the pain out when he finally let go.

'It must be tough to lose a business.'

Doyle pulled his head back and looked at Ben like he was going to impart something important, but he just shrugged his shoulders.

'One man's loss is another man's gain. I drive a taxi now, mostly drunks getting fecked out of the pubs at the weekend. Very glamorous, no? I have a wife and three hungry lads who would eat you out of house and home. They're all GAA players, and they'd demolish a sliced pan and a package of ham each in the one sitting.'

'Sport makes you hungry all right,' Ben said. Doyle was still staring at him like he was deciding whether to swat him out of the way or not.

'Life makes you hungry, but sometimes you have to settle for less, isn't that right?' He turned to Deborah, who was looking on.

He kept looking at her, and she met his gaze without flinching. Ben knew that Deborah had dealt with all types over her career as a crime reporter and was not easily intimidated. It was something he took secret pride in.

'So you're going making a health shop out of the place, full of scented candles and them little wind chimes.'

'There'll be a little more than that,' Deborah said. 'It's a health food shop, so we'll be selling every type of health food. People are more aware of what they're eating these days and the effect it has on their body.'

'So I suppose meat won't get a look in is what you're saying. Not good enough anymore, is that it?'

'Each to his own. There'll be a market for meat as well.'

'Just not here. Well, we'll see how smart ye are at the

end of the day.' He turned to leave. Ben felt relief to see him turn away. He noticed that the kids had stayed silent throughout the interaction. *Even Molly seems intimidated by this guy,* Ben thought.

'And what about the rotting meat in the freezer?' Deborah asked just as Doyle reached the door. Ben felt himself inhale sharply.

Doyle turned slowly to look at Deborah. His mouth was twisted into a grimace. 'Oh, so you want to kick a man when he's down, do you? I'd say you'll do a good job of cleaning the place out yerselves.' He stalked out of the shop before she could say anything else.

'Charming,' Deborah said.

'I suppose it was his livelihood,' Ben replied.

'Not really our problem, but he obviously sees it differently.'

They locked the door and walked back around to the main street.

'Who's for ice cream?' Ben asked the kids.

'Sure,' Jack said. Molly said nothing.

'I think I could do with an ice cream,' Deborah said with a wry grin.

There was a newsagents in the middle of the main street with a giant plastic ice-cream cone outside. It was a long shop with two aisles and a smattering of customers. Ben approached the counter, and the middle-aged female assistant stepped forward to help him. She surveyed the rest of the family as she did, passing an eye over each, then returning to look at Deborah again.

'Can I help?' she said to Ben, but kept her eyes on Deborah, a smile beginning to widen her lips.

'I think we're in need of ice creams,' Ben said, looking back at the kids.

'Four?'

'Yes, please, ninety-nines, I think, and don't hold back on the sprinkles.'

The woman laughed. 'It's been that kind of day, has it?'

'You could say that, but no doubt it's about to take a turn for the better, and the ice creams are going to play a starring role.'

'You're the one from the telly, aren't you?' the woman said to Deborah as she let the ice cream drop in folds into the first cone.

'Maybe,' Deborah replied.

'People said you were coming. You're the crime reporter.'

'That's me, or should I say, that was me. Not anymore.'

'Well, you did your job, and you did it well. Takes guts to take those criminals on.'

'I did have a supportive organization behind me.'

'Still, it's not for the faint hearted.' The woman handed Deborah the first cone. 'This one's on the house.'

'No, there's no need at all,' Deborah said. 'We're glad to be here, get away from it all.'

'No, I insist.'

Another customer, a swarthy, brown-haired man, approached the counter.

'Here, Mossy,' the woman said to him. 'This is the woman from the telly, the crime reporter.'

'Well, we like to keep ourselves to ourselves around here.' Mossy said without changing expression and handed the woman the price of a newspaper before leaving.

'That's Mossy Hennigan, the owner of that lively pub across the road. He's a big player in our town, very involved in all our committees. He's having a table quiz for the GAA club on Wednesday night. You might think of dropping by.'

'I think that would be a marvellous way to meet some of the locals,' Ben concurred.

They walked the town with their ice creams, and to Ben, it all felt very homely as they peeked into the quaint shops with their brightly coloured exteriors. There was a music shop with a broad range of traditional instruments—accordion, fiddle, bodhran, flutes—which gave Ben a sense of solidity, as if they were finally in a place that was connecting with their own culture.

Before they left town, Ben and Deborah left the kids waiting outside and slipped in to the pub. It was busy with men in rough work clothes who talked in deep voices that sounded like they were used to having to communicate across distances, the product of living in wide-open spaces.

Ben worked his way into a gap in the bar and smiled at Mossy Hennigan to get his attention. He didn't appear to see him for a few long, awkward minutes as Ben felt himself squeezed up against the men at the bar. From the corner of his eye, he could see Deborah shifting restlessly, no doubt thinking of the kids waiting outside.

Finally Ben reached over the bar as Hennigan was passing, to tap him on the shoulder. Hennigan turned, his expression one that looked like it could easily slip into anger at any moment.

'Sorry to trouble you, but we wanted to sign up for the table quiz on Wednesday night.'

Hennigan said nothing but slipped a sheet of paper towards Ben. On it there were lists of names with phone numbers beside them. Hennigan walked away, but Ben had no pen, so he waved a hand after him. Hennigan didn't seem to notice. Ben was suddenly feeling claustrophobic, hemmed in by the squash of bodies around him, but he didn't want to just give up. He wanted to make the effort to get to this quiz, to try to integrate with the community.

He turned and shouted to Deborah, 'Have you got a pen?'

'Don't think so, hang on.' Deborah searched through the loose leather bag she had over her shoulder. 'Here, best I can do.' She handed Ben her eyeliner, so Ben scrawled their names and number with it and left the sheet on the counter.

'He's not too friendly, that Hennigan guy,' Ben said once they were outside.

'Gruff country publican, conforming to type, I'd say,' Deborah said with a smile.

'Conforming a bit too well for my liking,' Ben replied and laughed.

They drove the half mile back to the house. It was on a slightly elevated site just past the outskirts of town. Ben felt it gave them just enough distance while being close enough to run their shop at the same time.

Pulling into the long, sloping drive, Ben felt that first real sense of ownership. His stomach fluttered with the excitement of the adventure they were embarking on. He squeezed Deborah's knee and smiled over at her.

'What's that?' Deborah said, pointing to the front door. Ben saw there was something flapping in the westerly breeze. It looked like a sheet of paper in some sort of plastic wrapping.

'Maybe someone left a note,' he said as they approached it.

Inside a plastic poly pocket, there was an A4-size sheet with a photograph on it. Ben pulled the sheet from the pocket. He could see it was a photo of their family and had been taken on their walk around town, just as they left their shop. The picture was blurry, and the photographer had captured full images of Deborah and the kids, but Ben was way off to the side, so only a small part of him was visible. On the top of the sheet, in the small white margin, was written the word 'Welcome' in thick black marker.

'That's odd,' Ben said, twirling it around in his hands to view it from different angles. He felt an unsettling feeling creep through him. The quality of the photograph was poor, as if someone had taken it in a hurry. The fact that someone had taken it and then gone to the trouble of posting it up on their front door was definitely strange. Writing 'welcome' was a token nod towards some sort of positive gesture, but whoever it was must have seen them go into their shop and then waited for them to come back out again. To Ben it felt like they were being watched.

'Kind of a weird welcome note,' Deborah agreed.

'It's probably someone who means well, but they've just gone a very peculiar way about showing it,' Ben said, trying to keep his tone light.

'Peculiar is the word,' Deborah said. 'Creepy might be another word.'

'And you're not really in the picture,' Molly said to her father as she breezed past and into the house.

4

Ben and Deborah spent a restless night in sleeping bags on bed bases without mattresses. There were just some leftover bits in the various bedrooms, so they all had to make do. Their own furniture wasn't due down until the following day, so the rooms were sparse, echoing, and uncomfortable.

Ben had tossed and turned in his sleeping bag and felt the uneven bumps of the bed base beneath him. Waking in the dark to the eerie stillness of the house, he had wondered about the photograph left on the door. He could only think it was an awkward, ham-fisted message of welcome, the photo taken badly, so he was sidelined in it. Still, combined with the reticent reception they'd had in their walkabout, he was left wondering if he had underestimated the whole cultural shift from city to country. Maybe the ideal of owning their own patch of land and small local business was going to be more complex than he imagined.

They'd been talking about it back in Dublin for a while. Ben had had enough of long, long hours working in finance, and crime reporting was taking its toll on

Deborah. The plan was to move some time over the next couple of years, but something suddenly made the move a lot more urgent. A major gang that Deborah had been reporting on had upped the ante in a big way. No one expected them to put a pipe bomb under a judge's car, but that was exactly what they did. They found bits of the car and bits of the judge scattered all over the road. The news every evening seemed full of figures with jackets over their heads being led out of court. It was hard to catch a glimpse of the faces underneath, but everyone knew what gang they belonged to. Deborah could name them all, and she said they were not going to stop until they had cornered the drugs market once and for all. There was a rumour they had a hit list, and there were journalist's names on it. One of her colleagues had seen a suspicious car outside his house.

Ben had never seen Deborah shaken by her work before, but he had noticed she had been surreptitiously looking out the front window to check the street outside at night. After one of those checks, their eyes met, and Ben said, 'You don't feel safe here anymore, do you?' Deborah had simply shaken her head. The next day they started putting the plan to move into action.

But one thought had followed Ben persistently as they made plans to travel west, set up a shop, and grow a few veggies on their own plot of land. What if the gang had decided retribution had to be carried out on reporters, too? Even though Deborah had left the game, maybe they were setting themselves up as a nice, soft target out in the isolation of the countryside.

He kept those thoughts to himself as they woke early the next morning to the sounds of farm animals and an apparent invasion of tweeting, whistling, chirping birds, some of which sounded as if they were stuck in their chimney.

Deborah shifted sleepily over to him when she opened her eyes, and they held each other, trying to get comfortable.

'Jesus, those birds don't half make a racket,' she said dreamily.

'Yeah, you come to the country for the peace and the stillness, and look what happens.'

'Hmmm.' Deborah snuggled into him. 'So who's going for coffee?'

'I wonder,' Ben replied with a laugh. 'Molly might volunteer to walk the half mile to the supermarket and come back with coffee and croissants. What d'you reckon?'

'Probably if not definitely, I'd say.'

'All right then.' Ben swung himself awkwardly from the mattress and slithered from the sleeping bag. 'I'd better get off that thing anyway, or I'm going to be making the local chiropractor rich.'

He returned forty minutes later with coffee, orange juice, and scones with butter and jam from the local supermarket. Jack and Molly were up and sitting on wooden benches at the picnic table outside. Molly had her earphones in and gazed into the middle distance like she was inflicted with an allergy to life in general and dared anyone to impinge on her bubble. Ben had been a little shocked when Molly suddenly withdrew somewhere near her thirteenth birthday. Initially he wondered had something happened, and then he went down the road of maybe she had been bullied or abused, but Deborah seemed a bit less taken aback and explained that it was hormones kicking in, and it might well stay like that for some time. She had never exactly been a daddy's little girl—even as a kid she had been sharp-eyed and occasionally caustic—but she had been affectionate, snuggling up to him as they watched TV or as he read Jack and her a story. He missed that affection and found it hard to tiptoe around her all the time, but he had learned to do whatever was needed to keep the peace.

He broke her spell by placing a scone and a paper cup of orange juice in front of her. Wordlessly she took the cup and sipped tentatively from it as if testing its allergy-inducing properties. It must have passed the test because she took another, longer sip, then began to give the same reluctant attention to the scone.

'Sleep all right?' Ben asked Jack.

'Not really. I kept hearing weird noises outside, like someone was walking around the house.'

'Was it accompanied by a tearing and chewing sound? Because I definitely heard cattle during the night,' Ben replied.

'I don't know. It was just weird,' Jack said conclusively.

'Country sounds,' Deborah said. 'You're going to be hearing a lot of them. No traffic or city noises to block them out.'

'Our stuff from Dublin should be down about lunchtime, so I suggest that you and Molly go to the beach. You can bring your fishing gear. The rocks down there are supposed to be good for fishing. That's what the estate agent told me, anyway. Harry could do with the walk as well.'

Jack got his fishing stuff out. Molly sat where she was, picking at her scone like an archaeologist expecting to come across a delicate historic artefact at any moment.

'You coming?' Jack asked her.

Molly stood suddenly and shook off whatever crumbs had escaped her forensic exploration. She didn't reply but exhibited the demeanour of someone who was at least ready to start walking.

'You know where the beach is,' Ben said. 'You go right just before the town and straight down. You'll hear the sea before you see it.'

But before they could take off, they all heard the sound of a car engine chug up the drive. Ben saw Jeremiah's battered, dirty green Jeep pull into view. He felt a tremor of something unpleasant flash through him. Harry ran over to the Jeep and started barking. Jeremiah sat in the driver's seat and looked out at them for a full minute before climbing out.

'Did ye want any help around today?' he asked, kicking at some little shards of gravel.

'I think we're fine, thanks, at the moment. We're waiting for the delivery truck to arrive, so we might need a hand later on.'

Jeremiah didn't respond to that but looked out past them to where the fields and trees marched towards the horizon. His gaze swept back towards the picnic table and the remains of their breakfast before stopping at Jack's fishing rods leaning against it.

'Is it yourself likes the fishing?' he asked Ben.

'No, that's me,' Jack piped up.

Jeremiah walked forward and handled the rod, looking along its length like a gunman might look the length of a barrel.

'Do you fish?' Jack asked.

'I do, surely. Gives you the peace and calm you'll not get anywhere else. You'll get plenty down below,' he said, jutting his chin in the general direction of the sea. 'But you'll need the right bait and lure, so you will.'

'I saw a fishing shop in town,' Jack said. 'I'll go down when I get my pocket money.'

Jeremiah smiled at him. 'You will surely. You're a

good man, so you are.' With that, he turned and climbed back into his Jeep to take off in a spray of dust and gravel.

'He's an odd one,' Deborah said as he took off.

'Takes getting used to all right,' Ben said with a smile.

'Like, he's a full-on hillbilly,' Molly said, and they all laughed at that.

Jack gathered up his gear, and he and Molly took off down the drive with Harry sniffing the ground around them as he followed, his short tail wagging with excitement.

Ben and Deborah were keeping half an eye out for the delivery truck, but then Ben got a text to say they wouldn't get down until three.

'Looks like we're home alone,' he said to Deborah after reading the text.

He ran his fingers up her back. 'Should we christen the place?'

'Maybe,' Deborah said. 'But where? On the bed bases? The rocking chair?'

'C'mon.' Ben led her to the bedroom and laid two sleeping bags out on the bed base. 'That'll take the worst of the pain out of it.'

They lay on the bags and started kissing.

'Hope they manage to find the beach,' Deborah said.

'Jack'll find it. You know, I suspect Molly turns into this jovial, gregarious outgoing social butterfly as soon as she leaves our sight. Do you ever get that feeling?'

Deborah laughed. '*That* is something I'd like to see.'

'Well, you were like that in college, weren't you? In every union and society that was going, always taking off on trips abroad. At least that's what you told me. Probably trying to make me jealous. I just did boring old business and played a bit of tennis at the weekends.'

'Poor you, must have been miserable, c'mere.'

Deborah pulled him towards her and started easing his trousers and underpants down. Just then there was a loud hammering on the door.

Ben pulled his trousers up again. 'Jesus, what the hell's that? Delivery guys couldn't be here yet. Shit, I'd better go see.' He got dressed and made his way to the door but not before there was another bout of hammering.

'Hang on, hang on. I'm coming.'

Ben pulled the door open to see Jeremiah standing there with a tin box in his hand. He proffered the box to Ben, who had no choice but to look inside and see a mass of wriggling black worms pointing their sightless faces up towards the air.

'Oh, Jesus.' Ben took a step back.

'It's worms, bait for the young lad,' Jeremiah said, looking proudly into the wriggling mass. He held the tin out for Ben to take it.

Ben moved back another step. 'It's grand, really. Maybe Jack could see them later. He's out.'

'So you don't want them?' Jeremiah fixed Ben with a cold stare.

'I wouldn't know where to put them, and my wife, well, she wouldn't like, well, you know, but thanks anyway.'

Jeremiah stuck the lid roughly back on the box. 'I'll leave them here on the windowsill.' He placed them roughly on the sill and marched back towards his Jeep.

'I didn't mean it like that,' Ben said, but Jeremiah had already gunned the engine and was taking off.

Deborah was walking down the hall towards Ben. 'What was that all about?'

'He had some disgusting worms for Jack. It was nice

of him, I suppose, but Jesus, did he have to just call unannounced like that?'

Deborah rubbed his back. 'Country life. This is what we signed up for. Now, we going back to bed?'

Ben shook his head. 'I don't think so. God knows who's going to turn up next. I think I'll stroll down to the beach and see how the kids are getting on. I might as well bring those worms down to Jack. He might actually have a use for them.'

Ben walked first the road and then the long, sandy lane that led down to the beach. He could feel the tension in his shoulders after the encounter with Jeremiah and his thwarted bed time with Deborah. He had hoped the break to the country would give them a lot more time together. *It's early days yet,* he told himself. *We'll settle in. The kids will settle in. We'll find our rhythm soon enough.*

Ben heard voices as he approached the beach. He turned into view to see a group of young lads facing Jack and Molly. Jack was standing on some rocks, fishing rod in hand. Molly was on the sand but still far enough away from the boys so they had to talk loudly. Ben decided to hold back in case they were in the middle of making some friends. He could see Harry off in the distance, barking and chasing after seabirds. He watched as the tallest of the boys, a good-looking, dark-haired guy of about fifteen, addressed Molly.

'So ye're the Dubs,' he said. The group eyed Jack and Molly as if they were livestock for sale.

'From Dublin, you mean? Maybe. Our reputation precedes us, then,' Molly said coolly.

'D'ye hear the big words there, Gav?' a sandy-haired guy with freckles said.

'Yeah, the likes of us thick country bucks wouldn't

understand them, not at all,' dark-haired Gav said with a sneer.

Ben didn't like the sounds of what he was hearing, but he decided to let it play out a little longer in case the tone changed. Maybe they were just going through the ritual teenage slagging stuff, testing the waters, before they could actually make friends.

'Which word do you not understand?' Molly asked. 'Or was it all of them?'

'She's smart, so she is,' the sandy-haired guy said.

'You're right there, Martin,' Gav replied. 'We might have to put manners on her.'

Jack started inching his way back over the rocks towards Molly.

'Look, here comes the cavalry. Watch out, lads,' Gav said with a laugh that was a bit too loud.

'Is this what you do all day?' Molly asked.

'What's that?' Gavin asked.

'Go around acting tough and giving people a hard time.'

'We're not giving no one a hard time, are we, lads?'

'Not yet anyways,' Martin replied.

Ben decided he'd heard enough, so he broke cover and started walking towards them. They didn't notice him, though, as they were so caught up in their mini drama.

'C'mon,' Molly said to Jack. 'Let's get out of here and give these assholes a chance to play chasing or whatever they normally do down here.'

'You've got a sharp tongue, Dub, but you're not bad-looking, and I like a bit of a challenge,' Gav said as they walked off.

'You seem fairly challenged all right,' Molly said.

Gavin tensed up, but then suddenly relaxed as quickly and started laughing. 'You're good, you are.'

Molly and Jack kept going, with Harry skipping around their feet. Ben walked quickly down to meet them. Molly looked up sharply when she saw him.

'What are you doing here?'

'I just came down to see you were okay.'

'We're fine. We can manage on our own.'

She feels humiliated that I came in the middle of their spat, like she can't look after herself, Ben thought.

'I needed to stretch my legs anyway, got tired of waiting for the delivery truck, and Jeremiah brought some worms for fishing.' He pulled the tin out and showed Jack, making sure to keep it hidden from Molly's view.

'Class,' Jack said. 'I'll use them the next time. That was nice of him.'

'Yeah, I suppose it was,' Ben said uncertainly.

5

The delivery truck was bigger than expected and didn't fit in the gate of their driveway, so they had to pull into the side of the road and block traffic on that side. The driver told Ben he wouldn't have time to bring everything all the way up to the house, so they would just leave it inside the gate. Ben gave Molly and Jack hi-vis vests and asked them to direct traffic around the truck.

'Dad, I look like a complete asshole out here,' Molly rasped, but Ben had no time to argue with her.

'We've got to do this, and fast,' he replied.

Ben and the delivery guys started pulling furniture out and leaving it just inside the gate. Traffic started to build on the road as people tried to get past the truck. Molly very reluctantly started waving people past on her side, and Jack did the same on the other side. Still, people were beeping and throwing angry looks as they squeezed past.

When the truck finally left, Ben heaved a huge sigh of relief. They still had to cart the stuff all the way from the gate into the house, not to mention finish clearing the house, but at least the strain and tension of holding up all the town traffic was over.

'That calls for a mug of tea and a sandwich,' he announced to Deborah. 'I'll fly into the supermarket deli.'

He took orders and went into town. While he was queuing at the deli, a middle-aged man with brown hair and an argyle-patterned V-neck approached him.

'Dave Breen,' he said, proffering a hand. 'I saw you back at the house, unloading all your stuff. Rather him than me, I thought to myself at the time.'

'Hope we didn't hold you up,' Ben said.

'Not a bit of it. I saw you had the whole family involved. It's nice to have the troops to call on if you need them.'

'Not sure how much I would describe the kids as troops. Militant maybe.'

Breen laughed. 'That's a good one. And you have Deborah there too helping out.'

Ben must have looked a bit surprised at his use of Deborah's first name because Breen smiled and winked at him. 'Best-kept secret around here. Not. Famous crime reporter from the telly is coming to live in our humble little town.'

'Yes, I suppose. She's hoping to leave all that behind now and start afresh.'

'Listen, Ben, there'll be a flurry of excitement for a while, but it'll die down.'

'Hope so. I'd better get the food here for the troops.'

'Of course, sure we'll see you at the table quiz anyway.'

Ben went to order four rolls, and as he waited for them, he was left to think over how much people in town had anticipated their arrival. He hadn't really thought of Deborah as a celebrity, but they obviously thought she was here. Then Breen had used his first name too before Ben had told him what it was. *And* he knew they had signed up for the table quiz. *So much for anonymity and slipping quietly into the background,* Ben thought, and he had to smile because he really hadn't expected this level of interest.

'Looks like we are regarded as celebs, I'm afraid. Well, you are anyway and the rest of us by association,' Ben said as they devoured the rolls.

'Oh, God, the horror of minor celebrity. You don't get the financial rewards, but you do get the attention. It won't last,' Deborah replied, wiping away a stray bit of mayo with a napkin.

'That's what the guy at the deli was saying.'

'So you've even been chatting about it.'

'Have to talk about something. It's too early to start talking about the weather.'

'True that. You'll have to wait until you're an established farmer, throwing wisps of straw in the air and seeing which way they float.'

'Give it a couple of weeks and I'll be spitting on my palm and shaking hands with the best of them.'

'Ooohh, gross,' Molly said with a curl of the lip.

'Right, let's get cracking,' Ben said. 'We've got to move all that,' he said, pointing to the pile at the end of the drive, 'in here.' He gestured towards the house. Nobody moved, so he started striding boldly towards the pile. When he turned, they were still watching him, so he threw his arms out in exaggerated exasperation.

'Okay, I suppose we'd better help,' Deborah said with a smile.

There was a lot to carry, and it was tough, back-breaking work.

'Where's Jeremiah when you need him?' Deborah asked.

'I texted him earlier, but he said he's busy with his County Council work,' Ben replied as the two of them heaved their double bed base up the gravelly path.

Jack and Molly started bringing some of the lighter stuff like lamps and the TV stand. They walked quickly up the gravel path, not officially racing but definitely trying to reach the house before the other. Harry followed in their wake, enjoying the movement and general excitement.

Ben and Deborah had to twist and turn the double bed to get it in the front door and then round the narrow hallway into the bigger one. Ben could hear Jack and Molly chasing each other down around the kitchen. Jack was shouting, 'It's mine,' and Molly was saying, 'I just want it for a few minutes.' This was followed by a crashing, cracking sound, and Ben instinctively said, 'Oh, shit.' Once they had the bed in place, he went down to the kitchen to find the two of them standing beside what had been the mother's rocking chair. The arm on one side was dangling loosely to the side.

'It was his fault,' Molly said before Jack could say anything. 'I just wanted to borrow his charger, and he wouldn't let me. I can't find mine in all the mess.'

'It wasn't,' Jack said sullenly. 'She dived for me and hit the chair.'

Ben felt completely flustered and didn't know what to say. He knew the chair was a family heirloom and probably important to Jeremiah, but he didn't want to make a big deal out of it with the kids. 'Oh, it doesn't matter. It was probably something we were going to do away with eventually anyway. Just leave it out on the skip for the moment, and we'll decide what to do with it later.'

Between them, they carted it out, darting accusing glances at each other as they went. 'I still want the charger,' Ben heard Molly whisper, but there was too much to do, so he just left them at it.

It was eight o'clock that evening before the house was in any sort of shape with the old stuff left out on the skip and their own Dublin furniture placed around the house.

'Thank Christ for that,' Ben said. 'I thought it would never end. Now who's for Chinese? We're certainly not cooking after all that.'

An hour later they were sitting around the kitchen table, wafts of noodles, sweet and sour sauce, and freshly cooked rice filling the air.

'It'll be good to sleep on a proper bed and mattress tonight,' Deborah said. She looked tired, holding her head up with one hand as she ate.

'And the Wi-Fi?' Jack asked.

'Tomorrow,' Ben said. 'First things first.'

'That would be a "first thing" for our generation,' Molly said.

Just then Harry, who had been sniffing around the floor, looking for any bits of fallen food, cocked his head and looked towards the side of the house. He let out a low growl and went to sniff around the bottom of the front door.

'Must be one of those foxes Jeremiah was talking about,' Ben said.

Harry let out a couple of short barks.

'You'd better go and see,' Deborah said.

'Yeah, Dad, you have to protect us now we're out in the wilds,' Molly said mischievously.

Ben got up, went up the hallway and opened the front door. It was twilight outside now, the sharp forms of daylight sliding out of focus to give way to thicker, more grainy outlines. Harry was straight out the door and round to the side of the house, where he took up the growling and barking once again.

'What's wrong with you?' Ben said as he followed him around. Everything seemed still and quiet outside. He could hear birds fluttering in the trees as they settled in for the night. When Ben rounded the corner to the side of the house, he could make out the solid bulk of the skip to his left, and then to the right of the skip, he saw a lone figure standing, holding something. Looking closer, he could make out the bulk and the many jackets of Jeremiah, and in one thick, meaty hand, he held the broken rocking chair. In the other hand he held something that Ben could not quite make out. He walked closer to see it was a rock, and Jeremiah was holding it in the air, looking at Harry as if daring him to make a move.

'Stop,' Ben shouted. 'Put the rock down. He's just not used to you yet. He's harmless.'

'What did ye do to it?' Jeremiah asked quietly. He didn't raise his head, but held the chair up higher for Ben to see its broken arm dangling.

'The chair? I'm very sorry. I forgot all about it. It was just an accident today when we were moving everything. It got damaged. I'm happy to pay to get it fixed.'

'There's no need. I'll do it myself. It was her chair. It meant the world to her, and I asked ye to keep it where it was, but ye didn't.' Jeremiah slowly lowered the arm that was holding the rock. He threw it against the skip so it made a loud metallic clang.

He turned and placed the chair carefully in the back of his Jeep before jumping in and taking off.

Ben watched him leave with a creeping sense of anxiety flooding through him. He felt he had underestimated the importance of the chair, and now he had got on the wrong side of Jeremiah, someone who could have been a possible ally to them.

Deborah had come out to see what was going on.

'It was Jeremiah,' Ben told her. 'He saw the chair in the skip, and he was mighty unimpressed. I forgot all about it, meant to get it back out again when we had everything done.'

Deborah looked after the Jeep as its headlights coursed a broad path through the falling darkness. 'Yeah, but what was he doing up here at this time of night anyway? Remember Jack said he thought he heard something or someone last night. Maybe we need to establish a few boundaries with our new friend.'

6

There is the proof. They have no respect for your mother's memory. He has no respect for her. Look what he did to the chair. That was her pride and joy. It meant so much to her. You can feel her spirit stirring. She can't be happy. These are her things. They hold her most precious memories, and they help her to forget about the bad thing that happened. You don't want her thinking about that, do you? You hear voices. You hear her voice. Of course you do. You want that to stop more than anything. The question is—how are you going to stop it? You know what to do. It is time to do it.

7

Ben spent a restless night waking constantly, listening for noises outside. It seemed to him as if every noise out there was circling their house. There was rooting, heavy shifting, loose stones tumbling, and sudden flurries of fluttering. He was left wondering at how active country life was at night. Finally, towards dawn he heard the sound of a rooster crowing, and that allowed him to relax enough to fall into a short, deep sleep.

'Right,' he said over morning coffee, 'it's chickens for us today. Don't forget, Molly, it's you who's going to be the guardian of the poultry.'

Molly observed him with a neutral expression as she cradled a mug of drinking chocolate.

At least it's neutral, Ben thought. *Anything short of a grimace is a victory.*

The whole family set off after breakfast to a farm that he had researched on an Irish farm fowl website. It was a warm day, and the green hills shone with an effervescent glow in the sunshine. The long steel exhaust pipes of tractors appeared like periscopes chugging along behind tall hedgerows. Cattle stood in mucky fields, their tails mechanically swishing flies away from their great haunches.

The farm was cheery and awash with hens of all varieties picking and scratching both inside and outside big chicken runs. The owner, a stocky, brown-haired woman with an outdoor jacket with little clusters of feathers all over it, was scattering food from a bucket to a group of hens that darted and pecked at the ground around her.

'Hello there. Ben, is it?' she said, looking up. Ben had been on the phone to her already.

'Yes, and we're here for a chicken run and some hens,' Ben replied.

'Obviously,' Molly said, looking around at the multitude of chickens and hens.

'Here, will you take over? Just throw a few fistfuls at them,' the woman said, handing Molly the bucket. Molly held it away from her body with a grimace, but the woman was already walking away and gesturing for Ben and Deborah to follow.

The hens clustered around Molly's feet, and Ben was amused to see her do a little dance with her trainers, trying to get away from them.

'Throw the food,' Jack said. 'Then they'll go.'

Molly grabbed a handful and threw it. The hens darted in a blur of red and brown after the food, then returned to peck around her feet. She threw another handful, and they took off again. This time she threw yet another before they had time to come back.

'I'm getting the hang of this,' she said with a smile. Jack reached into the bucket, and between the two of them they were laughing and throwing hen feed as quick as they could. Ben was relieved to see the two of them having a laugh for a change. It seemed like it'd been a while, and he hoped it might be an indication of more change to come.

Ben and Deborah picked out a long cage that was divided in two parts. One of the parts had wooden panelling and contained a half dozen brown hens who occasionally peeked out during the journey.

'Okay, we're good to go,' Ben said once they had the cage in the back of the SUV.

BACK AT THE HOUSE, Ben slotted the two parts of the cage together, then opened the door of the first bit so the hens could slowly emerge into the longer run part, where they walked stiffly as if they had just got up from a long sleep. They had a feeding and a watering part built into the wire mesh so they could be fed and watered from outside.

That evening Ben and Deborah went online and started ordering supplies for their shop. Ben had researched it well. He and Deborah had decided it was the best small business to set up, but he felt the onus of responsibility was on him. It was he who had pushed hard for the move out of Dublin. At the time he had said it was for their safety, which was true, but there was also a part of him that felt he had always worked such long hours he'd never really been there for the kids. He hoped this would give them more time together, a more regular family life.

He felt his years of business experience would serve him in good stead as well, although in previous times he was more used to managing other people's money, large quantities of it. Now it was their own money, and they had to get it right. They had set about sourcing the best local products they could find. They were surprised at how many small producers were dotted around the countryside in the West of Ireland. They found a traditional seaweed-processing company that produced everything from edible seaweeds to skin products to seaweed supplements. There was a chocolate company that used only locally sourced, organic products, a couple of different honey and jam suppliers, a coffee roaster, and, of course, multiple cheese producers, each with their own take on soft, hard, blue, Gubbeen, herb flavoured. It was hard to narrow down the choice. Then they had eggs from the woman they had bought the hens from. Some of it they had decided they would leave until they actually got there and checked out some farmers markets, so they just put in orders for what would make the shelves and fridge look stocked for the moment. There was a company in town that did shop fitting, so he arranged with them to be down later next day once they had the place cleared. The plan was to get a skip and clear it all out in the morning.

After dinner and after making sure the hens were back in their actual henhouse and not in the run part of their cage, Ben and Deborah set out for the town to join the table quiz. It was their first official social outing, and Ben was nervous. This was the first time they were going to be on display, as it were. He felt there was so much they had to learn about the town and the people, but he reasoned it was no different from so many other life situations he'd been in. He'd managed funds for clients over the years, and each time you were dealing with a whole new group of people, a fresh dynamic, complete with their own ready-made alliances and hostilities. He'd learned to ride it out until some sort of equilibrium was found. He hoped he could apply those skills in this new setting.

They walked in because they'd figured on having a couple of drinks. 'All things going well, we'll be singing our heads off in a lock-in at two in the morning,' Deborah said with a laugh.

They had both decided casual dress was the way to go, so Deborah was wearing a dark parka with a fur-trim hood and black jeans. Ben always thought she looked like Chrissie Hynde from the Pretenders, with her dark hair kept shortish but with a fringe hanging down over the left side of her face. She had strong features with sallow skin and deep, brown eyes. It was what had first attracted him to her, those relaxed, effortless good looks, and he felt she had kept them through the years just by being herself in a solid, laid-back kind of way.

There was a path of sorts into town. It started out skinny and barely discernible but grew into a full-blown pedestrian path as they got closer. The evening was cool with a soft wind that rustled leaves in the hedgerows they passed.

Once into town, they passed the big supermarket before the street started to dip down towards the old stone trough that still sat in the centre of the small square.

The pub was to the right, a short distance from the square. The door was open again, and they could hear the buzz of conversation from inside. Walking in, Ben noticed a drop in the level of chatter, but enough pockets of conversation kept going for it not to be uncomfortable. He put on his best cheery demeanour and looked across the sea of faces to find directions to the actual quiz. Mercifully he saw a badly drawn arrow with the word 'quiz' underneath stuck on a pillar. He took Deborah's hand and led her through the throng and up a stairs at the back until they emerged into a function room with long wooden tables. Ben recognized the guy, Dave Breen, he had met at the deli. He was sitting towards the front at a small table with piles of paper and a small money box. He had a proprietorial air about him and gave the two of them a half smile through thinly parted lips.

So that's how he knew we were going to the quiz, Ben thought.

'Well, hello there,' he said when they walked over. He gave Ben the briefest of glances before his eyes settled on Deborah. *Please don't say anything about her being a crime reporter,* Ben thought. Breen just stared at her and looked like he was going to come out with something but he just kept that thin half smile.

'Where should we sit?' Ben asked, breaking the staring spell.

'Wherever you like,' Breen replied, gesturing towards the tables. Most were already full, divided into teams of four. Ben saw one or two other couples, though.

'Will we try to team up with someone?' he said.

Breen made a kind of a grimace, like he had just eaten something sour. 'I think you're a bit late to the party, unfortunately. People have already teamed up.'

'What about those couples?'

'They'll be waiting for someone,' Breen said, the sour expression persisting.

Deborah tugged at Ben's elbow. 'It's grand. We'll see who else turns up.'

'Don't forget this. You won't be going anywhere without it.' Breen handed them an answer sheet. Other people were coming in behind them, so Ben turned to go.

'And the finances?' Breen asked. 'I thought you were a financial man, or have you gone native already?' He pointed at a sign that said ten euro per person.

Ben felt flustered, as there was a growing queue

behind him, and he couldn't think of anything lighthearted to say, so he rifled through his pockets, got the money from his wallet, and paid. He had been determined that this was going to be a light introduction to the townspeople but could already feel himself tensing up.

He and Deborah took a table on their own. 'I'll get some drinks,' Ben said and marched off downstairs towards the bar. The crowd there was quite solid, and again he had difficulty getting attention. There was a different barman on, but he was so busy that he only paused for microseconds in front of Ben.

'Could I have a Guinness and a rum and Coke?' Ben eventually shouted over a row of heads. The heads all turned around to look at him. 'I have to get up to the quiz before it starts.' This elicited no response from the heads, who just turned back again. The barman nodded imperceptibly in Ben's direction, though, and poured the drinks.

When he got back to the room upstairs, Ben noticed that the two sets of couples who had previously been without partners had now joined up. It made Deborah look very isolated at a big table on her own. Ben slid in with the drinks.

'Everyone looks to be fixed up apart from us newbies,' Deborah said with a shrug of the shoulders.

'We'll show them,' Ben said with a smile, and they clinked glasses.

The publican arrived and sat at the top of the room, looking very much the quizmaster. Ben considered how he had seen him a few times now but had never seen him smile. His expression was unfriendly, even dour-looking, but Ben had also noticed that others seemed to treat him with respect.

· · ·

'RIGHT, first round, pens at the ready,' the publican said, through a microphone that hissed with static. 'Local knowledge. Name the three church spires that can be seen from outside this pub.'

Everyone scratched busily at their sheets. Ben and Deborah looked at each other blankly.

'Two. In which year did the local GAA team get to the county final? We only did it once, so that should be an easy one.'

Again scratching and again Ben and Deborah looked at each other. 'Biased in favour of the locals, I'd say,' Deborah whispered.

The first round of questions stuck to the local themes, and Ben and Deborah scored zero. Dave Breen collected the sheets with a studied efficiency.

After scores were calculated, Ben and Deborah found themselves at the bottom of the table. Ben felt self-conscious. They were the only couple without a partner, *and* they were bottom of the table.

'Better luck next round,' Dave Breen said as he handed out the new sheet of questions. 'But sure you'd hardly need luck, a smart guy like you,' he said to Ben, that thin smile creeping back.

They scored a couple of questions in round two, enough to bump them off the bottom of the table. Ben felt relieved, and in round three, local history, they scored well. Ben had done his research into the area. Round four was celebrities, and Deborah, being media savvy, was able to answer most.

Round five was the last one, and Breen handed out the question sheets without saying anything or making eye contact.

They finished second in the end and got a small round of applause and a bottle of cheap red for their troubles. They went straight to the bar after. The bar was rammed, but they got two high stools a few feet away with a small ledge for their drinks.

Ben noticed Breen at the bar. He kept looking over at Ben and Deborah until he finally prised himself away from the bar to join them.

'Ye did well,' he said with a wink.

'Beginners' luck,' Ben replied.

'You'll need that around here,' Breen said, and that sneer of a smile returned.

'Why is that?' Deborah asked.

'Vested interests, old grievances, all sorts of stuff going on, but you have a good man at the helm here.' He nodded at Ben.

'And a good woman,' Ben said.

'You don't need to tell me about Deborah,' Breen replied. 'I suppose, like a lot of people, I've always found the world of crime and crime reporting fascinating. I suppose you found a lot of them interesting yet disturbing at the same time.'

'You could say that,' Deborah said. 'Most of it is sad and comes from desperation.'

Ben thought about the gang who had blown the judge's car to smithereens. He didn't ever think about them coming from a sad and desperate place. He just thought about what a bunch of ruthless savages they were. They were going to get whatever they wanted and get rid of anyone who was in the way. Ben felt very much that Deborah had been seen as 'in the way'. He tried to play it down now that they had moved, but he kept wondering if the gang thought there was unfinished business to be settled.

'But it must give you a thrill hunting the bad guys down,' Breen persisted.

'You start to wonder who the bad guys are after a while. Desperation, as I said, is the main motivator.'

'But the murders. I mean what would drive a person to do something like that? You know, there's no turning back from that, is there?'

'Fortunately there's not too many of them.'

'Not too many. But you never know where the next one's going to spring up, do you?'

Pat Doyle, the butcher whose shop they had bought, stuck his ruddy face into the conversation. 'Hope I'm not intruding.'

'Not at all,' Ben said, moving aside so he could step into the circle.

'We're talking crime, of course,' Breen said with a knowing nod towards Deborah.

'I see, and have you mentioned our own little mystery case, connected to the house you're in and all?'

Breen shook his head. 'We haven't gone that deep yet.'

'Ah, maybe I'll leave it for another time, then,' Doyle said. 'Sure we don't get out to let the hair down much these days. Not me anyway. Run ragged I am trying to feed the hungry hoors at home.'

'We should go anyway,' Deborah said. 'The kids are at home, and it's all still a bit strange for them.'

'Of course it is. There's plenty of strange people out there. I could tell you stories. The taxi is like the confession box, but then I've taken the vow of silence, haven't I?'

'We weren't going to look for a taxi home, then,' Deborah said as they started the walk home.

Ben laughed. 'Quite the cast of characters all right. Wonder what Pat Doyle is holding back from us.'

'Probably nothing. It's something I learned from crime reporting. People like to mythologize both the crime and the criminal. It makes them feel better about their own cosy world.'

'Yeah, I'm sure you're right.'

But later that night Ben noticed his phone vibrating on the bedside nest of drawers. When he checked, there were multiple texts all saying just the one word, 'Welcome'. The caller ID was blocked.

He found it hard to sleep after that. It was almost certainly the same person who had left the photo on their door, and it could just be some harmless prank. But Ben wondered why whoever it was seemed to be homing in on him. It was probably some weird rite of passage they put newbies through, but it had an eerie personal touch to it. *Where did they get my number?* he wondered, but then he remembered he'd written it down for the pub quiz and left it on the counter for all to see. Thoughts of the gang from Dublin pushed their way in to his head, but he brushed them aside. He shifted in the bed and found himself listening out for any strange noises before falling into a restless sleep.

8

Next morning as Ben was making coffee, he heard a piercing shriek from the direction of the henhouse. He dashed out to find Molly clutching something small in her hands.

'Look, Dad, it's an egg, an actual egg that our hens have laid.'

'And here's another one,' Jack said, holding out a feather-covered, off-white egg.

'Wow, that's fantastic,' Ben said. 'That didn't take long. He looked over at the henhouse and the hens scrabbling about in their enclosed run and felt an overwhelming sense of relief. He'd been terrified when he heard the shriek and could still feel his heart racing. *Jesus, I have to stop this,* he thought. *I'm getting completely wound up.*

'That's so cool, kids. Now you're well on the way to being chicken farmers.' He gave Jack a hug and patted Molly on the shoulder.

'So I'm going to end up looking like that woman on the chicken farm, covered in feathers. How cool is that,'

Molly drawled, but Ben could see she was secretly proud of her find.

He and Deborah drove down to their shop after breakfast. Ben had ordered a skip, and it was waiting outside. They both pulled on overalls and work gloves, then set to clearing the place. Ben had brought extra thick black refuse sacks, and he used one of these to cover the rotting meat they had found. He felt like retching having to handle it and smell its rank, cloying odour, but he managed to put on a brave face for Deborah's sake.

He'd brought a wheelbarrow down from the house, so he set a plank of wood against the skip and ran the barrow up the plank and into the skip with everything from the freezer to the old shelves and glass display cases that the butcher had used.

The shop fitters arrived and set shelving up on both sides and a large refrigerated unit at the back. They put a flat wooden stand in the middle of the shop. Ben and Deborah had wicker baskets to place on either side of this, which they would fill with fresh fruit and veg. Beside those, Ben had figured they would put wooden boxes with pulses and rice so people could scoop out whatever they wanted themselves.

'We're going for sustainability here,' he had said to Deborah.

'You bet,' Deborah had agreed. 'Anything to get away from the mountains of plastic you see in supermarkets.'

Stock started to be delivered throughout the afternoon. Ben put a call in to Jack and Molly, who came down from the house to help stock the shelves. Once they had the dry food on one side, the creams and essential oils and supplements on the other, and a few bits and pieces in the fridge, Ben felt it was taking on the appearance of a bona fide health food shop.

'Looks good,' Molly said without a trace of irony.

'We're getting there,' Ben said, surveying the place. 'We're going to have to order a lot more stuff, but this will do for a kick-off.'

Ben got rolls from the supermarket, and they sat on upturned boxes to eat them with paper cups of tea.

'So are you going to employ us, like, as minimum-wage slaves here?' Molly asked.

'Do parents have to employ their kids as slaves?' Deborah replied. 'I think we can just command you to do our bidding and not give you a cent.'

'Not in these times,' Jack said earnestly. 'We've got children's rights. We learned about them already.'

'Well, maybe we'll have to find a loophole, then,' Deborah said, with a wink at Molly.

Suddenly the light inside the shop grew dimmer. Turning towards the shopfront window, Ben saw why. A gang of youths had pressed their faces against the window and were leering and pointing in. Ben recognized the dark-haired guy, Gavin, in the middle.

'They're the assholes we met down at the beach,' Molly said.

'Just ignore them,' Ben whispered.

'They've nothing better to do than slag us and have a good gawk. Bunch of losers,' Molly said acidly.

'I'm sure they're harmless,' Deborah said.

They started banging on the window, though, and laughing, so it was hard to ignore. Gav was there in the centre of them, although he wasn't doing the banging or laughing. Finally Ben stood and started walking towards the door. He could feel the blood rising through him, and he felt himself clench his fists. He saw Deborah get up suddenly as well. She moved to block him from getting out the door, but Ben kept going. He wasn't going to have a gang of punks bully his children like that. Just as he went to open the door, the group scattered and ran, laughing up the street, looking back at Ben as he stood red-faced at the door.

'We should probably go, or they might be back,' Molly said after a while.

'No, don't let them bother you like that,' Ben said, but Molly was already throwing her wrappers in the bin.

'It's okay, Dad. We'll go check on the chickens and Harry, make sure he hasn't broken in and eaten them.'

Jack and Molly left, and just as they did, the ruddy face of Pat Doyle peered into the shop.

'Well, what have we here?' he said, walking in. 'The height of sophistication no doubt. Gone are the days of the classical retailer. It's all the newfangled stuff nowadays.' He picked up some of the products they had put on the shelves and twirled them in the light as if he might elicit some hidden information from them.

'We'll give it a go, anyway,' Ben said.

'I'd say you'll do that all right and more power to you,' Doyle said with a nod, still sweeping his gaze around the shop. 'I'd say you'll do that all right. Show us poor country fools how it's done.'

Ben could feel the anger hopping off him. *His butchers must have really gone belly up and left him in the red*, he thought.

'It's just trying something new. No harm in that,' Deborah said with a hint of impatience coming into her tone.

Doyle looked at her and shrugged his shoulders, then turned to leave.

'Before you go,' Deborah said. 'You know what you were saying in the pub last night about something mysterious being connected to our property. Is that something we should know about?'

Doyle turned and brought a hand up to his chin like he was thinking about it. 'That'd be David Mertens,' he said eventually. 'Disappeared the fuck off the face of the planet, he did, some years back.'

'And how is that connected to our property?' Deborah asked.

'He stayed with Jeremiah when it was the family home before the mother died, Lord have mercy on her.'

'And who was this David Mertens?'

'Good question. A Belgian, turned up from fuck knows where and decided he wanted a life in our little town. Well, he didn't last. Had a run-in with Mossy Hennigan, the publican, and he's not a man to mess with. Disappeared the night after, like vanished, and never saw him again.'

'Does Jeremiah know anything?'

'Sure, he's half simple. People said the Belgian was just using him as a soft touch. He has his own troubles going back, does our Jeremiah. The mother held him guilty as charged for killing the da, but sure it was only an accident. Now, I think you've heard enough of the dark history of our lovely little town for one day. I'll leave ye to transform our lives with your city magic.'

'Creepy or what?' Deborah said after Doyle left.

'Weird all right, but sounds like it's history. He said it was a few years ago; nothing to concern us, I'd say.'

But Ben couldn't help mulling it over that evening. *What if there is something connected to our house? Could that be the reason we're getting a strange reception in town? This person who left the welcome note and is texting me, are they in some way connected to whatever happened? Is there someone who wants to scare us out of the house altogether?* Ben felt the possibilities were endless. *It could even be the gang from Dublin letting us know they've tracked us down.*

They had the house Wi-Fi connected, so he was able to distract himself and go online to order stuff for the shop, and that proved a welcome distraction. The kids and Deborah watched back episodes of some drag queen reality show, and he could hear shrill voices and canned laughter in the background.

He and Deborah were tired after their first day of work, so when they went to bed, they fell into a deep sleep.

Ben was woken by the sound of Harry barking just as the first rays of light were slipping under the curtains. He had to shake himself to remember where he was.

'Harry,' he called, 'go to sleep.' Harry had taken to sleeping in the kitchen near the stove on the woolly fleece that was his official dog bed.

Ben could hear him snuffling around in the hallway between barking sessions. Deborah shifted in the bed, but she was still asleep. Ben didn't want to shout at Harry again and risk waking her, so he slipped out of bed and stumbled out the door.

Harry wagged his tail when he saw Ben, but he went back to snuffling at the bottom of the front door. Ben went to the kitchen and pulled the curtains back, but he couldn't see anything. It was still half dark, so he could only really see a few feet in front of the house. He went to a basket beside the stove and pulled out a poker, then went to slowly open the front door. Harry dashed outside but didn't bark. Ben could hear him snuffling around again.

He put on the torch on his phone and did a quick sweep of the immediate area in front of him, but saw nothing. He heard a noise and stopped. *What was that?* It sounded like something scratching in the soil. Ben went forward, poker held up at the ready, torch sweeping the ground in front of him. The scratching noise was getting louder.

He saw something move in front of him and stopped. It was on the ground, a living creature, moving slowly, legs scratching helplessly at the soil but unable to do anything else. It was one of the hens, and he could see something dark ooze from its neck. Ben immediately swept his torch over to the henhouse. The wire in the run was torn open, and he could see one hen outside pecking at the ground. He leaned down to the hen in front of him, then drew back in revulsion. Her head was hanging by what looked like a sliver from her neck, and the dark stuff oozing out was blood. She stopped scratching just as he pulled back.

He went closer to the henhouse, looking around him as he approached. Whatever had happened had been very recent. Whatever or whoever had done it could still be around.

It's probably a fox, he thought.

Getting closer to the ripped wire, he could see that a large hole had been torn in it. The wire had been strong. *Could a fox do that much damage?* he wondered.

He saw feathers scattered around the gap in the wire. He grabbed the hen that was pecking outside and placed her back inside the wire, then pulled it back together. He took the lace off his shoe and used that to tie the wire back up again. It just about held it closed. *That'll have to do until morning*, he thought. Then he searched the area around the house, poker held high again. About twenty yards away, he saw something on the ground. Shining the torch, he could see the body of another hen, but it was only the body, no sign of the head.

Christ, he said to himself, *what the hell has happened here?*

He searched around but found nothing else, so he went back in the house and got a refuse sack and some work gloves. He used these to pick up the dead hens, put them in the bag, then place that deep into the skip. He couldn't let the kids see what had happened. He didn't look forward to telling Deborah either.

Jesus, this isn't the way it's supposed to be, he told himself. *Christ, we're only here a couple of days and this has happened. What or who might have done it?*

He spent the rest of the night sitting up in an armchair near the stove, and his thoughts drifted inexorably into what sort of place he had led his family to. They'd had to move when the judge's car was blown up. They had both agreed on that, but Ben had pushed the move all the way to the west as far from Dublin as possible.

It was all a bit rushed in the end. Ben had lost money in the crash of 2008, and he could have done with a few more years of building the nest egg back up again, but they had just about enough to set up a shop, stock it, and wait it out a few months before the sales started ticking up. Now he was starting to feel under siege. 'What is this weird shit that's happening?' he whispered to himself. Whatever forces were turned against them, the old walls of the house were giving him no answers. He looked at them—solid, silent, mysterious—and wondered what secrets they held.

He threw a couple of briquettes and pieces of wood into the stove to warm the place up, then dozed off on the chair. He woke sharply as soon as he heard Molly walking down the hall.

She looked at him as he rose quickly from the chair.

'Is there something wrong? How come you're in

here?' she asked. 'I got up early to see if there were any eggs.'

'There was a bit of an accident last night,' he replied. 'I heard a noise, and Harry was barking, so I went out to check.'

Molly already had her hand up to her mouth like she knew what was coming.

'Something tore the wire on the henhouse, and I'm sorry to say two of the hens are gone.' He went to hold her, but she stiffened in his grasp.

'There's something wrong with this house,' she whispered and pulled away from him.

'It's not that, Molly. It's probably a fox. Remember Jeremiah said there were foxes here.'

'Jeremiah?' Molly said. 'That freak?'

9

Ben had planned to be at the shop that morning but instead found himself back at the hen farm, where he purchased an even stronger chicken run and two more hens.

'It can happen,' the farm owner said. 'Unusual though for a fox to be able to tear that wire. It was pretty sturdy. Usually the fox would kill them all if it had time and carry off one or two. Something might have startled it.'

'Our dog was barking all right.'

'Maybe that did it. Anyway, hope you have more luck with these two.'

Ben felt a pang of guilt looking at this cheery, red-faced country woman who obviously knew how to look after her stock. Here he was, the oaf from the city who had already had a tragedy.

Molly was in sullen humour as he set up the new run. Deborah had already gone to the shop, as they were waiting on deliveries.

Ben took Jack aside before he left.

'I think Molly needs a bit of looking after today, so

try to do something with her. You can come down to the shop later when we have things set up if you like, maybe even serve a few of our first customers.'

'I was going to go fishing,' Jack said.

'Perfect, take Molly and Harry with you. Make like it's an adventure.'

Jack looked doubtful. 'I'll try, but Molly isn't really into fishing.'

'Yeah, but if you catch something, tell her you can cook it up later.'

Jack still looked doubtful, but he nodded in agreement.

Ben walked to the shop, as Deborah had taken the car. He had time to appreciate the fresh country air and to let his vision stretch over the fields and take in the sweet smell of blooming flowers in the hedgerows. But hovering like a dark shadow over all of this was the nagging doubt that he had led his family into a place they never should have ventured. Was it just a couple of unfortunate incidents that made it look like a bad start? He wondered about Jeremiah and his obsession with his mother and her stuff. What was the 'incident' that Doyle had referred to from his past? Had he been blamed for the death of his father? Did he have some strange obsession with the house? Apparently it had been left as an heirloom to his older brother, who had decided to sell it. Was Jeremiah bitter and vengeful over the sale? And then, thoughts of the gang from Dublin were always looming in the background. Would they follow Deborah this far?

So many questions that Ben had floating around in his mind, but he pushed them aside and put on his best cheery face as he walked into the shop.

'Wow, looking good,' he said, throwing his arms open in appreciation. The shop was indeed looking good, with all shelves now stacked, and the refrigerated unit was now also full. Ben put an arm over Deborah's shoulder, and they surveyed it together.

'I think we've managed to keep the old-style shop feel while blending in our cutting-edge new age products.'

'Even if you say so yourself,' Deborah said. Her expression turned suddenly serious. 'You don't think that was anything malicious with the hens last night, do you?'

Ben felt himself pause for a little too long. 'No, fox probably,' he said, but his voice sounded higher than he would have liked.

Deborah looked at him. 'You're not feeling spooked, are you?'

'No, why would I? Just a couple of unfortunate things, but lots to be positive about.'

Deborah hesitated. 'Do you think this is going to be tougher than we thought?'

'It was always going to be tough at the start. Things will settle down.'

'I hope so. I know we tried to shield the kids from that stuff with the gang in Dublin, but they definitely picked up on some of it. The last thing they need is to be feeling scared again. You don't think this is anything to do with the gang, do you?'

'No, why would they bother us here? How would they know where we've gone?' Ben tried to sound as convincing as he could, but the worry was there in the back of his mind.

'I don't know what's going on,' he said after a while, 'if there's anything at all, but don't worry, the kids will be fine, and we'll ride the tough bits out together like we always have.' Ben rubbed Deborah's cheek, and she leaned her head on his shoulder. He could feel the soothing warmth of her body against him, making him feel grounded.

'The signwriter is due about now,' Ben said, to change the subject. 'He said it would take about an hour to do. You still happy with Garden of Eden as the name?'

'As long as I don't have to be Eve.'

'Why, were you going to tempt me?' Ben held her close again and ran his hand over the curve of her bum.

Deborah turned her face up to his and gave him a long, lingering kiss. 'Later, love, we'd better keep ourselves focused here.'

AFTER LUNCH THE 'GARDEN OF EDEN' sign was up in white writing on a green background. They opened the door of the shop and waited. Deborah had got a couple of aromatisers, and the smell of lavender quickly infused the entire shop.

'That'll banish any lingering smells from Pat Doyle's meat,' she said with finality.

Ben was happy to see people wander in and help themselves to the plates of free flapjacks they had left out. They looked around the shelves, picked up the odd item and generally left after their inspection.

They sold a few packets of brown rice, some tofu, buffalo mozzarella, oat milk, rye bread they had sourced from a bakery in the neighbouring town, and then a big batch of seaweed-based skin products to some French tourists. The till was beginning to look respectable. The card payments were building up.

'Not too bad,' Deborah said during a lull.

'Yeah, you could see it picking up. Tourist trade will be important.'

'The locals might be slow adaptors,' Deborah whispered, and they giggled.

'Maybe, but you'll see, once we have our website up and running, we'll get plenty of online business too.'

Just then Dave Breen strolled in and picked products off the shelves with his usual proprietorial air.

'Not my kind of thing, but nicely laid out,' he said with a slightly patronizing tone. 'I just wonder if you've pitched it right for the local trade.'

'We've had a fair few tourists in,' Ben said.

'Ah yes, but that won't last. They'll be gone by September.'

'Maybe we'll be rich enough to retire by then,' Deborah said.

Breen chuckled at that and put down whatever product he was holding.

'Which brings me neatly to the subject of accounts. Any change of heart there? Do you want Dave in the driving seat? As I told you, I manage the accounts for most businesses in town. Local knowledge. I know how things work around here.'

'Well, we're coming in with our ideas and our way of doing things, might just freshen it all up.'

'Suit yourselves, then. Don't come crying to me if it all goes belly up.'

He took two pieces of free flapjack, stuck them both in his mouth, then looked pointedly at Deborah. 'On second thoughts, you can come crying to me anytime you want,' he said before grabbing another flapjack and ambling out the door.

'What a creep. Ugh,' Deborah said, throwing her eyes to heaven.

'Yeah, figures he rules the roost around here. He's probably had the run of the town for too long.'

THEY WERE EXPECTING Jack and Molly to drop down in the afternoon, but by four o'clock there was no sign. Ben gave Molly a call.

'I'm at the house with Harry,' she said.

'Where's Jack?' Ben asked.

'He's fishing.'

'On his own? That's not safe.' Ben felt his pulse begin to race.

'No, like, we met those local guys again, so he's with them.'

'Does he have his phone?'

'No, he thought it would get wet, so he left it here.'

Ben wasn't at all reassured by what Molly had told him, but at the same time he didn't want to panic. Maybe Jack was okay with that group of guys, but it seemed like very early days for them to be hanging out together. When he had seen them at the shop, they didn't seem too friendly, but maybe it was just them acting like teens.

'Right, you stay home, then, and let me know when he comes back.'

Ben did his best to put the uneasy feelings he had to the side. He didn't want to unduly alarm Deborah on their first day of trading and after the incident with the hens the night before.

'Looks like the kids won't make it down for a while,' he said to Deborah without giving any details.

They dealt with a slow trickle of customers through the afternoon, largely tourists but some local trade too. By five thirty Ben was very concerned there had been no call from Molly to say Jack had arrived back, so he called her again.

'Still no sign?'

'No.'

'Were the guys being okay with him? Did it look like they were having a good time?'

'Yeah, but one of them was weird with me. The bigger guy, Gavin, he was chatting to me, and then he asked me out, but I said no way, so he went off all angry.'

'Right, I think I'll head back now just to go down and check.'

'I'm just going to go back and check on Jack,' he said to Deborah after he finished the call. 'He's still out fishing.'

'I'm sure he's fine, but yeah, I'll manage if there's a last-minute rush,' she said with an ironic smile. 'You take the car. I could do with the walk.'

Ben jumped in the SUV and drove quickly back to the house, his mind racing as he did. *It's probably me just getting worried after all that's happened,* he thought, *but Jack isn't a good swimmer, and he's a bit innocent.*

Pulling up the long drive of the house, he hoped to see Jack's fishing gear resting against the house, but he didn't. Molly came out to the car with Harry behind her.

'He hasn't come back,' she said.

'Okay, bring me down to where they were. Jump in the car.'

They drove the half mile to the beach, parked up and jumped out. Ben scanned the area. The tide was far in up the beach, so only the tops of some rocks were visible.

'They went over in that direction,' Molly said, pointing off to the right.

Ben looked closely at a clump of rocks sitting about a hundred yards out. He thought he saw movement on them and ran down to the shoreline. The sea was choppy, and waves threw themselves at his feet, sucking at the sand as they pulled back out again. Looking closer, he could definitely see movement on those rocks. It was a person, and he was waving frantically.

'Oh, shit,' Ben said. 'That's Jack stuck on those rocks.' Ben ran to the edge of the choppy water and saw that Jack was standing on about two feet of rock sticking out of the water, and the tide looked like it was still coming in. Ben tore his shoes, socks, and trousers off and ran into the sea. He felt the freezing water sting his legs and stomach as he waded in. He was quickly up to his chest, and the cold was making his breath come in short, sharp gasps.

'It's okay, Jack. I'm coming,' he shouted, but his voice felt small and lost in the churning waters. He could see Jack's pale face looking desperately over at him. 'It's okay,' he shouted again, but a high wave sent freezing salt water rushing down his throat, so he choked and had to spit the salty water out.

Shit. This is useless, he said to himself. *What am I going to do when I reach him? He'll be too panicked to swim back in.* Then he remembered that he had a length of rope in the car. He felt he had no choice but to start turning back. 'I'll be back in a minute. Wait. You'll be okay,' he shouted at Jack. All he could see was Jack's face get paler as he stood on the diminishing piece of rock.

He struggled back in shore and ran to the car to get the rope.

'What the hell are you doing, Dad?' he heard Molly shout after him, but he was back with the rope in seconds.

'Here, put this around your waist,' he said to Molly. 'Then pull when I give the signal.' He dived back into the water with the other end of the rope in his hand.

Progress was slow through the heaving water. As he

got nearer, he could see Jack was shivering so badly his whole body shook.

'C'mon, Dad,' Ben heard him shout. 'Hurry.'

Waves slapped into Ben's face, and he could taste salt water at the back of his mouth. Finally he reached the rock and pulled himself up against it. His breath was coming fast with the effort. The water was so cold his fingers were white and numb.

'It's okay, Jack. I'm here now. You're going to be all right.' Even as he said the words, they seemed weak with the force of the grey, churning sea slapping at the small piece of rock that was left.

'Grab hold of this rope. Wrap it around your arm, and when I signal, Molly is going to pull you in. I'll be beside you, but don't let go of the rope whatever you do.'

Jack looked at him, his face rigid with fear. He didn't move. 'I can't,' he said weakly.

'You have to, Jack. It's not that far. Molly will pull you. It's okay. I'll be beside you all the way.'

Jack stayed where he was. Ben went closer. He prised Jack's hands loose from the rock and pulled him into the water, then waved a frantic hand to Molly. Nothing happened for a few seconds; then he felt the rope go taut. He put it in Jack's hands and closed them around it.

'Just kick a little with your feet. You'll be fine.' Even as he said that, Ben looked around at the grey, relentless, churning sea and knew they were not fine, but it was the only chance they had. The rope pulled tighter again, and Jack started moving towards land. Ben swam beside him as best he could and shoved him from behind. He saw Jack's legs kick.

Thank Christ, he thought, *at least he's moving*.

They made about twenty feet before a big wave

surged up behind them, and Jack's mouth filled with water. He let go of the rope and started flailing. The rope started moving away quickly with Molly pulling and no weight on the end of it.

Oh, shit, Ben thought. He had to make a quick choice between Jack and the rope. He chose the rope first and lunged for it, grabbing it before it disappeared. He quickly turned to find Jack struggling to stay afloat. His hands were smacking the water helplessly. Ben grabbed him and pulled him over. He held him and the rope like that for a few seconds until Jack calmed down. Then he wrapped the rope back around Jack's arm and clamped his hands over it.

Jack started moving through the water again. Ben was exhausted, struggling to stay afloat himself, but he pushed on until finally he felt ground beneath his feet. Once he could walk, he put both arms around Jack and heaved him slowly towards shore. Jack was able to find his feet a couple of minutes later. He stood, panting and shivering at the same time.

'Keep going,' Ben said over the noise of the sea. He was afraid Jack would get hypothermia and freeze up altogether. They still had fifty yards to go.

'Come on. My arms are killing me,' Molly shouted from shore.

Finally they were just up to their knees in water, and Jack started to walk without holding the rope. He moved like a zombie, water spilling from his sopping clothes. His face was pale and immobile, staring sightlessly ahead.

He collapsed on the sand when he reached it, breathing heavily and sobbing quietly. 'I thought I was dead,' he said eventually between sobs.

Ben lay beside him and held him. 'You're all right now. You're safe. Let's get you home and dry off.' Ben resisted the urge to convulse with the cold himself. The freezing water had ebbed into every pore in his body, but he could see real fear on Jack's pale face. Out there in the swollen waves, he'd felt like he could really have lost Jack, that he could have slipped under the grey water never to be seen again. He rubbed Jack's shoulder and whispered whatever words of comfort he could find. Finally, he decided they had to get to the warmth of the car.

Ben put an arm around Molly when he stood up. 'Thanks, love. You were an absolute hero there. We couldn't have done it without you.'

He saw some movement up ahead in the sand dunes. A group of young lads, the same group he had seen outside the shop, were standing there pointing at them and laughing. Ben felt a surge of red-hot blood flush through his freezing body. 'You bastards,' he shouted and took off across the sand towards them.

'Dad, come back. Stop,' he heard Molly shout, but he kept going. They scattered and disappeared into the dunes, their laughter trailing behind them. Ben kept going but realized it was useless, and he was standing, sopping, in his underwear. He walked sullenly back to Jack and Molly.

They drove the short journey home in silence with the heating in the car at full blast. Jack was shivering and silent. Deborah was waiting when they pulled into the house.

'Oh, my God, what happened?'

'It's okay. We'll talk later. There was a bit of an accident. Jack needs to get warm and dry fast.'

Ben put the stove on in the kitchen when they got back. Jack sat shivering beside it. Molly was sullen.

'I thought we were getting rid of the creepy stuff in the house,' she said, nodding at the Saint Brigid's cross.

'This is hardly the time to bring something like that up,' Ben replied tersely, but he took it down and leaned it against the stove.

Ben and Deborah sat down with Molly and Jack once their son was changed and had stopped shivering. Deborah had wrapped a warm blanket around Jack and sat him beside the stove in an armchair. Molly related what had happened.

The young guy, Gavin, had chatted her up, and then when he had enough, he headed down to the beach where Jack was fishing on the rocks. Jack took up the story from there. He had been having a bit of banter with one of the others about fishing. Gavin got that young lad to bring Jack further out and keep him distracted while the tide came in. The young lad had then dived into the water and swum off, leaving Jack stranded. Jack thought he could just wait until the tide went back out, but it kept coming in, and he got more and more stranded.

'So basically those young guys could have drowned him,' Molly said succinctly. 'That guy Gavin, the one who chatted me up, is the publican's son. He thinks he's some sort of big shot in town because of that.'

Ben looked over at Deborah. She looked worried. They both knew what Pat Doyle had said about the publican: *you don't want to mess with him.*

'We're going to have to think about this,' Ben said. 'It would be stupid to rush into anything. We've just landed in the town. Nobody is going to be on our side.'

'Jack lost all his fishing gear too. You have to do something,' Molly protested.

'We will when the time is right.'

'Which is, like, basically never,' she said, and stormed off to her room.

'Molly's right,' Deborah said. 'I know we need to be

careful, but at the same time we can't let those kids push Jack and Molly around. That was very dangerous out there today. Jack could have been in serious trouble.'

'I'm going to bed,' Jack said finally.

'I think we all need an early night,' Deborah agreed. She brought Jack up to his bedroom.

Ben stayed up a little to mull things over. This was a delicate situation that could spiral out of control if they made the wrong move. He was very wary of the publican. Maybe he needed to get more involved in town life. He'd heard there was a Chamber of Commerce that was chaired by the publican. That might be a good point of entry. With that in mind, he got up to follow Deborah to bed. He saw wisps of smoke coming from beside the stove and, looking down, he saw the Saint Brigid's cross had got singed on one side.

Oh, shit, he thought, *Jeremiah is very attached to that. First we broke the rocking chair; now we've burned the cross that was so important to his mam.*

He put it back on the wall, with the singed side facing in so it wasn't visible. He checked the hens—the new sturdy run looked reassuringly strong—then went to bed.

10

They opened the shop at nine next morning. Ben spent the first hour unpacking and arranging a delivery of honey from a local producer, whose bees were kept up near a field full of heather. Ben and Deborah had sampled it, and they agreed that it both smelled and tasted of heather.

'I think this is going to be a really good seller,' Ben had said. With that in mind, he spent time arranging it in the shop window as their front of house display. It attracted quite a bit of attention from the get-go. A group of English walking tourists dived in and took about half their stock.

'That's a good start to the morning's takings,' Deborah said.

'Yep, we're going to need some more of that.'

'I think I'll pop back up to Jack and Molly,' Ben said after a while. 'They'll need a bit of TLC after yesterday, and I thought I'd give the two of them something to do—they can make a scarecrow for the veggie field.' He had hardly slept the night before, running over and over what had happened that day.

He kept seeing images of Jack's pale face bobbing just above the grey water. Even as he saw this image, he felt how easily his son could have just slipped away out of reach forever. *It didn't happen. He's okay now,* he told himself over and over again, but even as he did, another voice came in and said, *But what if it did happen? What if it did?* That troubling voice kept him from sleeping, made him pace the hallway of the house, wondering what sort of hell he had got his family into. Had he done the right thing getting them out of Dublin to the 'safety' of the countryside? *Doesn't look so safe now*, he thought. *Jack nearly drowned, and somebody, something is out there with a thirst for blood or vengeance or fear, or what?*

Ben did his best to dismiss all the fears that crowded into his mind. He wanted to try to do something fun with the kids. Putting up a scarecrow should be just that. He dropped into a charity shop on the way home and bought a man's jacket, shirt, and trousers. He got a couple of wooden poles in the hardware and some extra rope. Then he picked up some pastries at the local bakery and headed home.

The kids were initially exhausted and reluctant when he did a general 'rise and shine' call around the house, but warmed up when they saw the goodies and heard about his plan.

'We'll get you some new fishing gear soon,' Ben said to Jack as they devoured the pastries.

'I'm scared of fishing now,' Jack said as he took a chunk from a chocolate croissant.

'That's understandable, but I'll go with you so you won't have to worry.'

Jack looked unsure, but the melting chocolate inside the croissant he was eating soon took up his attention.

'Right,' Ben said. 'Let's get cracking.'

They took the gear from the SUV, and Ben brought it over to the field where they were going to dig.

'So the mission is to construct something that'll keep those pesky birds away. He gestured towards the trees at the far end of the field from which crows could be seen to rise lazily and drop back down again.

'Meantime I'm going to start digging. Jeremiah will be here soon to help.' While he appreciated having someone with experience like Jeremiah to help, he also felt trepidatious about having him around the house after what had happened to the hens. He had wondered if Jeremiah could harbour that much of a grudge about them living there. Ben felt he couldn't answer that, but from what he'd heard in town, and from what he'd seen, Jeremiah wasn't very stable. They needed someone to help them out, but their own safety had to come first.

Ben started on the field by getting a long length of rope. He got four strong lengths of bamboo he'd bought and stuck them in the ground to mark out a big square area, then tied the rope around each of the four bamboos.

There we go, he thought, *first step towards veggie self-sufficiency.* He got some wellies and old trousers from the house, then grabbed a shovel. *Jesus, it's a while since I've used one of these with any real intent, and now I'm about to dig a small field.*

The kids were laughing and messing with the scarecrow clothes, trying them on and chasing each other around the field.

Ben positioned himself in one corner of the roped-off area and jammed the shovel in the ground. It went in, and he released a moist sod of earth, which he then chopped up with the side of the blade. *One sod down*, he thought, *just another thousand to go.*

Harry started barking an hour later to herald the

arrival of Jeremiah. He walked with solidity and purpose across the field, a shovel in one hand, pitchfork in the other.

'I brung the chair back. It's in the car,' he said by way of introduction, then started straight in to releasing massive sods of earth that left Ben felt made his own efforts seem positively infantile. Once he had a good batch of them dug, he returned to attack them with equal ferocity with the pitchfork until they had crumbled into even layers of moist, dark-brown soil.

He certainly knows what he's doing, Ben thought as he watched him, *and he seems to have the strength of ten men.*

The kids were still messing with the scarecrow clothes. Jack had put the pole across his shoulders and the jacket over that. He ran up to Jeremiah and shouted, 'Boo,' at him. Jeremiah laughed and slapped his knee. But as soon as Jack turned away, Ben noticed Jeremiah's expression quickly became dour and impenetrable again. *It's like he's carrying the weight of the world on his shoulders*, Ben thought.

An hour later Jeremiah was still tearing into the soil. Ben was making his own slower, more modest impression, and between the two of them, they had a good bit of the soil turned and raked.

'Right. I'll need to get back to the shop soon,' Ben said. 'Do you fancy a cup of tea before you head off?' He felt obliged to ask even though he had no idea what he'd talk to Jeremiah about if they actually ended up sitting in the kitchen together.

'Not a bit of it. I need to get back to work too,' he replied, to Ben's great relief.

They went back to the house, and Jeremiah carefully unloaded the now-repaired rocking chair from his Jeep. He placed it lovingly back in its previous spot beside the stove and gave it a little nudge so it rocked back and forth a few times. Jack and Molly were watching. Molly looked on disapprovingly.

'Dad?' she said, nodding towards the chair and then up at the cross. Ben shrugged his shoulders and opened his hands in a gesture of helplessness. Jack went over and rubbed the sleek arms of the rocking chair.

'I think it's really cool,' he said. 'You don't see these around anymore.'

Jeremiah patted his head. 'You're a good young man, so you are. We'll have to get out fishing one of the days.'

'I lost my fishing gear,' Jack said.

'He had a bit of an accident,' Ben said.

'It was no accident,' Molly blurted. 'A gang of thugs led by that Gavin guy left him stranded on the rocks. He nearly drowned.'

Jeremiah frowned and took a step back. 'They done that to a lad like you? Bastards, to treat a young boy like that. Bastards they are. Young boys need to be protected.' He was frowning, and his lower lip was trembling. Ben was afraid he was going to start crying. 'They need to be protected, so they do,' he repeated.

'It's okay,' Ben said. 'We're putting it behind us. I'm going to get new gear for Jack.'

Jeremiah had a hand on the back of the chair and was rocking it compulsively, staring glassy-eyed ahead as if he were in a trance.

Molly was twirling her finger round, pointing it at her head to show Jeremiah had a screw loose. Ben wagged a finger at her to indicate she should stop.

Jeremiah looked suddenly up at the Brigid's cross. 'That's on all arse ways,' he said and took it down so he could adjust it. Ben held his breath as he watched Jeremiah turn it over in his hand until he saw the burnt and blackened other side. Jeremiah froze. His mouth dropped open.

'What's after happening?' he asked quietly.

'I had to take it down for a minute and accidentally left it against the stove,' Ben said. He could feel a slight nervous shake in his voice. *This is ridiculous*, he said to himself. *I'm actually nervous telling him about the stupid straw cross.*

'That's bad,' Jeremiah said. 'Bad it is. The only two things of hers in the house and look.' He looked up at Ben. Ben felt nothing but a deep, chasm-like chill in the stare. Jeremiah's eyes were expressionless, void of feeling for that moment. It felt like they had entered a place where anything could happen.

'I'll try to clean it up. I just hope she's not looking down on us. She'd be angry, she would. Angry.' His face grew suddenly red, and he spoke in a sharp, scolding voice. *'You're nothing but trouble. You've brought only ruination on our family. Ruination. You're a pup, a useless bloody pup.'* He stared at the cross, and his breathing was heavy. Ben sneaked a glance at Jack and Molly. They were standing stock-still, hardly daring to breathe. Finally the red colour drained from Jeremiah's face. He held the cross up and looked from Ben to Molly to Jack, then turned and left the house.

Harry snuffled after him and barked as he left.

There was an awkward moment between Ben and the kids in the silence that Jeremiah left in his wake. Ben clapped his hands to break the spell.

'The stuff belonging to his mother is obviously very important to him,' Ben said, almost apologetically. The kids said nothing but stared out the window as they heard Jeremiah's Jeep take off.

'Right, I have to get back to the shop to help your mum,' Ben said eventually, 'and you know what? You guys can come with and give a hand.' He didn't want to leave them on their own after what he had just witnessed.

'Jesus, what a freak,' Molly muttered.

'But what about the scarecrow?' Jack said.

'Don't worry, he won't be going anywhere in a hurry,' Ben said, and they laughed.

11

I told you it was time for action, and you didn't believe me. Now he's gone and burned her cross. She had such devotion to that. I understand you've a soft heart and you're fond of the boy, but think of your mother. It's her and the voices that you want to stop. I am here to help you. I told you from the start that was the mission. He is in your house, wrecking the memory of your mother. You were so close to her. It's like you were one. Until that day. Now is your chance to get that feeling back. She is watching over you and waiting for you to do the right thing. It's not a time for being soft. There's plenty of time for that later, when you finally have freedom from those horrible thoughts. They have tormented you for too long. It's time for you to make them stop.

12

Ben had been shaken by the encounter with Jeremiah and the straw cross. He had seen Jeremiah tumble suddenly into a dark place where he looked capable of doing anything. They were going to have to cut ties with him and fast.

They did a little more work in the field that evening, and the kids finally put the scarecrow together and stuck it in the middle.

'Not bad for some city slickers,' Ben said as they surveyed the work.

'Seeds on Saturday, was that the plan?' Deborah asked.

'Yeah, apparently because it's kind of late in the year, we're going to have a limited range of things to grow, but we should see some lettuces sprouting in the next couple of weeks.'

'And then the plague of rabbits will descend?'

'Like in *Father Ted*,' Jack threw in.

'Yeah, the one where Bishop Brennan has the rabbit phobia,' Molly said. She pretended to find *Father Ted* naff, but somehow she knew a whole lot about each episode.

'Right,' Ben said, 'I think we deserve a good feed after our work, and then we'll turn in early like proper farmers.'

'I think proper farmers get up in the middle of the night to pull sheep out of drains, too,' Deborah said.

'Well, we're only starting. We're not quite there yet.'

'And never getting there, we hope,' Molly said.

They ate a feast of Chinese that Ben had got in town. The kids repaired to their devices. Ben and Deborah watched some news. At some stage they heard Harry barking outside, but they were too comfy to stir.

'I'll check in a few minutes,' Ben said. 'Myself and Molly, who is taking care of the hens, have to throw a bit more food into the hens as well. Isn't that right, Molly?'

Molly was enraptured by her screen and either didn't or chose not to hear Ben.

'Right,' Ben said after the weather forecast had delivered their temperate mixed bag of summer fare, 'let's get moving.'

Molly stayed in situ, her face a pale green study of still life with the screen light. Ben cleared his throat demonstratively beside her, and she looked up.

'Hens?' Ben asked tentatively. 'Those little egg-laying creatures for whose lives we have taken full responsibility.'

Molly slid off her chair and trailed Ben to the front door. Ben grabbed a healthy fistful of corn from a steel container. Molly followed suit. Ben expected to see Harry sniffing around as usual but no sign. *He must have wandered around the back,* Ben thought.

They opened a door in the wire mesh and threw the food in. The hens scrabbled busily for it, pecking furiously around each other's feet.

'Prehistoric,' Ben said while they watched them.

'Hmmm?' Molly enquired.

'Dinosaurs. These guys are direct descendants, apparently. Some of them even have spurs on the back of their legs, and that's an indicator.'

'They wouldn't have survived very long as dinosaurs,' Molly said incredulously.

'Well, I'd say they were a couple of feet bigger, and those spurs were nice and sharp and a few inches longer.'

'Creepy,' Molly said and turned to go back to the house.

Ben walked around the back to look for Harry. He didn't see him. The light was starting to fade, but he could still see fifty or sixty yards quite clearly.

'Harry,' he called. No response. *Strange*, Ben thought. *He's not the type of dog to wander off.* He looked over into the field they had dug and saw nothing but the scarecrow with its sleeves flapping in the breeze.

With a chill rising from the pit of his stomach, he went back into the house and down to where Deborah was scrolling through Facebook.

'I can't see Harry,' Ben tried to whisper, but Jack and Molly looked up simultaneously, suddenly gifted with superfine hearing.

'What?' Jack said. 'Harry?'

Jack and Molly had argued as kids whose dog Harry really was, with Molly saying he was hers because she was older and able to look after him. Jack said he was his because he was the baby of the family and the one who most needed a pet, but they both adored him equally.

'I'm sure it's fine,' Ben said hurriedly. 'He's probably just following a fox scent or something.'

'Harry always stays close to us,' Molly observed,

and Ben found it hard to contradict her. Harry was a real family dog. Over the years he had taken turns sleeping in the kids' beds. First couple of years it was Molly, then he moved on to Jack, as if he was giving them both a turn. Molly hadn't been happy about it at first, but as she hit the pre-teens and started having make-up and things she didn't want disturbed, she had become reconciled. Still, she could be quite possessive of Harry when it came to snuggling up beside him on the couch.

'Here, I'll help look for him,' Deborah said, getting up.

'Me too,' Jack and Molly said simultaneously.

Ben grabbed two torches, gave one to the kids and kept one for himself and Deborah. They scoured the land around the house, calling his name as they went, but there was no sign of him. Ben felt that chill in his stomach rising quickly. He couldn't help flashing back to the scene with Jeremiah and the burnt cross and that cold void that had entered Jeremiah's eyes. He had to force himself to try to sound upbeat for the kids. He could sense their growing panic.

'He's wandered off the property altogether,' Ben said. 'Maybe he got confused and thought we were at the beach or something. You guys wait here and keep an eye out, and we'll jump in the car,' he said to Jack and Molly.

Ben and Deborah scoured the beach, which was grey-blue under the light of the moon. Waves lapped lazily up to shore, and he could hear the cries of seabirds out by the rocks, but there was no Harry.

'What do you think could have happened to him?' Deborah asked. 'He's hardly wandered into town. Do you think he might have chased a fox or a rabbit and then got lost?'

'I haven't a clue,' Ben said. 'I just know we'd better find him. Jack and Molly won't sleep until we do.'

'We should probably report him just in case somebody sees him and hands him in.'

'The nearest Garda station is a couple of miles away on the outskirts of the next town. I don't want to leave the kids too long, so we'll pick them up first.'

They collected a reluctant Jack and Molly, who didn't want to leave the house in case Harry came back, but Ben was feeling uneasy after all that had happened, and no way was he leaving them alone.

Ben pulled up outside the Garda station, which was in what looked like a small, pebble-dash house right on the edge of the next town. The only clue it was a Garda station was the patrol car outside and the small blue Garda sign that hung like a lamp from the wall. The kids waited in the car while he and Deborah went in.

Inside there was a short, wooden counter and some frosted glass with a hatch in the middle. After a couple of eerie seconds of silence, the hatch was opened by a smart-looking young Garda with short, dark hair.

'Well, what can I do for you?' he asked, running his eyes over the two of them.

'Our dog has gone missing,' Deborah said.

The Garda raised his eyebrows with what looked like surprise.

'We've only just moved into the area,' Ben added. 'He doesn't know his way around, and we thought someone might hand him in, so it was best to report it.'

'When did he go missing?'

'A couple of hours ago,' Ben replied.

'Hours?' the Garda said, this time with the eyebrows raised higher to indicate definite surprise. 'I think you'd need to give it a bit longer before you start worrying.'

Ben suddenly felt foolish standing there reporting

something that must have seemed very trivial to the Garda. He leaned in closer. 'There's been some other unusual stuff going on since we arrived.'

The Garda said nothing to this but looked at Ben, waiting for him to explain.

'Our henhouse was ripped open, and some of the hens were killed. Somebody took photos of us while we were in town and stuck one on our door. I got strange texts in the middle of the night. Our son said he heard someone outside the house at night. There's a bunch of young lads, one in particular, have been giving our kids a hard time. They put our son's life in danger when he was fishing.' As Ben went on, he could see the Garda starting to tap his pen on the counter with impatience. 'I know it sounds strange, but it seems like there is somebody stalking us or something.'

'Did you want to press charges in relation to any of the incidents you have recounted?' the Garda asked, looking sharply at Ben.

'Well, no.' Ben felt truly flustered now. 'I just wanted to inform you. We've been worried by the events all coming together like that. We've only just moved to the area, as I said.' Ben felt his words hang in the space between himself and the Garda.

'Would you like to give me a description of the dog?' the Garda asked abruptly.

Ben went on to give a hurried description of Harry. The Garda tapped his pen on the counter again. 'Garda Byrne is my name. We'll inform you if there are any developments,' he said, and closed the glass panel back over.

'He thinks we're nutjobs,' Deborah said as they walked towards the car.

Ben had a sinking feeling as they drove back towards the house. The Garda was most likely just going to throw the report at the very bottom of a big pile and move on to what he considered matters of actual importance. He was thinking that as the lights of their car swept up the drive towards their house, but there, in front of the house, he could see the form of what looked like Harry lying on the ground. He felt an initial surge of elation, but that was quickly followed by the feeling that something was terribly wrong.

'Look, it's Harry,' he heard Jack cry excitedly from the back.

Ben pulled the car over to the side so the back of it was facing where they saw Harry lying down. He wasn't bounding towards the car like he normally would. In fact, he wasn't moving at all.

'Hang on a second,' Ben said as he pulled the car in. He saw Jack and Molly jump out, so he jumped out too and ran to stand between them and Harry.

'I think something is very wrong,' he said desperately. Deborah climbed out and looked over at Harry. The light had almost completely faded now, but his pale shape was still clearly visible lying immobile on the driveway. She looked at Ben, and he could see a grimace of worry twisting her lips.

'I think it's best if you all go in the house while I see if he's okay.'

'Your dad is right,' Deborah said. 'It looks like there might have been an accident.'

The two kids stood where they were.

'But Harry,' Jack said, and Ben could hear tears choking his voice.

'C'mon, it's best if Dad checks first, and then we'll see what we can do.' Deborah put an arm around each of the kids and eased them towards the front door. They kept looking behind, their feet dragging in the gravel.

Once they were inside and out of sight, Ben

approached the prostrate form slowly. He felt a tingling on the back of his neck like a cold breath of air. First he touched the dog, and he felt warm but unmoving.

'Harry,' he whispered. 'Are you okay? C'mon, boy, you can get up.' He pushed at him to try to get him to move, but the dog stayed immobile and unresponsive. 'Oh, shit,' Ben said out loud, 'what the hell has happened to you?'

Desperately he put his arms under Harry to try to lift him, and that was when he felt a mass of something wet and sticky sliding across his fingers. 'Jesus Christ,' he said and lurched backwards. A metallic smell of blood wafted up to fill his nostrils, and he dry retched. *He's dead. He's fucking dead. His stomach has been cut open. I have to do something*, he thought. *Deborah will only be able to hold the kids inside for so long.*

His whole body shook as he ran towards the car. There was a pair of work gloves there. He had to get them and fast. He had to move Harry no matter what. He put his hands under him again, trying not to feel the guts and innards that were sliding under his grip. He dry-retched and staggered back, staring in disbelief at the body on the ground, but he had no choice. He bent down again and slid his hands underneath. This time he lifted, trying to ignore the stench that was blasting up his nostrils. The dog came with him in his arms, but when he looked down, he saw a part or parts of him had been left behind. The four legs had been neatly severed from the body and lay there exactly as the dog had been laid out.

Ben stared in disbelief at the ground; then he retched fully to the side and retched again. 'Oh, shit,' he said. 'Oh, shit. What have they done to you? What have they done?'

He stumbled with the body of Harry but managed to

carry him to a low stone wall, then placed the body carefully on the other side so at least he would be out of sight. He went back then and collected each of the legs and brought them over to place them carefully on the body.

He heard the front door open and the sound of footsteps hurrying across the gravel. Molly and Jack appeared. Luckily the light had almost completely faded now, so the bloody mess that had been under Harry was barely visible.

Ben took off his gloves and went to hold both the kids.

'I'm sorry, guys. He was in some sort of terrible accident. It's best you don't see him.'

'But, Dad, we have to see him. It's Harry. What happened?' Molly said and started crying hysterically. He could feel her shaking against him, and he held her close. No matter what, he couldn't let her go. Jack just stood there staring at the ground where Harry had been. There was a dark stain visible in the moonlight, and the stench of death lingered in the air.

That was no accident, Ben thought.

13

'We need to tell the Gardai,' Deborah had said when the kids had finally gone sobbing back into the house and Ben had a chance to tell her the state that Harry had been in.

'I know, I know,' Ben had said, 'but I don't want to go rushing over and spook the kids even more.'

Deborah had drummed her fingers on the side of the car as she listened to him. 'Okay, we'd better go back in. The kids are in absolute bits.'

'First we need to bury him. We'll wait until morning. For the moment I'm going to put him in one of those canvas sacks we got the hen feed in and leave him in the shed so no animals get at him. I'll take a photo to show to the Gardai.'

He went out, climbed the low wall, pulled his phone out and took a quick shot, hardly daring to look at the image; then he slid the body into the sack. The feeling of retching had left him. Now he just felt hollow inside. *Who could do such a horrible thing to us? What sort of twisted mind is targeting us?* Those thoughts brought him straight back to the look in Jeremiah's eyes as he looked at the burnt cross. They were cold, empty, devoid of any feeling.

Neither of them slept that night. Every time Ben turned restlessly in the bed, he saw Deborah either sitting up and reading or checking her phone or turning restlessly herself. In the morning they both had bags under their eyes, and Ben had to drag himself down to the kitchen.

The kids wouldn't touch any food. They both stared vacantly into the middle distance.

'We're going to bury Harry in the corner of the vegetable field,' Ben said.

Neither responded. Deborah arrived and tried to lighten the mood. 'At least he'll have a nice resting place.'

'Harry was only six years old,' Molly said bitterly. 'He had so long to live, and we were going to have this great adventure with him down here, and now he's gone.'

Neither Ben nor Deborah could think of any consoling words.

Wearily, Ben got a shovel and the bag with Harry from the shed. He dug a deep hole in the corner of the field and placed him carefully inside before throwing enough soil over so he was completely covered. He went back to the house where Deborah and the kids were sitting in silence.

'Do you want to come down and we'll say some words?' he asked.

Deborah rose first, and the kids dragged themselves reluctantly from the kitchen. They shuffled down to the corner of the field and stood around the hole Ben had made. Tears streaked both their faces, and Ben could see they wouldn't be able to say anything.

'We'd like to say thanks to Harry,' Ben began, 'for

being our friend and keeping us company all these years. He was a real friend to all of us.' Ben could hear both Molly and Jack sobbing. He wasn't sure how to continue. 'We just hope he's happy wherever he is.'

'And that we find out what happened to him,' Molly said between sobs.

Ben threw some more soil on top. He put a wooden stick in the ground to mark the spot. 'We'll get something carved and put in a proper marking later,' he said.

Molly and Jack stood there staring at the pile of earth. Their shoulders heaved with sobs. Deborah put an arm around each and coaxed them gently back to the house.

They didn't want to leave the kids alone, so they brought them down to the shop, where they sullenly fingered products on shelves, and it was only when customers came in that they were able to shift their mood.

Ben noticed Molly perk up when a young woman called Sophie popped in. Ben had met her already. She worked in a bookshop up the road, and her mum was the woman who had sold them the ice creams. Sophie was in her early twenties and had her hair dyed orange and cut in a bob with a high fringe. To Ben she was the most glamorous creature he'd seen yet in town. It looked to him like Molly might concur because she ambled over to the till to help serve her.

'Not sure what I want,' Sophie said. 'I think I just like being here with all the healthy, natural smells. Right, I'll pick up a bit of fruit and some of this kick-ass yoghurt and make myself a breakfast bowl.' She gathered her produce, humming to herself as she did.

'So, how are you settling into this crazy little town of ours?' Sophie asked Molly.

'Not so good. Our dog was killed yesterday.'

'Your what? Your dog? Killed? Jesus, that's awful.' She put a hand out to rub Molly on the shoulder. 'How? What happened?'

'Well, we're not sure yet.' Molly's face was turning red. Ben was afraid she was going to start crying. Sophie kept rubbing her shoulder.

'But how? Was it some sort of accident?' She drew back then, seeing that Molly was only getting more upset. 'We have dogs, and I know exactly how much they mean in a family. I'm really sorry to hear that.'

'Thanks,' Molly said diffidently.

'No need for thanks. I just know how much they mean. If I can help in any way, let me know.'

Ben took for the goods and Sophie left.

'She's very nice,' Deborah said. 'Her mum is the one who sold us the ice creams on day one. First nice family we've met in town.'

'It won't be the last either,' Ben said. 'Don't worry, things will pick up for us.'

That statement was greeted by a stony silence. Ben could find nothing else to say. He felt so bad about Harry and at the same time worried. Very worried. Someone had done that to Harry. Why? What were they trying to achieve? It looked like they were sending a message, telling them to go before something worse happened, but why did they want them out of the house, out of the town even? Had they done something since they arrived, or was it because of something that had happened before they came? Could it be Jeremiah? The gang from Dublin? They would kill a dog no problem, and do much worse, but he didn't want to think about that.

That evening he and Deborah stood in front of Garda Byrne from the previous night.

'So you arrived home to find your dog dead,' he said slowly.

'That's correct.' Ben had decided to be as succinct as possible.

'Were there any visible injuries on the dog?' The Garda spoke quickly like he was on the verge of losing patience.

He obviously doesn't think a dead dog is worth reporting, and we are just wasting his time, Ben thought.

Ben took his phone out and showed the picture he had taken. 'He seemed to have been mutilated. His legs were cut off.'

That caused the Garda to pull his head back and scrunch his features in surprise.

'Where did you find him?'

'Right outside our house,' Deborah said, 'on the driveway, just lying there. Ben got the kids into the house so they wouldn't see him.'

'Was the dog left free to roam during the day?' the Garda asked.

'Of course,' Ben said. 'But he was always just outside our house.'

'As far as you are aware,' the Garda said.

'Our dog was no trouble to anyone.'

'As far as you are aware,' the Garda repeated. 'A city dog coming into a rural community could worry farmers, and if he was seen as a threat to sheep or livestock, I'm afraid some farmers have very little patience.'

'But to kill and mutilate a dog?' Deborah asked.

'As I say, some farmers have been seen to take things too far in the past. I'm not in any way condoning or justifying it, and we will look into it, but sometimes they can just close ranks, and that makes it difficult for us.'

'Listen,' Ben said, 'this may sound far-fetched, but the son of the family we bought the house off, Jeremiah, has been acting very strange since we moved in. He's very possessive of his mother's things, and he seems like he just doesn't want us there. It could have been him who killed the hens, and then when that didn't work, he decided to kill the dog.'

The Garda looked at him and tapped his pen on the counter again. 'Are you making an accusation against this individual?'

'No, not an accusation. It just seems like he really doesn't want us there, and to be honest, he doesn't seem the most stable. Someone mentioned that there had been an incident in the past that has left him in some way disturbed.'

'We deal with facts here, not speculation. As new people in this area, I would advise caution before jumping to any conclusions. We will follow all lines of enquiry into the death of your dog and will let you know in due course should we find anything of concrete value.'

'He doesn't sound like he's going to do very much,' Deborah said as they walked to the car. 'He did look shocked at the mutilation, but then he kind of rowed back all right. I shouldn't have gone into that rant about Jeremiah, but who else could it be?'

Later that evening, over a cup of tea, when the kids had finally gone shakily off to bed, Deborah turned to him.

'Do you think this has all been a mistake? Do you think we have bitten off more than we can chew and we should just cut our losses?'

Ben was taken aback by the frankness of Deborah's statement, but those thoughts had certainly gone through his own mind already, so he had an answer of sorts.

'No, we've made a commitment here, and we deliberately left our past life behind. This needs to work, and we are resourceful people who have been very successful in what we did before. We can and will get through whatever is going on here.'

'I don't know, Ben. Whoever killed Harry is obviously disturbed. I know we can't go back to Dublin, but maybe we just picked the wrong spot here.'

'But, Jesus, Deborah, we bought the house; we've set up the shop. We have to make this work. There's no way back.'

'There's always a way back. We have to put the kids first.'

'We'll find whoever did this to Harry, and we'll sort this out. You have my word.'

Ben felt like a vigilante on patrol that night. He spent ages walking around the perimeter of their land, looking for anything suspicious. He watched all headlights that pierced the darkness and waited until they had slid past their house. He checked and rechecked the henhouse, made sure every window in the house was closed: the kids had a habit of opening windows to let cooling air in at night. He didn't want to spook them completely by saying there was no way they could do that, but at the same time, just for tonight he wanted to make sure every window was closed.

That night, as he lay sleepless, he resolved to do something that would bring him into the community so he could figure out what the dynamic in the town was, and he could get close enough to find out what had happened that would cause someone or some people to attack their family.

14

Ben had seen a notice about a Chamber of Commerce the night of the pub quiz. It was taking place a few days after the quiz. He had initially been wary of joining when he was such a new arrival, but he felt the events of the last few days had left him with no choice.

It was taking place in the upstairs room of the pub where the quiz had been held. Ben held his breath, then climbed the stairs at the back of the pub and entered the big meeting room. Immediately inside the door was Dave Breen sitting beside a big ledger with names listed on it.

'Ah, Ben,' he said, 'you decided to drop by.'

'Yeah, well, I guess I need to know how things run around here, and maybe I can make a positive contribution with my own skill set.'

'Maybe you can,' Breen said ambivalently. 'The city slicker, huh?' he added with a sneer. 'Probably best to keep your powder dry for tonight though, get a little insight into how we do things local.'

Just then the publican dashed up the stairs and saw

Ben standing there. He nodded at him but didn't say anything, then moved to sit at the top of a row of three small tables that had been lined up together. A group of locals were sitting on either side of these tables. Pat Doyle, the butcher, was the only one Ben recognized, so Ben squeezed awkwardly in beside him. The publican looked down the table at him, and he suddenly felt very conspicuous packed in with the locals.

'I see we have fresh blood, as it were, this evening,' the publican said.

Ben waved at the assembled cast. 'Ben Higgins. Myself and my wife, Deborah, have opened the Garden Of Eden health food shop.'

'I'd say everyone knows who you are,' the publican said abruptly. 'We take pride in knowing what goes on in our little town.'

'I was hoping I could contribute in my own way,' Ben said. 'I worked in finance before.'

The publican didn't respond to that. Breen slid in beside him at the top of the table.

'The note-taker has arrived,' Breen said. 'Your every word will be taken down and may be held in evidence against you.'

'I wanted to bring up the issue of vandalism,' Pat Doyle said. 'This town is going to hell with the graffiti being sprayed all over the place.'

'Duly noted,' Breen said.

'Noted, yes, but what's going to be done about it? I drive a taxi, as you all know, and it's a bloody embarrassment at times when you have to drive visitors around.'

'It's some families can't control their young ones is what it is,' the publican said.

Ben couldn't help thinking about the publican's own son, Gavin, who had left Jack stranded and then taunted them. He seemed like a likely culprit for graffiti writing, but nobody said anything.

'There's a lot of pissed people wandering around too, and I don't just mean late at night,' Pat Doyle added.

The publican looked down at him, his face red and humourless. 'I hope that's not any reference to publicans and the way they do their business.'

'Who said anything about pubs?' Doyle asked defensively. 'I just said there are people pissed, and it doesn't look good.'

'Were you ever pissed yourself, Pat?' Breen asked, and everyone except the publican sniggered.

'Ah, piss off and go to hell, the lot of ye,' Doyle said angrily. 'Youse all know what I mean.'

'Listen,' Ben said, and he was surprised to hear his own voice rising over the din, 'maybe we should talk about what way we can make a positive impact rather than focusing on the negatives. Have people been encouraged to put up window boxes and paint their shopfronts, for example?'

A stony silence hung over the room, and Ben could almost feel his words echo off the walls.

'With respect, Ben, we have our way of running the meetings, and we like to hear the views of our members first,' Breen said.

'You probably think you can come in and run the show with your sophisticated ways,' Doyle said, 'but we have our country ways, and you might need to start learning them fast.'

Ben felt ganged up on, so he said nothing for the rest of the meeting and listened to them wrangle and gripe about how badly run the town was. At the end, as everyone was leaving, Ben still felt he hadn't gleaned any information, so he went over to Breen.

'Listen, I'm going for a pint straight after, if you'd like to join me.'

'Sure, why not,' Breen said. 'Maybe you can confer some of that city wisdom on me.'

They got two stools in an alcove slightly away from the mill at the bar.

'Tread softly because you tread on my dreams,' Breen said as they settled in. 'Yeats, wasn't it? Talking about some woman he was obsessed with. That was a love poem, but sure it could apply to the chamber meetings, as you just found out.'

'I thought it would take a more positive direction. Surely it's not run like that all the time.'

'There's some people very stuck in their ways. Tread softly, as I said.'

'Our dog was killed this week,' Ben said after a pause.

Breen grimaced and turned his head so it faced Ben at an angle. 'That's tough. I heard something happened all right.'

'What did you hear?' Ben asked.

'Just that something nasty had happened to the dog.'

'We don't know what happened, but he was in a bad state. The kids are absolutely gutted.'

'They would be. They get very attached, don't they?' Breen said, looking around the bar. His face showed no trace of emotion. It was something Ben had noticed about him. He always seemed at one remove from whatever he was saying.

Ben decided to probe and see if Breen had heard anything. 'Who would do a thing like that?' he asked.

'You wouldn't know. People can just get an idea in their heads. Someone might have seen him as a threat.'

'What? Our little springer spaniel and all the big sheepdogs people keep around here?'

'Those dogs know the country ways is what some people might think, rightly or wrongly.'

'What sort of twisted mind would think it's okay to kill a pet dog like that? And our hens were got at during the week too, and a couple of them were killed.'

'And they haven't ruled out foul play?' Breen slapped Ben hard on the shoulder at the joke and laughed until tears formed in his eyes. People at the bar turned to look at the two of them. Ben suddenly felt self-conscious, so he changed the subject.

'Someone said that bad things had happened to Jeremiah in the past, and it might relate to our house.'

'Bad things all right,' Breen agreed.

'Like what?'

Breen looked at Ben, his face turning serious again. 'His dad was killed in a car crash when he was coming back from giving Jeremiah a lift to football practice. The ma blamed Jeremiah even though it was nothing to do with him. Some drunk who was still steamed from the night before did it, but Jeremiah sort of took all the blame on himself and saw himself as the protector of the ma from that day on.'

'He's been very funny about her stuff in our house. He seems to see us as intruders or something.'

'You wouldn't know what's going on in people's minds some of the time. That's for sure.' Here he made prolonged eye contact with Ben as if to emphasize the point.

'But do you think he could do something like kill our family dog?'

Breen sat back to put some distance between himself and Ben. 'Oh, God, I wouldn't go rushing to conclusions of any description. Not at all.' He smiled then and leaned back in closer. 'Now it's time for me to ask the questions. What's it like being married to a celeb like Deborah?'

'She's not really a celeb, just a face that a few people know.' Ben had been used to people getting a bit excited just because Deborah was a known face from the TV. He had expected a bit of it here as well, so he wasn't put off by Breen's question. His tack was always just to play it down as much as possible, make it seem so mundane that their fascination dwindled away.

'More than a few, I'd say. Sure, half the town here was talking about her before you came. She did some very interesting cases indeed. That one of the two fellas who were having an affair with the same woman and didn't one decide to kill the other. Knocked him stone dead with a lump hammer, then cut him up and buried him in the septic tank. A small country town. You wouldn't think something like that would happen there.'

Ben could see that Breen was on a roll. He wanted to get into the gory details and see if Ben had any inside information. Ben had met people like that before. They wanted to go down the dark little rabbit hole and revel in the evil that resides in other people's souls.

'I suppose human nature is full of surprises,' Ben said, 'not all of them good. Now, if you'll excuse me, I'd better get going.'

As Ben made his way home, he reflected on how he hadn't got very far in his quest for information. Maybe it was just small-town politics, but he felt very much on the outside looking in. It almost felt like there was some secret that was being kept from him. Deborah had asked if their whole enterprise in moving here was a big mistake. He needed to prove it wasn't, that they could make a go of this new life they had chosen, but he needed to keep his family safe at the same time.

15

'We don't want him coming here anymore, do we?' Deborah said early next morning as they lay in bed.

'I agree. I was thinking the same thing myself, but we need to go about it carefully,' Ben answered. 'If we just go and ban him from the property, then that may have all sorts of repercussions. If it wasn't him, then it might well turn him against us, and we need all the allies we can get.'

'You'd call Jeremiah an ally?'

'No, not as such, but for now we can't be sure he is an enemy.'

'Jesus, listen to us talking about allies and enemies. You'd swear we were in the middle of a war. This is getting ridiculous, Ben.'

Ben looked up at the ceiling, a blank canvas with no answers. 'I'm doing what I can without upsetting the whole apple cart,' he said finally.

'That meeting didn't seem to produce much last night.'

'No, but it's a start. We need to get people on our side; then we can figure out what's going on.'

'But if it isn't Jeremiah, then who is it? He's the one with all the reasons and what looks like a massive grudge that we are here in his house crapping all over the memory of his mother.'

'I'll only have Jeremiah over to work when I'm here. As I say, I don't want to go completely back on the deal we made. He's getting a small allowance to help us out as we start up. We can put security lights around the house, and although I would be very reluctant to go that far, we might think about putting in CCTV.'

'So we'll be living in Fort Knox in the country.'

'I know it's not what we wanted, but we've invested so much in this we need to stick it out. It will get better.' Ben felt he was convincing himself as much as Deborah. It seemed like the walls of the house were closing in around them. He had to find a way out, and he had to stop things before they got any worse.

They had a chat with the kids and explained that they would be texting them every now and then to make sure they were okay and that they were to come down to the shop later in the morning.

'That sounds like a real blast,' Molly had said in response. 'The freedom of the countryside and all that crap we were talking about before we came.'

'It's just for the moment,' Ben said. *I'm starting to say that a lot*, he thought.

'We could really do with some help in the shop anyway,' Deborah said.

THEIR MORNING in the shop was brightened by the arrival of Sophie and her mum, Maureen, who had served them ice cream the first evening.

'Sophie told me I absolutely had to come down. She's always raving about this place,' Maureen had said. 'It's a far cry from the ice creams that I'm selling up above.'

'We've got our own ice-cream equivalents,' Deborah said with a laugh. 'This organic chocolate is produced in the south-west, and it's to die for. The banana bread there is from a local baker, sugar-free but lots of local honey to sweeten it.'

'I'll take some banana bread to go with my morning coffee. Mmmmm, the smells in here,' she said, picking up some lavender soap. 'You feel like you could eat everything. How are you settling in?'

Ben and Deborah exchanged glances.

'We're doing okay,' Deborah said. 'We had a couple of setbacks, but we're trying to put them behind us.'

'I heard about your dog. That was really awful,' Maureen said, shaking her head.

Just then Molly and Jack arrived. Sophie turned to greet them with a smile. 'Well, look who it is.'

Molly and Jack shuffled self-consciously in front of her. 'Are you coming down to help out?' Sophie asked.

'Kind of,' Jack said.

'I'm sure you're just being modest. Listen, if you're not doing anything at the weekend, I have a friend who has a pet farm with all sorts of animals, big Vietnamese pigs, goats, rabbits, horses. I usually help out on a Saturday, if you want to come with me.'

The kids looked up at Ben and Deborah, who both nodded enthusiastically. 'That'd be lovely, Sophie. Thank you so much,' Deborah said.

'Okay, here's my number, so just give me a shout

Friday, and we'll arrange it.' She scribbled her number on a piece of paper and left it on the counter.

Ben arranged for a company that does security lights to call over later in the afternoon. They checked the place but said it would be a few days before they could do the actual installation. He didn't like the sound of waiting for 'a few days', but at the same time he didn't want to seem too panicky about it with Deborah. He felt there was an onus on him to try to dial things down as much as possible.

He got a wooden plaque inscribed for Harry with the words 'Harry, our beloved dog, much loved, much missed'.

They replaced the wooden stick that was marking his plot with the plaque. Jack and Molly collected some wildflowers, tied them together in a bunch and rested them against the plaque. Ben couldn't help but feel responsible for the scene. This was something his kids should never have experienced. He felt he had failed them as a father.

'Did we find out what happened to Harry yet?' Molly asked.

'That's going to take time. Hopefully the Gardai will come up with something.'

'So it wasn't an accident,' Molly said.

'Well, we're not completely sure what happened yet, so we don't know.'

'Then why are you waiting for the Gardai to come up with something? Surely we can find out ourselves,' Molly said.

'Yes, you're right, but we don't want to rush into anything.'

'If I were a superhero, I'd catch them, and then they'd be sorry. I'd treat them the way they treated Harry,' Jack said quietly.

Ben instinctively wanted to say *that wouldn't solve anything*, but when he saw how upset Jack looked, he decided to say nothing.

Ben got some diced lamb in town and made a hearty stew with it. He was trying to lift their spirits. It had been a family favourite before, but the mood was flat during dinner.

'That sounds like fun, going to the pet farm with Sophie,' he ventured at one stage, and that did get an enthusiastic 'yeah' from both kids, but the conversation died on its feet straight after. They sat down together and watched some repeats of *The Office* on Comedy Gold. The kids flicked nonchalantly at their own screens as they watched. At one stage Molly went out to check on the hens, and Ben watched her from the window. He didn't want to march out after her and make it look like he was being overbearingly protective, but at the same time he wanted to make sure she was safe.

They went to bed sometime after twelve. Ben felt absolutely shattered and, for once, fell into a deep, unwavering sleep.

The first intimation that something was wrong was a knock on their bedroom door. Ben experienced it as part of a dream where someone was drumming on the roof of his car, and he couldn't get the door open. Slowly the drumming turned into a knocking, and as he pushed the last threads of dream aside, he realized it was their bedroom door, and it was Jack who was standing inside their room and knocking to wake them.

'Mom, Dad, I hear something strange outside. Listen.'

Ben could feel Deborah stir awake with a sleepy 'mmmm' sound beside him. She raised her head to look at Jack. Molly came like a ghost in the dark to stand beside Jack. Ben listened carefully. He could hear something strange all right, but he couldn't figure out what it was.

'It's Harry,' Jack said. 'Listen.'

'Don't be silly,' Ben said, relieved that it was just the kids getting scared after all, but then he stopped and listened carefully. He could hear what sounded like a bark, then another bark, then a whimper. Both he and Deborah bolted out of bed and hurried down the hall. The noise was coming from outside. Ben grabbed the poker from beside the stove. He gestured for Deborah and the kids to stay inside as he carefully unlocked and opened the front door. He stepped into the night. There was a slight wind that rustled the trees and bushes.

He peered out into the gloom, not wanting to turn on the torch in his phone yet in case he gave himself away. This time, if there was someone, he wanted to catch them and solve this mystery once and for all.

There it was again, a barking, Harry's barking. It couldn't be, yet there was no mistaking the sound. He knew that bark so well. *What the hell is going on?* He shook himself as if to check whether he was still dreaming. Then the barking stopped, and there was whimpering, then a howl, followed by a long, high-pitched whimper and then silence. Ben braced himself and stepped forward, the poker raised. His eyes were getting accustomed to the dark now. He could see clear outlines of his car, the henhouse, the bushes around their house.

The noise stopped. He stood stock-still. There was a fluttering from the henhouse that came and went. Ben walked slowly in the direction he thought the noise had come from. He couldn't be sure, but it had sounded like it came from some bushes behind the henhouse. He heard a sudden thumping, shuffling sound somewhere over to his right and froze until he heard the deep breathing of what sounded like a cow. He kept looking in that direction, but the deep breathing stopped again. He could just see the outline shapes of some cows just the other side of the wall.

He rounded the henhouse and could feel the light wind stir the hairs that were rigid on his neck and scalp. His skin felt cold, and he gripped the poker so tight his fingers hurt. Suddenly he heard the barking start up again. It was definitely closer now, clearly audible, the same sounds—barking, followed by short whimpers, followed by a long whimper. Ben peered at the bush the noise was coming from. He could see the branches and leaves sway in the gentle wind, but nothing else. Still, he raised the poker so it was over his head, ready to come crashing down on anyone who moved.

'Who's there?' he said, and the sound of his own voice frightened him. He heard the hens flutter and cluck again. Nothing moved in the bush. He crept closer. The barking started up again. Now it felt like he was right beside Harry, like he could almost touch him.

'Come out,' he said, louder this time. Nothing stirred.

'Ben,' he heard Deborah call from behind him, 'be careful.'

He stepped forward so he was right up against the bush, half-expecting someone to leap out and grab him. The poker would be useless now, as he had no way to swing it, so he put it back against his side. His heart was banging in his chest as he pushed the branches of the bush aside so he could see clearly, but there was nothing, just a view out the other side to the gloom of the fields beyond. Ben reached for his phone and flipped on the torch. The light was sudden and intense as it flashed through the soupy darkness.

He turned the beam of the torch around the bush.

Nothing. He waited and could hear only the occasional clucking from the hens behind him as they settled back down again.

Then he heard the familiar bark and the whimpers. He flashed the torch towards where he thought it came from. There below, hidden in the bushes, he saw something dark and rectangular. Reaching down cautiously, shining his torch closely at it, he saw a small speaker. Picking it up, he could see no wires. *A Bluetooth speaker*, he thought. *Jesus, what type of sick joke is this? Somebody must be controlling this, and whoever it is can't be too far away.* He felt a surge of rage flash through him. What sort of sick bastard would kill a dog and then taunt the family? He gripped the poker, determined that whoever it was would pay dearly for this. He flashed the torch from his phone around the field but saw nothing. The cows over to his right started suddenly and moved heavily away.

Ben held the speaker in his hand and waited, but the barking didn't start up again. *Whoever it is has seen me, and they've stopped.*

'Hello,' he called into the darkness, but he heard nothing. There was a low stone wall on the other side of the bush, so he crept towards it and sprang up suddenly to shine his torch on the other side. Nothing. But then he saw what looked like a dark figure at the end of the field. His phone torch wasn't strong enough to be sure, so he turned the torch off and listened. There, the sound of a car engine being turned on somewhere in the distance. He darted out and ran down his driveway to look up the road in the direction of the car but too late. There was only the faint sight of headlights brushing the trees far down the road.

'What was it?' Deborah and the kids had come to

meet him as he walked back up the drive. He showed them the Bluetooth speaker.

'So it was whoever killed Harry,' Molly said slowly.

Ben said nothing.

'I wish I could have got them,' Molly said.

'Yeah,' Jack agreed, but his voice trembled as he said it.

'THAT WAS JUST PURE MALICIOUS,' Deborah said as they lay in bed an hour later. 'Are we dealing with a sadist?'

'I don't know is the answer. I am trying to compute what type of person would do a thing like that. They know the effect it would have on the kids.'

'That's what I'm saying, a sadist. Who'd be nasty enough to do something like that? The gang from Dublin? Yeah, they'd be nasty enough, but would they bother? That's a question I ask myself too much, Ben. They scared the shit out of me. I'm still living on the edge of my nerves and now this. We need to sort this shit out and fast.'

'I'm going back to the Gardai with this. They have to do something to help. As well, I was thinking we can try to flush whoever it is out. Surely someone capable of doing this has been noticed in the area. If we put up posters saying we are looking for information into the 'accident' our dog had, then maybe somebody who knows something will come forward.'

'And what about our kids in the meantime? How do we know they're safe?'

'We'll have to keep them close by until this is over.'

'That's not what we came here for, Ben. We came to give them a better life, more freedom, to be safe, not to be shackled to us.'

'They'll get all of that. This will work. We've invested so much in this. We need to make it work. This is probably just some madman who has got a very strange notion into their heads, and somehow we are the focus of that notion. Let's not forget Jeremiah is our number one suspect. We just need to be vigilant. We'll find out who this is, and our troubles will be over.'

Later that night, as dawn was creeping in, Ben saw his phone vibrate. Checking it, he saw another message with caller ID blocked. It said: 'Barking up the wrong tree. Ha ha.'

He took the speaker to the Gardai later that afternoon. Garda Byrne twirled it in his hand.

'Malicious all right to do something like that, but do you think it's any more than just some sort of prank?'

'Are you joking? If someone is prepared to record the death of a dog and play it back, is that just some prank? I've been getting texts at night as well, caller ID blocked, teasing kinds of texts but nasty. Look.'

He showed the Garda the texts he'd got.

The Garda nodded. 'We can try to trace where this speaker was purchased and see if that leads us anywhere. Meantime all I can say is be careful and try not to react. Whoever this is might just be goading you, trying to get you to do something you shouldn't. If anything else happens, we are your first port of call.'

Ben felt dissatisfied afterwards, but at least the Garda seemed to be taking him seriously. If they could get any more evidence, then maybe a proper case could be put together.

16

That evening they printed off a series of A4 posters with a photo of Harry that said simply 'Our dog was unfortunately killed in an accident this week. If you have any information on what happened, we would be most grateful and are offering a small reward'.

They taped them to lamp posts around the town.

'That will get some reaction, anyway,' Deborah said. 'Somebody must know something, or at least it will get people talking.'

Ben decided to sleep on a mattress in the front room. He wanted to be first in line if anything happened, but nothing did. They received no information about Harry the next day but got a few expressions of sympathy in the shop. The Gardai phoned Ben later in the day and told him the speaker that was used had been on special offer in one of the chain supermarkets over the last couple of weeks. A large number of them had been sold, and it would be impossible to narrow it down to one individual. All Ben could say was thanks for the help, but they were left feeling very much on their own again.

That night the publican, Mossy Hennigan, was celebrating his sixtieth birthday, and he had put out an open invitation to everyone in town.

'It's a good idea if we go,' Ben had said to Deborah. 'Everyone in town will be there, and they'll be drinking. Loose tongues and all that.'

'You're right,' she agreed. 'We need to get up close and personal with some of the locals if we're going to find out what's going on. The kids will have to come though. No way I'm leaving them alone.'

'Of course,' Ben said, and he immediately felt guilty that he hadn't been the first to say it. He felt he was getting too caught up in the whole thing and forgetting what he was here for in the first place: to keep his family safe and give them a better life.

Molly whined, but she allowed herself to be dragged along as long as it was for 'just an hour'.

'We'll go early and leave early,' Ben promised.

They arrived just as Hennigan was giving a speech. Jack and Molly got some minerals and sat on their own in a quiet spot. Looking around the bar, Ben figured a lot of the crowd had got a head start, judging by their bleary-eyed expressions.

They found some seats at a small table and listened to Hennigan.

'… and this town has meant so much to me, welcoming me in as a stranger all those years ago. You didn't know what you were dealing with.'

'We do now,' someone shouted up.

'But sure you're in control of the beer taps. Most important man in town,' someone else shouted to raucous laughter.

'Anyway, I hope you'll lower a few in my honour,' the publican said, 'and move fast 'cos the free bar is on a timer.'

There was a rush to the bar the second the speech was over. Ben could see a lot of faces he recognized from around. One of them was the son, Gavin, who was helping out behind the bar.

Ben went up when the mill had calmed a little. He ended up standing right in front of Gavin, but the young lad moved off quickly. He eventually got the attention of the regular barman. By the time he got back with the drinks, a slightly bleary-eyed Dave Breen was sitting on his stool, talking to Deborah. He got awkwardly up when Ben arrived.

'I was just talking to your better half about the world of crime. I suppose it's that question we all ask ourselves, like, what makes a killer? What turns someone into that madman who'll kill someone and drive up the mountains to get rid of the body? Then they resume normal life as if nothing ever happened.'

Deborah was looking somewhere between bored and uncomfortable. Ben knew it as a familiar refrain at dinner parties once guests got sozzled enough to start delving into the dark side of humanity. Deborah said it was kind of like being a doctor in reverse. Instead of being pestered by relatives about the slight throbbing just over where they imagined their liver to be, people asked her about the most grisly crimes she had ever been at and what she saw, what the criminal was like, how she felt, etc. until she usually politely, or not so politely, suggested she needed a refill or a pee and toddled off.

Ben was used to playing point man on such occasions, and he stepped right into the breach. At the same time he felt, with Breen obviously the worse for wear, it was a good time for a little fishing.

'Nice do. I suppose he's a popular guy, Mossy.'

Breen looked at Ben from under a raised eyebrow. It

looked to Ben like part incredulity and part attempt to focus.

'Tom Hennigan? Popular, maybe, or feared maybe.'

'Feared?' Ben asked.

Breen smiled a smile that slid right across his face. 'Yeah, as someone said, he's got his hand on the beer taps.'

'But he doesn't seem like a character you would want to cross.'

Breen looked all serious again, like he was trying to compose himself. 'No, not a character to cross, as that Belgian fool found out.'

'Oh, what happened there? I thought he just disappeared.'

'Disappeared, yeah,' Breen said with a guffaw. 'After a little argy-bargy with you-know-who.' Breen reeled backwards and grabbed a bannister nearby for support. He swept an unfocused, reptilian gaze around the heaving sea of faces. He smiled down at Deborah and pointed a finger at her as if he was going to say something, but then he just kept that lazy smile and shook his head.

'What was the argy-bargy about?' Ben asked. He wanted to press the point while Breen was so pissed. He might let slip some valuable information.

'Argy-bargy?' Breen looked genuinely surprised, as if he had no clue what Ben was talking about.

'With the Belgian,' Ben said. He could see Pat Doyle walking towards them, a big grin plastered across his face as he saw the state that Breen was in.

'Belgian?' Breen asked, a look of deep confusion furrowing his brow.

'Steamed to the gills,' Doyle said, nodding at Breen. 'Can't hold his drink, the money man. Same with all you office types, first puff of wind and you blow over like a feather.' Doyle's red complexion was a couple of shades brighter than usual. He held a pint in one hand and a whiskey in the other.

'Making the most of the free bar, then,' he said to Breen, who took a couple of steps back and had to reach for support again.

'Fuck are you talking about, with the two drinks in your hand?' Breen slurred.

'I see the accountant has the claws out,' Doyle said with a laugh.

Ben sat down with Deborah and threw his eyes to heaven. Doyle moved over to his right so he was standing, hovering over the two of them.

'I saw the signs up for your dog. Poor creature. I hope someone comes forward with something on that. Rumour has it he was cut bad, the poor thing.'

'What rumour?' Deborah asked.

'Oh, look at the crime reporter in action,' Doyle said. 'I don't know, just rumour. You wouldn't know what to believe in this town.'

'Do you have any information that might help us?' Deborah asked.

'Me, the humble taxi driver, be able to help the high and mighty likes of yourselves. That'd be a big ask.'

'Well, maybe you should shut up and keep your rumours to yourself, then,' Deborah said. 'C'mon, let's get out of here.' They picked Jack and Molly up on the way out.

'That was quick,' Molly said with a look of surprise as they hurried back to the car.

'Yes, I think we've heard enough BS for one day,' Deborah said tersely.

They drove home in silence, a sense of defeat sitting uneasily between them, but as they pulled into their drive, both let out a gasp.

'Oh, shit,' Ben said and drove cautiously up towards the house. Jeremiah's Jeep was parked at an angle at the top of the drive.

'Don't panic,' Ben said quietly. 'I'm sure everything is perfectly okay. You guys wait here, and I'll see what's going on.' Deborah didn't listen to him. She stepped out of the car as well. They approached the house cautiously.

'There's lights on in the kitchen,' Deborah whispered.

Ben crept slowly towards the window. The curtains were open, and he could see movement inside. Suddenly Jeremiah's frame filled the window. He was holding a hammer.

'Oh, shit,' Ben whispered, and he gestured for Deborah to pull back into the shadows.

Jeremiah stood still, the hammer held loosely by his side. *If I go straight to the door, it might startle him*, Ben thought, *and then Christ knows what he might do*. Instinctively he looked back to check the kids were still sitting in the car. They were.

Deborah moved quietly up beside him. 'What the hell do you think he's doing?'

'I don't know. Wait a second, and we'll see what he does.'

They waited, but then Ben heard the car door open. Molly and Jack were getting out. He had to do something before they got any closer. He ran to the window and knocked loudly. Jeremiah whirled his head round to look at him, but he didn't move. Ben could see the hammer dangling loosely in his hand.

'I'm going in,' Ben said with determination, partly because he was afraid Deborah would try to go in first. With a trembling hand, he managed to get the key in the lock, turn it and push the door open. He half-expected to see Jeremiah standing there, hammer in hand, but he wasn't. Ben rushed down the hall and into the kitchen.

'What are you doing here?' he shouted.

It was then Jeremiah pointed to the Saint Brigid's cross. It was back up on the wall, and there was no sign of any burn marks at the sides.

'I cleaned it up, so I did,' Jeremiah said softly. 'I kept thinking about Mam and how angry she'd be. Suddenly his face turned red and distorted. *'What do you think you're doing, young man? What have you gone and done now? There's no teaching you, is there. None at all.'* As quickly as it had become distorted, his face flashed back to his normal shifting, furtive look. 'I can't think about Mam being angry with me. Not anymore.' With that, he turned and walked slowly up the hall and out the door. Ben heard his Jeep start up; then Deborah, Jack, and Molly appeared.

'What was all that about? I heard him shouting,' Deborah said.

'He came in to put the cross back up.' Ben nodded towards the cross. 'He's scared of his mam. He hears her voice.'

'Jesus, he is a fruitcake,' Molly said as she brushed past.

'He still has keys to the house?' Deborah asked with raised eyebrows.

'I'll deal with it. When the time is right,' Ben said. 'It felt like he could have done anything there.'

'All the more reason to get the keys ASAP.'

17

Next day the security company came and put the lights in.
'That's a bit of a relief,' Ben said. 'At least it'll put people off coming near the house at night.'

'And make us feel even more like prisoners,' Deborah replied. 'This is getting ridiculous, Ben. When was the last time the two of us actually kicked back and relaxed? This is our country idyll, and look at us. We can't let the kids do anything. We haven't got any closer to finding out who killed our dog. There's something very weird here, and I don't like it, and you don't seem as concerned as you should be.'

Ben put an arm around her shoulder, but she froze at his touch, and he felt her shoulders tense up. 'I am concerned. Of course I am. I'm just trying to keep a level head at the same time. This has to work, Deborah. We can't go back. If the gang get wind that we're back in Dublin, they'll definitely take action. We'll make it here. We have to.'

'But at what cost?' Deborah asked quietly, almost like she was talking to herself.

Back in the shop, business was starting to pick up. Ben felt that was a welcome distraction from the tension that just kept dogging them. What Deborah had said was true: at what cost would they keep going, hoping things would take a turn for the better? He really did want it to work, but what damage was it doing to their relationship, to the kids?

One new idea they had for the shop was doing home deliveries, and people were buying into it. Orders came in either by phone or online—people who lived outside town and liked the convenience of getting a healthy box of veg and brown bread delivered.

'Right, finish off part of the field this evening, and then we can get some seeds planted,' Ben said. He was doing his best to be upbeat despite Deborah's recent comments.

He got the kids out to help. It was a pleasant summer's evening with small birds—including sparrows, finches, blue and grey tits—darting in and out of the hedgerows. Swallows swooped low across the fields to snatch some unwary insects dancing in the sun. Sheep called to their lambs as the sun was starting to slip towards the horizon. Ben watched the kids raking over the soil, and he felt that if they just held onto their vision, things could really work out.

'Hey, look what I found,' he heard Jack say and saw him lift something small up. Ben went over to investigate. It was a leather wristband with the initials DM carved into it.

He turned it around in his hand. It was dirty but didn't look that old.

'And look.' Jack was holding up a plastic tobacco pouch with what looked like Dutch writing on it.

'Looks like our Belgian friend left some stuff behind him in our field,' Ben said when he and Deborah were looking at the two things later on, but in the back of his mind, he was piecing two and two together.

'It's probably his all right,' Deborah said.

'Well, yeah, it's got the initials DM on it. His name was something like David Mertens, and then there's the tobacco with Dutch writing. Makes sense, no?'

'Which is no big deal, I suppose, given he was a friend of Jeremiah,' Deborah said reflectively.

'Except he went missing without a trace, and somebody wants us off this land. Could that be the reason? Is there more to discover here?'

'One thing I learned from crime reporting is that you don't jump to conclusions; you get the facts and work from there.'

'He had some connection with the publican, and he has been nothing but hostile towards us since we arrived.'

'Again, we can't jump to conclusions. People come and go. It doesn't mean anything bad happened to him. In any case, if it did, it might have nothing to do with whoever wants us out of here. Jeremiah is the one with the biggest reason. I think we are agreed on that.'

'Yes, but what if there are multiple reasons, if it's not just as simple as Jeremiah's fixation with his mother?'

They had been walking the land around where the things were found, partly so Ben could show Deborah the spot, but also because they didn't want to the kids to hear the conversation.

Deborah stopped and looked out over the rolling hills that stretched towards the dropping sun. 'I'll check out this Belgian guy. I'm reluctant to go back to my former contacts, but we need to sort this shit out.'

That night the security lights tripped as Ben was falling into a deep sleep. Ben struggled out of bed and grabbed the poker. He stopped to listen just inside the hall door. No sound, so he opened the door slowly. The night was breezy with wind tossing the dark shades of leaves against a moon that skidded behind rushing clouds.

'Hello?' Ben called into the night, but he felt his voice carried away by the wind. He pushed out a little further and peered around the corner of the house. No sign of cars or anything unusual. He ventured out further again, walking slowly over towards the henhouse. As he neared it, he saw a small shadow dart like quicksilver and disappear with the fluidity of liquid over the wall behind the henhouse.

A fox or a weasel, something small and quick, he thought, letting the poker drop by his side. He listened, but no sound emanated from the henhouse, so he shone his phone torch around the wire and saw no sign of rips or tears. The hens were silent, probably sleeping, oblivious to the danger that lurked outside.

'It's nothing, just a fox or some small animal,' he said wearily to Deborah as he climbed back into bed. As he tried to get back to sleep, Ben was left thinking, *If this happens a few times a night, I am going to be good for nothing within a week*. Mercifully nothing happened again that night, and he was able to get some proper rest.

18

On the Saturday morning, as arranged, Ben dropped Jack and Molly up to Sophie's house. She was heading out to her friend's pet farm just outside town. Molly and Jack were full of excitement, and Ben felt such overwhelming relief that they were actually doing something enjoyable with a young person from the town. It normalized things in his mind and gave him hope that there was a positive side to the move, and they just needed to keep their heads down and stick with it.

Sophie lived with her mum in a detached house on a small piece of land that was on a rise and looked back into town. It was only a five-minute walk from the centre but still far enough out so they got a view and had enough land for a couple of brown donkeys that peered over a stone wall.

'You can expect them to be tired,' Sophie said. 'Saturday is a busy day, so lots of animals to feed and water, and they'll need someone to help out with the pony rides. They'll put a lunch on up there, so don't worry about food. I'll drop them back up when we're finished.'

'Thanks, you're a star,' Ben said to Sophie. In reality he felt like getting down on his knees and thanking her with all his heart, he was so grateful.

'No worries at all,' Sophie said as she ushered the two of them into her house.

Ben went down to open the shop then, and he was even more grateful to Sophie for what she had done because when he arrived, the words 'Molly is a slut' had been written in crude black marker across the wooden border at the side of their shop window. It was written in shaky writing, looked like it had been done in a hurry, but still the intention was there, and he was so happy that Molly hadn't been there to see it.

Ben got a damp cloth from inside, and it was just a question of wiping it off, but it left him feeling deflated again. *Must be that gang of young lads*, Ben thought, *led, of course, by the publican's son—Gavin.* And the publican had been the one giving out about people having no control over their kids. Ben tried to push it to the back of his mind and get on with business. *It's just the kind of crap that stupid teenagers got up to if they fancied someone*, he told himself.

By the time Deborah had arrived, he had managed to get a cheery face back on, telling her how much the kids were excited by the day ahead.

'It's nice to have something positive for them for a change,' Deborah said. Ben felt there was a bit of a sting in the tail of the comment, but he chose to ignore it.

'Absolutely,' he agreed, 'hopefully it'll be ongoing, something for them to look forward to.'

'Maybe, we don't want to crowd Sophie out either. They need to make friends their own age.'

'Of course, but it's a start.' Ben could almost feel the desperation in his own voice—trying to put a positive spin on things. He said nothing about the graffiti on the shopfront.

It was a busy day in the shop, and that took their minds off things. Deborah was moving between taking orders for home delivery and serving people in the shop. Ben was stacking shelves and serving customers.

'Jeez, we actually need Jack and Molly on a Saturday, which is good news,' Deborah said once they got a bit of a lull.

'Yeah, anything to keep them busy helps. Now, I'd better get around to doing some of those home deliveries.'

Deborah gave him a list of addresses and what they had ordered. Ben packed up the cardboard boxes and set off. It was late afternoon, and the shop was quiet now, so he felt okay leaving Deborah on her own. *Jesus, I shouldn't even be thinking like that,* he told himself. Soon, as he wound his way through country lanes and up to isolated farmhouses, he began to appreciate the beauty of the countryside in summer with lush curtains of foxglove and honeysuckle dripping from the hedgerows. The smells were a heady combination of sweet scents from the flowers and pockets of sickly-sweet manure from the fields. He could hear sheep calling their young and the distant chug of a tractor. Surprisingly he caught the smell of a turf fire burning somewhere. *But then some of these houses use just the solid-fuel stoves for cooking, heating and everything else,* he thought.

It was early evening by the time he got to his second-last call. There was an address but no mobile contact number. *Some people are still just working off their landline*, he thought.

The house was at the end of a bumpy lane, secluded on the right by a row of pine trees. To the left it looked out over stony, unkempt fields. There were old curtains hanging askew in the windows. Looking up, he could see tiles missing from the roof. At the side of the house he could see the rusted hulk of an old Jeep. *Whoever lives here keeps to themselves*, he thought. Through some of the deliveries he'd done, he had got used to seeing houses that looked thrown together and ramshackle on the outside, but then the door would be opened by someone elderly but well-turned-out.

As he approached the front door, he noticed it was slightly ajar. It had frosted glass on the upper half and plastic underneath. The frosted glass had a long diagonal crack running through it. The doorbell was hanging by some wires, so he knocked loudly on the door. There was no sound from inside. All he could hear was the gentle soughing of wind in the tall pine trees over to his right. He knocked again and waited. No answer and no sound from inside.

'Anybody home?' he called. Still no answer. *They must be out*, he thought. He didn't fancy waiting around any longer, so he decided to knock again, and if there was no answer, he would just leave the box inside the door, and they could collect payment another time.

After knocking and getting no answer, he leaned against the door to push it slightly open. The bottom half scraped the ground as it moved, making a loud screeching noise that startled him. There was something spooky about the place that made him want to rush away, but at the same time he didn't want to mess up on an order, so he stepped inside the narrow porch. From there, if he craned his head, he could just see into the kitchen. It looked tidy, with a brightly coloured oilcloth covering a wooden table. On the table he could see some large photos laid out. He decided to leave the box on the table and glance at the photos, as they might give him a clue who lived there.

'Hello?' he called again, just to make sure no one was going to suddenly appear before he walked over to the table. Ben plonked the box in the middle of the table, then looked at the photos. His heart began to race as he did. There, on the table, were A4-size photos of his family, just like the one that had been pinned to their door before. It showed them walking around town, outside their shop, standing on the drive of their house, different places, different vantage points, but the one thing all photos had in common was that his image had been neatly cut out. All of them showed just Deborah and the two kids. A creeping sensation began to move up his spine, turning him rigid. He suddenly became hyper-aware of all his movements, of standing there in that kitchen, isolated, far from help. There was nothing else on the table, no words, no message. He put the box down and turned slowly. He had the sensation that he was being watched. Ben tried to act casual as he turned and walked back towards the door. He had only one thing in mind, and that was to jump in the car, gun the engine, and get the hell out of there, but he felt he had to act with caution. If this had been set up for him, then he needed to show that he wasn't going to panic.

When he reached the front door, he looked left and right. Nothing was moving out there. His car was about fifteen yards from the door, ground that he could cover in a matter of seconds, but it seemed a million miles away. His throat was dry, and every muscle in his body was taut.

He fumbled for the car keys in his pocket and, trying to look calm, he walked towards the car. It was then he noticed. Both tyres on this side of the car were flat, with large gashes running from one end to the other.

They've been slashed, he thought, and at the same time he heard something crack off the body of the car. When he looked to where the noise came from, he saw a dent. *Oh, shit, someone is shooting at me.* He turned and dashed for the front door of the house, jumping in just as another sound cracked off the frame of the door. He slammed the door shut, the screeching sound of the frame tearing high into the air; then he threw himself on the kitchen floor.

Instinctively he reached into his jacket pocket for his phone, but it wasn't there. *Shit,* he thought, *I left it on the car seat.*

He crawled towards the base of the kitchen window, leaned against the wall and looked desperately around the room. He needed a weapon. The kitchen sink was to his left, and under that were the cutlery drawers. *How long has this house been abandoned?* he wondered. *Will there be anything in the drawers? Is it worth exposing myself?* But he knew he had no choice. Whoever it was could come through the door any second. He slithered across the dirt floor on his belly until he was under the drawers; then he reached up. Just at that second he heard a noise, the sound of footsteps outside. Looking back towards the window, he saw a shadow flit by, all black, no features.

Shit, they're coming for the door, he thought, so he jumped up, pulled the drawers open but nothing. They had been cleaned out, and all that was there were some filthy old food wrappers. He heard a movement outside again, so he grabbed a chair and shoved it under the handle of the front door and wedged it shut. He ran from the kitchen into a long hall that led into a bedroom at the back. There was a big window in the bedroom. He tried the handle. It was open. From the window he could just see the front of his car.

At the same time he heard the glass in the front door smash. Then he heard the chair fall back on the floor and the shrieking scrape of the door as it was pushed slowly open. Ben knew he had only one chance. He counted to three, which he figured gave the person enough time to step inside the house; then he opened the bedroom window, jumped out, ran at a crouch to his car, pulled the door open and climbed in. Keeping his head low to the dash, he pulled his keys out and, with a shaking hand, turned them in the ignition. The engine roared as he stamped his foot on the accelerator, rammed the gear into first and released the handbrake. The car shot forward, and he turned the wheel sharply to the left, his head still low. He couldn't see where he was going, but he knew a sharp left would bring him in a circle to face the driveway out. Only when the car had completed the circle and he had his back to the house did he raise his head. As he did, he saw what looked like a shadow race from the house towards the car. Again all he could see was a blur of black, the person hooded. He heard a crack and saw his wing mirror splinter into a thousand tiny pieces.

Ben pressed his foot harder on the accelerator. The wheels ground hard against the rocky surface, scrambling for purchase without their tyres. Finally the car lurched forward, Ben raised his head and let the car tear down the laneway, bumping hard against the ground. The car kept lurching to the right, and he felt it scrape off one of the stone walls, but he kept his foot to the floor, not even risking a change of gear. The engine whined in protest, but the car kept moving. He thought he heard another crack as he neared the end of the lane, but he didn't look back, just kept going until he was out on the open road and chugging nosily, with both tyres flapping against the road.

Back in town, he pulled into the supermarket car park and let his head rest on the steering wheel. His heart was still fluttering madly in his chest, and his fingers were white where he gripped the steering. Small gasps of breath came in sharp, irregular puffs. Sweat dripped from his forehead and trickled from under his arms. He could feel his body start to convulse, so he stepped from the car and took a deep breath. The cool air swept across his skin, and he began to focus again.

19

'Air gun pellets.' Garda Byrne let a small, round piece of metal roll around in the palm of his hand. He had searched the ground around where Ben's car had been parked and found a couple of metal pellets. It was late morning, the day after the incident.

'It was a gun,' Ben said. 'Someone was shooting at me.'

'I am fully cognizant of that fact. For example, if this were a .22-calibre bullet, it would be a very different matter.' The Garda looked from the little pellet to Ben to make sure he had grasped the information.

Ben ran his hands through his hair. 'I don't see the significance of that. Someone endangered my life. Surely that's all that matters here.'

'Correct,' Garda Byrne said with a definitive nod. 'But at the same time, this could be some young lads winding you up rather than someone trying to hurt or kill you. You mentioned before that you'd had a run-in with some local lads.'

There was another, younger Garda there as well. He

was walking around the old house, looking at windows, surveying the crime scene. He had short red hair and a flushed complexion but was tall, with an athletic build. Each step he took covered a lot of ground.

'This was Sweeney's place, wasn't it?' he said to Garda Byrne.

'Got it in one.'

'They fecked off to America, the lot of them, didn't they, and left the poor ma alone. She's gone to the nursing home a long time now. Wouldn't you think they'd have some pride and keep the place up?' He was shaking his head as he viewed the shabby exterior.

'They'll leave it until she dies; then they'll sell up,' Garda Byrne said succinctly.

The younger Garda nodded in agreement, then shook his head again.

'So you'll follow all lines of enquiry and let us know how you are progressing.' Deborah addressed Garda Byrne. She had insisted on coming up. Ben had wanted her to open the shop and let him deal with it, but she had left Jack and Molly in charge. A mechanic had fixed the tyres and cracked wing mirror, but they had brought them to the Garda as evidence.

Garda Byrne looked quizzically at her. 'Of course we will follow every line of enquiry, and we will pursue it until we have a successful outcome. The problem with the gun is that air guns are ten a penny, whereas a .22 would be traceable. That may hinder us, but be assured we will do our best.'

Deborah didn't look too reassured to Ben. She kept looking at the Garda as if expecting more, but he just tossed the pellet in his hand and looked towards the house.

'Okay, we'd better get back to the shop,' she said impatiently.

As they were driving back to town, Deborah asked, 'Do you think they're just a bit lazy, or do you reckon there's something else holding them back?'

'I was thinking the same thing. Is it just that we are newbies, and they are trying to see how genuine we are, or is it that they are so proud of the area that they don't want to admit bad stuff can happen here?'

'Or is it because someone with influence is putting pressure on behind the scenes?'

'That thought had crossed my mind, but I think it's a conspiracy too far. Maybe they're just not used to dealing with serious stuff and it's taking a while for them to warm up to it.'

'Well, they'd better warm up pretty fast because I am reaching breaking point. This is getting too much, Ben, no matter what we have invested here. You know me. I am a determined person and not easily put off, but this is starting to scare the shit out of me. If we can't make a decision together, then maybe one of us needs to make that decision.'

Ben had no answer to that. He had been badly shaken by the incident and felt his own determination to see this project through was starting to waver. Whoever was doing this was not giving up. They were determined to see it through. *But who is it,* he wondered *and why are they doing it?* This incident was well thought out. It made him think again of the gang from Dublin. But would they stoop to using air guns? If they wanted to take him out, they would have had more than one person on the job, and they would have had proper guns.

Somebody out there was thinking all this through very carefully. It seemed like they wanted to give him a bad scare without actually killing him. He wondered if Jeremiah would be capable of that level of planning. He found it hard to buy into the idea that the gang of teenagers from the beach would be behind something like that, but at the same time he felt he couldn't be sure. All he knew was he had to resolve all this, and fast. He could feel Deborah's patience was running out.

THE MOOD LIFTED MOMENTARILY over a dinner of roast ham glazed with the heather honey from the shop. Molly was in particularly good form.

'We had a great day yesterday with Sophie at the pet farm. She's really sound.'

Ben had rarely heard Molly address anyone outside the virtual world as being 'sound' or indeed anything that could be construed as complimentary.

'I was in charge of the pony rides,' Jack said breathlessly. 'I got to give them their rewards when they behaved well, carrots and stuff.'

'Sounds like you had a blast,' Deborah said.

'Yeah, Sophie and her friend really get our generation, which makes a nice change,' Molly said.

Ben thought he picked up a needle in his and Deborah's direction but was very happy to overlook it, seeing a lingering smile on Molly's face.

'I heard back from some of my ex-colleagues,' Deborah said later that evening when the kids were out of earshot. 'They were able to give me a bit of background on the David Mertens guy. Seems he was involved in some heavy-duty drug smuggling.'

'That's interesting,' Ben said.

'Yeah, he was involved in a shipment that got intercepted off the south coast. They were in some sort of inflatable, and it started sinking, so they ended up in the water and got pulled out by Customs and Excise.

Mertens was in that group, and he ended up getting a hefty prison sentence.'

'So he was a seasoned con, by the sounds of it.'

'Yeah, a career criminal. He had smaller charges in different countries around Europe.'

'So he was involved in some sort of cartel?'

'Maybe, certainly working on the fringes of one, but there was something else of interest that came up. There were people on shore as well who were supposed to direct the boat in and help unload the shipment. A couple of them got away, but some didn't, and one of those who didn't was a Tom O'Sullivan, who was described as being a barman.'

'Right, and how is that relevant?'

'Well, the publican's name is Mossy, which is slang for Thomas, or Tom for short.'

'Yeah, I heard Breen refer to him as Tom all right, but his second name is Hennigan.'

'It is possible to change your name by deed poll, and the fact that he's a barman stands out for me. It's a well-trodden path from barman to publican.'

Ben shook his head. 'That all sounds very unlikely. This guy is a respected member of the community here.'

'Yeah, but remember the speech at his sixtieth? He said something about the town welcoming a blow-in. It means he came in from outside.'

'Still, that's a very spurious connection.'

'The timing is the other thing. Mertens got fifteen years, but he served ten. This Tom O'Sullivan guy got four years and served two. This all happened over twenty years ago. We don't know exactly when this trouble with Mertens was, but if it was a few years back, maybe eight or nine years back, then it might just dovetail with the time that Mertens was released.'

Ben nodded. He knew Deborah was thorough in her

work and her research. She'd won multiple awards in her time as a crime reporter. 'Yeah, we have a bit of digging to do there, but as you say, there are a few elements that point in the same direction. I guess then the theory is that Hennigan has something to hide, i.e., his past. He didn't want Mertens hanging around, so he did whatever he had to do to get rid of him.'

'And that's the key question. What did he do to get rid of him? If we found some of Mertens' belongings here, then did something very nasty happen on this property?'

'Which is why Hennigan is so apparently hostile to us and could be behind all the crap that has happened. Maybe Jeremiah is somehow involved as well. Remember, he was a friend of Mertens. If the family home was sold suddenly and they are afraid there is still some evidence here, maybe the publican wants to get rid of us before we discover any more.'

'And if that's what he wants and he is a ruthless criminal, then we are in a very dangerous position.'

'True,' Ben said, 'but we are still very much in the realm of speculation here. As far as we know, he is who he says he is and may have no connection at all to the smuggling. Mertens was obviously deeply involved in criminality, so maybe he tried something desperate to get money.'

Ben was left thinking about it all. The incident the night before had really frightened him. He'd tried to play it down as much as he could with Deborah, and they had said nothing at all to the kids, but he had been really shook. It had been well thought out with the photos on the table, the slashing of the tyres, and then the attack from the trees with the air gun. He didn't go along with Garda Byrne's view that this could just be the young people who had been harassing their kids having a go at him. It was too well orchestrated. It scared him enough that he wondered should they just call it a day, but something in him didn't want to give in either. He'd developed a steeliness that had served him well in the world of big business, and he wasn't going to be pushed around and lose the dream of a new life. And then where would they go anyway? Dublin was too dangerous, and they had put so much money into this place. They had to make it work.

There was another Chamber of Commerce meeting the next night. It would be chaired by Mossy Hennigan and would have the usual cast of characters present. Surely there was some way he could get some more information, something that would lead to a definite clue, something that he could bring to the Gardai as evidence.

20

He sat through the chamber meeting, listening to all the local gripes. He made a couple of innocuous comments about trying to get more tourists into the town just so it looked like he was making an effort. At the end of the meeting, he saw Pat Doyle head for the bar, so he followed him.

Ben ordered a pint and sidled over to Doyle, who was chatting to a couple of locals. Ben drew him aside as if he had something important to say.

'So how do you feel the meeting went this evening?' Ben asked, and Doyle looked perplexed by the question.

'Same old shite that's been going on for years. Sure they couldn't organize a piss up in a brewery, this crowd.'

'Must get frustrating,' Ben said, and Doyle rose to the bait.

'Oh, yeah. I've had plenty of ideas shut down just like that.' He snapped his fingers. 'Just because I'm the poor butcher who saw his business go down the swanny.'

'Through no fault of your own, I'm sure. If they'd given you a bit of help, it might have been different.'

'Now you're talking,' Doyle said with an emphatic nod. 'Miserable shower of bastards wouldn't give you the steam off their piss.'

'Still, I suppose there have been bumps along the road for everyone. Now, take Hennigan, whatever that messy business was with the Belgian.'

Doyle looked at Ben for a beat, then shook his head. 'Hennigan's not one to cross, and nobody knows what that Belgian did, but he sure riled our Tom. Nothing nasty happened that we know of or that Tom is telling, anyway. You'll not get much change out of Hennigan.'

'But surely someone knows something.'

'As I said before, it was only Jeremiah who was pals with him. Everyone else stayed clear once they seen Hennigan's attitude. The man who pulls the pints calls the tune. Now, I'd better get back and talk some proper shite with them lads. The missus has me on the clock.'

He walked back over to his companions, so Ben finished up his pint and headed home.

He filled Deborah in on the events of the evening and how he didn't get anywhere in the quest for new information.

'The lack of openness makes you feel there is a lot more to it,' Deborah said.

'I know, but it's how to get them to open up. It's like Hennigan has them all afraid to speak. And then what part did Jeremiah play in it all? It's getting very frustrating. You'd love to shake them up a bit, get them out of this torpor.'

'Well, we need to find out what part we are playing in it all. That's all I care about, so that the crap that is happening to us stops. On that note, I did a bit of prowling around online to see if I could dig anything up about that Tom O'Sullivan who was caught with Mertens. Seems he was a bit of a boxing star in his youth because he made it into the papers. No photos though. He didn't make it that big, never quite got to the nationals.'

Ben thought about Hennigan with his gruff, red face and a nose that was pushed over to one side. He could have been a boxer, but he looked like a man who wouldn't be shy about using his fists anyway. Still, they had to keep an open mind on anything that would help them.

The conversation finished on that uneasy note, and Ben went over to do accounts on the laptop while Deborah vegged out in front of the TV.

About an hour later the headlights of a car swept across their windows, and they heard it stop outside their front door. Two doors opened and shut; then there was a loud knock on the door.

'Jesus, who the hell is that at this hour?' Ben asked, and he had a familiar sinking feeling in his stomach. Through the frosted glass of the door, he could see the outline of two uniformed Gardai.

Maybe they have some information for us, he thought.

He opened the door to Garda Byrne and his red-haired sidekick. The red-haired Garda shifted from foot to foot, his hands buried deep in his pockets. Garda Byrne said nothing initially, just looked curiously at Ben as if he was waiting for him to answer a question.

'Well,' Ben said eventually. 'Did you make any progress?'

'On?' Garda Byrne asked.

'On the case up at the house or our dog, of course,' Ben replied impatiently.

Garda Byrne looked down at a notebook he was holding. 'Not as such. We came about another matter.'

'What other matter?' Ben could feel the impatience rising. He knew he had to try to check it.

'You were in the pub this evening,' Garda Byrne said.

'That's right. I had one pint and walked home.'

'Walked which direction?'

'There's only one way from the pub to our house,' Ben said. Deborah had come to stand behind him in the doorway. The younger Garda nodded in her direction.

'Did you pass the supermarket?'

'Of course. That's on the way. What's this all about?'

'It's about young Gavin Hennigan,' the Garda replied.

'What about him?' Ben asked, and again he knew his tone was too sharp.

Garda Byrne looked at him with a studied, neutral expression. 'He was assaulted,' he said suddenly.

'Assaulted? Is he all right?'

'Depends on what you call all right. Bruising, mild concussion, swollen eyes.'

'That's terrible. When did it happen?'

'Well, now, that's the million-dollar question.' He turned to the younger Garda, who smiled back at him and nodded.

'Whoever it was came out of nowhere and gave him a right going-over, so he's confused, doesn't know exactly when it was, just knows it was up around the car park in the supermarket after he'd left his friends. He was having a smoke before he went home 'cos the da doesn't know he smokes, you know the way. Well, he doesn't know how long he was there, but out of the blue.' Here the Garda smacked his notebook off his hand, making a sound so loud that Ben jumped back.

'That's terrible, but you don't seriously think it was me, do you?'

Garda Byrne looked back at the younger one again, who shook his head and pursed his lips. 'We are examining all lines of enquiry. You had a run-in with the young man.'

'I would never do a thing like that. That's outrageous.'

'You'd be surprised what a man would do to defend his family. And sometimes rightly so.'

'I'm a professional. I own a business in the town. What sort of fool would I be to get involved in something like that?'

'You would be surprised by behaviour in extreme situations is all I will say. In my years as a Garda, I won't say I have seen it all. That's what you would call a cliché, but I have seen people do things they would normally never dream of.'

Ben looked from one Garda to the other. 'And have you found anything about who might have been taking shots at me up at the house? Is that of equal importance? Have you been doing house-to-house enquiries about that? Or our dog that was savagely killed?'

That led to a prolonged silence from the two Gardai. The older one flipped his notebook in his hand. 'We treat all incidents with equal seriousness, but if we have someone capable of carrying out a brutal assault on the son of a respected town member, well, I think that would be considered a matter of urgency. You have young children yourself. I'm sure you understand.'

With a final flap of the notebook, the two Gardai left, walking slowly to the car, looking around the grounds of the property as they did. The car ground across the gravel of the driveway, and Ben watched the headlights streak a path into the night.

He turned to face Deborah in the hall. 'Jesus, what is wrong with those guys?'

'I suppose that young guy Gavin had it coming,' Deborah said.

'I'm sure he did, but what about whoever was taking potshots at me? That would seem like a far more serious incident.'

'Not in their minds, apparently. Weird the way someone just attacked him though. That time he was outside our shop, he looked big enough. Must have been someone a lot bigger, like an adult.'

There was a pause there in the conversation, and Ben wondered if Deborah was subtly insinuating that it might have been him who attacked Gavin. He searched for clues in Deborah's demeanour, but she seemed to be lost in thought, so he decided to address it himself.

'I hope they get whoever did this quickly,' he said.

'Why?' Deborah asked.

'Well, because rumours will start, and people will be more likely to blame the outsiders than one of their own.'

'They seem to be blaming us for everything else, so, yeah, you're probably right.'

Another pause.

'It wasn't me, by the way,' he said eventually.

'Oh, God no. I didn't think it was. You didn't need to tell me that.'

'Well, I'm just not sure what is being thought or believed at the moment.'

'No, I wouldn't think you were capable of that. Not the Ben I know.'

There, Ben thought, *is she trying to tell me that the Ben she knew wouldn't do something like that, but maybe things have changed so much that the new Ben would be capable?*

'I think I'll take a little walk,' he said. 'I need to clear my head. Fancy coming?'

'Don't you think we should tell the kids what's

going on? The police have just come to our door. We'd better let them know why.'

'Of course.' Ben felt bad for not having been all over that. Naturally, the kids would want to know why police were calling to their door at night.

'So somebody beat the crap out of that guy Gavin?' Molly asked with what Ben thought looked like a smirk of appreciation.

'Yes,' Deborah said. 'Which is very serious, a young person getting assaulted like that. He could have been seriously hurt.'

'But, like, I'm sure he probably deserved it,' Molly continued.

'Yeah, he nearly got me drowned. Even Jeremiah said nothing like that should happen to a young lad like me,' Jack said.

'Jeremiah,' Ben repeated. 'Yes, he did say something like that all right, didn't he?' He felt something click in his head.

Later when it was just Ben and Deborah talking, he asked her, 'Do you think it might have been Jeremiah?'

'Possibly. I suppose.'

'If it was, then it points a finger in his direction in terms of what happened to Harry. At least we know Jeremiah is capable of violence.'

'If it was him. But the publican's son?'

'I'm not sure Jeremiah is someone in control of his actions. The look in his eyes when he saw the burnt cross. That was scary. The way he blurts stuff out like he has this constant conversation going on in his head. It's like he isn't really there half the time. He seems to like Jack, and he knows that Gavin nearly drowned him.'

'I really don't know,' Deborah said wearily. 'I need to sleep.'

She looked tired as she shuffled off to bed. Ben

stayed thinking in the low light of a lamp in the kitchen. As he sat there, he felt his phone vibrate. His hands shook as he picked it up and tapped into messages. In his inbox, from a phone with caller ID blocked, was a message: 'We can end all this. There is an easy way out. Check your phone tomorrow at 3.'

21

The mood was uneasy between himself and Deborah the next day in the shop. She went about the work in a functional, self-contained manner. Ben made a couple of attempts at brightening things up, but she seemed exhausted. She was normally the vibrant one, pushing projects and fun things to do. Ben couldn't recall seeing her this deflated before.

'It's just one thing after another,' she said at one stage.

'It'll pass. We're bigger than this,' Ben had said, but his words somehow rang hollow.

He said nothing to her about the late-night text, judging the mood and figuring it was just something he was going to have to deal with. Maybe whoever this was had decided enough was enough. It could have been the assault on Gavin that tipped it over the edge. Ben had decided that whoever it was and whatever solution they proposed, he was going to go along with it for the moment. He'd wait until the dust had settled and he and Deborah were back on an even keel, and then he'd start looking for justice for all the bad stuff that had happened to them. There was no point risking an immediate confrontation. That might just set things rolling again. What he and Deborah needed now was some normality, some time and space to be relaxed, to get to know this new life they had chosen.

Ben watched his phone once three o'clock came. There was no text. Maybe the person was just winding him up. It could be another way of keeping him on edge. Maybe they were going to do something else while he was distracted watching the phone. He did his best to act normal with Deborah and whatever customers came in, but inside he felt agitated. Why the hell would they just not text?

Finally, as they were approaching five o'clock and they were starting to clear up, he felt the phone vibrate in his pocket. When he got a chance, he slipped it out and checked the message. It said: 'Meet me at the viewing point car park tonight at nine o'clock. I'll be in a blue car with tinted windows.' That was it. This could all be resolved by tonight. Ben felt his heart race with excitement and nerves. Whoever it was was capable of doing some nasty things. He would have to be on his guard. Ben started thinking about whom he had seen in what car in town. Certainly, he had only seen Jeremiah in his battered Jeep, but that didn't mean it was the only car he had access to. Pat Doyle drove a seven-year-old hybrid as his taxi, but again, he could have access to something else. He hadn't seen what Mossy Hennigan drove.

The viewing point was a couple of miles out of town and was at a place where the road rose steeply and twisted in a series of sharp bends to give views out over a deep, glaciated valley. On a clear day, you had an uninterrupted 180-degree view of lush farmlands straight ahead, the sea over to the left, and far off to the right the mountains that Ben had seen as they drove down. Ben had passed it on occasion when he was doing home deliveries, so he knew it well.

But the arrangement was for nine o'clock that night, so he couldn't pretend to Deborah that he was doing a home delivery. It was too late. He had only one other possible excuse for going out at that hour.

'There's another chamber meeting on this evening,' he said over dinner. Deborah had maintained her quiet, distant mood over the course of the day. He felt like she was trying to figure out what the next move should be, but, worryingly, she wasn't sharing her ideas with him. That call from the Gardai the night before had obviously thrown her. Ben didn't have the heart to bring it up yet. He decided he'd wait until the meeting that night. Maybe he'd finally have some good news to bring to her.

'Another one? After last night?' She looked surprised.

'Yeah, must be some issues suddenly came up. Best I show my face anyway.'

'Whatever you think,' she said, toying with a bit of salmon on her plate. She was peeling some of the silver skin off a small piece she had left. To Ben it seemed she was putting far more effort into that than into her conversation with him.

'We still have to get that fishing gear for you,' he said to Jack, deciding to change the subject. Jack looked blankly back at him.

'You know, after losing the stuff that you had.'

'I'm not so sure about the fishing here,' Jack said with a furrowed brow.

'Don't let those guys put you off,' Ben said. 'I'll go with you the first few times until this all settles down.'

'If it settles down,' Molly said.

'Well, look at the positives. You have a friend now in Sophie, and more good stuff like that'll happen. You'll see.'

Deborah was still playing with her food, not really taking part. Ben felt, again, like he was the one left doing the defending and the explaining. He started feeling annoyed at her, but he stifled the annoyance as best he could. He had to get out there tonight and do what was needed to fix this. Then he would get the opportunity to express his disappointment at her lack of support.

'Okay, I'd best be off,' he said at eight thirty, giving Deborah a peck on the cheek.

He checked the henhouse on the way out and was glad to see that they, at least, were clucking happily from inside.

He drove into town first and parked up near the square, thinking he might see the car taking off and get some clue who was driving, but, after sitting there for ten minutes, he started feeling conspicuous and hadn't seen any car that matched the description. He checked his phone again. No new messages had come in, so he figured the arrangement must stand.

It took him fifteen minutes to reach the viewing point. He drove past it first just to check that everything looked normal. It did, and even better, a car of exactly the description was sitting there facing out towards the valley. It was the only car at the point, which didn't surprise Ben, as it was starting to get dark.

He drove half a mile up the road and found a place to turn. As he came back down, he could feel his hands grip the steering wheel tighter, and his mouth started to go dry.

Who am I going to meet here, and what are they going to say?

He had no answer to that question, but this was something he had to go through with. He had no choice, so he pulled slowly into the viewing point, keeping a good distance from the other car. He looked over towards it, but as the text had said, the windows were tinted, so it was impossible to see in from that distance. Ben sat where he was, deciding it was best to let them come to him; then he would see if they had a weapon or what their intent was.

Time passed, and there was no movement from the car. He stepped out of his own and leaned against the bonnet, just as if he were somebody up to have a look out over the darkening valley. Still no movement from the car. He thought he heard a radio or music coming from inside, so there was definitely somebody there.

Leaning against the bonnet, he could feel the fresh night air cooling the sweat that had broken out on his forehead. It was hard to stand still knowing that there was somebody there watching him. Maybe they're just making sure I haven't called the Gardai or set up some sort of trap for them.

He could hear a dog bark somewhere in the distance, its sound carrying easily across the valley. It made him think of Harry and the terrible way he had been killed, but he had to put those thoughts aside. He was here to put an end to it all, nothing else.

It was getting much darker now, and he didn't want to leave himself exposed, alone up here in this isolated spot, so he decided he had to do something. He approached the car slowly. The sound of music from inside grew louder as he got closer. Going around to the front of the car, he glanced in. The tinted windows in the half-light made it impossible to see anything. He was getting more nervous, beginning to wonder if there was going to be a sudden attack, so he went right up to the front of the car and looked in.

He could make something out inside but wasn't sure what, so he looked closer again, shielding his eyes with his hand. There was definitely something moving in there. The movement stopped suddenly, and the driver's door burst open. Ben instinctively jumped back. A young man with tight brown hair and a square jaw jumped out. His shirt was open to the waist. He was lithe and strong-looking, and he dashed over to stand toe to toe with Ben.

'What the fuck you doing, you perv?' he spat in Ben's face.

'I got a text to come here,' Ben said weakly.

'Really, is that a fact? Well, pervs like you understand one thing only, isn't that right?'

Ben heard a rush of wind and at the same time felt a jarring blow to his right cheek. He staggered back and held his face.

'Fucker.' The young man was on him again, sent a fist smashing into his nose, then another to the ear. In the blur of pain Ben heard the passenger door open and a female voice.

'Robbie, stop. I know him.'

Ben looked over and saw a familiar figure standing there. It was Sophie from the shop. She was rearranging her clothes.

'Stop, Robbie,' she pleaded with him. 'It's okay. It must be a mistake. I know him.'

'That's no mistake. D'ye see how close he was to the windscreen, getting a good eyeful?'

Sophie was standing beside Robbie now, holding him back. 'It's okay. Forget it.'

Robbie was breathing heavily, his fists still tightly

clenched. Sophie started easing him back towards the car.

'That was no mistake,' Robbie repeated, but he started going back with Sophie.

'You'd better go,' Sophie said hurriedly to Ben.

'I was supposed to meet someone else here,' Ben said, but it hurt his jaw to talk. He felt warm blood oozing from his nose. He turned and staggered back to his car, turned the ignition on, backed hazily out of the car park, and drove back towards town. His head throbbed, and the blood from his nose was coming in a steady flow.

He pulled in a couple of miles down the road. His ear was warm, and his jaw was starting to stiffen. Ben looked for a tissue in the glove compartment and pushed it against his nose to stop the flow of blood. Looking down, he could see dark red stains all over his shirt. His body trembled with the adrenaline that still rushed through him.

Shit, he thought, *that was a disaster. I am truly screwed. How am I going to explain this? Who is going to listen to me? Word will be out that I'm some sort of perv. And Deborah? The kids? Who will they hear about it from?*

He drove back into town, unsure what to do, not able to face the prospect of going home and explaining himself. *Jesus, on top of this humiliation I have the deception with Deborah to deal with.*

Parking up in the square again, he saw a light on in the newsagents shop. It was just approaching ten. They'd be shutting soon. He walked past and saw someone he didn't know was serving, so he zipped up his leather jacket to hide the stains on his shirt and walked in, trying to look relaxed and casual. There was a freezer towards the back of the shop, and that was where he went to pick up a pack of frozen peas. With his head down, he approached the cashier, paid quickly, and left. Back in his car, he held the frozen peas against his jaw until it felt numb with cold. As he sat there, he felt his phone vibrate in his pocket. *Probably Deborah wondering when I am back*, he thought, but when he checked the message, it was from the same person—caller ID blocked—and the message simply said: 'Ha, ha.'

He threw the phone onto the passenger seat in anger. 'Bastard,' he said aloud and gripped the steering wheel. His anger was palpable. It coursed through him like an unstoppable current. *If I got hold of that bastard now, what I would do to him.*

Then he heard an engine approach and turned to see the same car with the tinted windows passing by. Sophie was getting dropped home. It was time for him to go home too and face the music.

22

Ben went breezily in the front door as if nothing were wrong and shouted, 'Hi,' down the hall to the kitchen area. There was no response, so he kept going on up to the bedroom, where he got a change of clothes and stuck his bloodied shirt deep into one of his drawers. He went into the bathroom and surveyed the damage. His jaw had started to swell visibly, and the beginnings of a yellowy-blue bruising coloured the swollen area. He washed off any of the dried blood that still caked the area around his nose.

He walked as jauntily as he could into the kitchen. The kids looked up from their screens. Deborah looked up from her book, but there were just a couple of lamps on, so nobody seemed to notice anything.

'How was the chamber meeting?' Deborah asked.

'Grand,' he replied, 'nothing important after all.' Ben knew that he would have to tell Deborah what had happened, but he'd have to wait until the kids were out of earshot. He'd spent time on the drive up to the house thinking through all the horrible consequences of what had just happened, and, surprisingly, the one that upset him most was the knowledge that Sophie would probably want nothing to do with their family any more. That meant no pet farm for the kids, and it meant that the one friendship they had managed to nurture was gone.

After making himself a cup of tea, Ben said to Deborah, 'Think I'll go and make sure the hens are okay, if you want to come out for a bit of night air.'

She looked up, then shut her book lazily and followed him to the door. Ben could feel his heart fluttering in his chest. He took a deep breath once they were clear of the front door.

'I have something to tell you,' he said with a voice that sounded weak and shaky.

'And what's that?' Deborah asked, her tone weary.

'There was an incident this evening involving Sophie and what I presume is her boyfriend.'

'What?' Deborah had stopped walking and was looking at him like he was some sort of alien species.

'It's a long story, but I was tricked into going up to the viewing point outside town. I thought it was the person who's been stalking us. I got a text to say he wanted to end everything and I should meet him up there.'

Deborah's mouth was open, but she said nothing.

'I didn't want to drag you into it, so I just went up on my own. He sent me a text last night. I really thought I could resolve the whole thing and come back with some good news.'

'So where does Sophie come into this?' Deborah asked.

Ben's jaw was stiff. It pained him to talk.

'He told me the type of car he'd be in, but it was really Sophie's boyfriend's car, so I was looking in the window because it was tinted.' Ben stopped there because he wasn't sure how to continue. How could he explain the stupidity of staring in a car window at two local people who were making out?

'And?' Deborah said impatiently.

Ben turned so his jaw was clearly visible under their security lights.

'Oh my God,' Deborah said and took a step towards him. 'That's badly bruised. What happened?'

'The guy thought I was some sort of perv, and he jumped out of the car and hit me a couple of times.'

Deborah didn't say anything in response to that. She kept looking at the jaw and at his face like she was looking at a puzzle.

'The worst thing about it is the female passenger of the car was Sophie and, well, the two of them were making out.'

It took a few seconds for that information to sink in. 'You absolute arsehole,' Deborah said after her short deliberation.

'What?' Ben was surprised by the suddenness of her change of tone.

'You absolute arsehole, going up there, doing something without telling me, and now somebody has made you look like a complete fool or a complete pervert depending on how you look at it, but either way you have gone and shat all over the one friendship our kids had made.'

'I know, and that's the bit I feel worst about.'

'You should,' Deborah said, 'and I'll give you the honour of explaining it to the kids because they were all fired up about going back to the pet farm this Saturday.'

'I know it was a stupid thing to do, but I really believed it could bring an end to all this.'

Deborah just turned and walked back into the house. Ben was left alone in the night with his throbbing jaw and a burning sensation where the guy had hit his ear. He was left to think through who the hell was behind this and what they wanted. The most likely person was Jeremiah. He had the grudge against them for taking over his mother's house and both breaking her chair and burning her straw cross. Plus he was obviously unstable, and he had been a friend of the Belgian guy. That brought Ben back to thinking about what the connection was between the Belgian guy disappearing and what was happening now.

He felt the whole thing was spiralling out of control and, somehow, he had to rein it back in again. He had been so obviously set up, but Deborah had just stormed off on him. *She's had enough*, he thought. The only consolation he felt was that whoever did it had local knowledge. They knew that Sophie would be there around that time. That meant it couldn't be the gang from Dublin. So he felt he knew for sure it was somebody local. He wondered again about the Belgian guy and Hennigan. That was an avenue he felt needed more exploration, and he had an idea how he could do some digging.

The idea of the boxer—Tom O'Sullivan—was still floating around in his head. He had noticed a stack of filing cabinets at the chamber meetings that Hennigan put the minutes of the meeting into. He only ever used the top drawer. There were three other drawers, and Ben wondered was there anything in there that might give them some clues. Maybe they were worth checking out to see if there were old newspaper clippings or just something that would give him a positive lead.

Meantime he had to try to figure out some way to tell the kids that their relationship with Sophie was jeopardized. Somewhere in the back of his head, he was hoping that Sophie would understand that it was just a mistake, and she would turn up at the shop like she always did, maybe a little more circumspect than usual, but that wouldn't matter. He could get a chance to explain to her that it was a genuine mistake.

But Sophie didn't turn up. One day passed and then the next and then the next, and there was no sign of her. The kids were around the shop, helping out, and they noticed.

'Haven't seen Sophie in ages,' Molly remarked one afternoon.

Deborah threw Ben a look but said nothing. She hadn't been saying much at all to Ben. Worse, the shop had been quiet, and that had led Ben to speculate that word had got around town about the incident. Ben knew that Deborah would be thinking the same thing, and he had developed a permanent knot in his stomach. He thought he might make things even worse if he went looking for Sophie to explain it was all a mistake.

With the customers who did come in, he was too effusive, and now he was afraid of a pall of desperation starting to grow in their shop, and it would all be his fault for taking such a foolish bait without consulting Deborah.

He had managed to pass off the bruising on his jaw to the kids as the result of a fall when he was out checking the hens at night. He'd kept going with the frozen pea treatment at any opportunity, and he'd even used a bit of light foundation to cover the worst of the bruising so he'd be presentable in the shop.

'I have something to tell you guys,' Ben said eventually.

'About Sophie?' Jack asked with a worried look.

'Yes, well, she comes into it.' Both kids now looked worried. Ben took a deep breath. There were no customers in the shop. He had no choice but to tell them.

'You know all the bad stuff that's been going on, like with Harry and the henhouse and the speaker outside. Well, it looks like someone is trying to give us a very hard time. We didn't want to say too much about it in case you guys got worried. The other night someone texted me to say we could end all the bad times if I met them. I really wanted that to be true so we could just start settling in properly and leading a normal life. But it turned out to be a lie and, not only that, it was a deliberate trick. The person said they'd be in a particular type of car, but when I went to that type of car, it was Sophie and her boyfriend, and they thought I was some sort of weirdo, so the boyfriend jumped out and, well, he hit me.'

Ben exhaled after he finished. He really hadn't wanted to get the kids involved, but now they knew there was a connection between the different incidents.

'I will never be able to set foot in this town again,' Molly said with her head hung low.

'You mean there is definitely somebody out to get us?' Jack asked in a quavering voice.

Ben put his arms around Jack. 'It could be just somebody playing a lot of foolish pranks and giving us a bit of a scare because we're new in town.' He held Jack tight and hoped that there was reassurance in his voice, but he had begun to doubt everything, especially himself.

'They're very scary pranks,' Jack replied.

'You were such a dork to go up there,' Molly said, her face reddening. 'This place stinks. The whole lot of it. Sophie was the only good thing here, and now she's gone.'

'When I see her, I can try to explain. She's such a nice person; she'll understand.'

'You will do no such thing,' Molly said sharply. 'I think you've done enough damage.'

Deborah sat there and looked at him. She said nothing.

23

There was a brief moment of positivity a couple of days later when Ben noticed the first sprigs of lettuce and broccoli pushing through the surface in their veggie field. He called Deborah and the kids out.

'Looks like the scarecrow is doing his job,' he said, pointing at the growing veg.

'Yeah, he is,' Jack replied with some enthusiasm until he saw Molly's dour countenance and decided to say nothing else.

'These should be ready to pick in a few weeks, then we'll have our own veg, and we'll even be able to sell some in the shop.'

'To our dwindling number of customers,' Deborah said wryly.

Ben felt his enthusiasm flagging, so he didn't pursue it any more. He had noticed that Deborah was happy to spend less time in the shop and more time either at home with the kids or out in town. Ben felt increasingly that the shop was becoming his baby, and he had to find a way to make it work.

One morning he arrived to open the shop, and he found an A4-size brown envelope shoved under the door. It had just the name 'Ben' written on it. It was mixed in with the other bits of post. He felt that familiar sense of dread looking at it and began to open it reluctantly. If he left it, Deborah might be down, and if it was more bad news, then he wanted to deal with it before she came.

Peeking inside, he could see another of those A4 photographs that he had seen before, but this time, as he slid it fully out, he saw something very different to the previous ones.

It was a picture of Deborah on the banks of the river that flowed through the town, in a secluded area where people sometimes went to walk. There were wooden benches that were carved from old bits of tree trunk, and Deborah was sitting on one of those. With her was a younger man with dark, curly hair, and he seemed to be listening intently to Deborah. In the white margin of the photo was written the words 'Best watch your back'.

Ben dropped the photo on the counter. He felt his eyes mist over and his vision start to blur. *Who the hell was Deborah talking to without telling him? What was going on? An affair? Talking to a solicitor about a possible separation?* He knew things had been bad in the last while, but did she think they were actually much worse?

Ben spent the day in a fog of confusion. He didn't know what he was saying to customers. He could only go through the motions, but always on his mind was the photo. What was he going to say to Deborah when she arrived?

She came in after lunch, but he found he couldn't say anything. Several times he tried to pluck up the courage, but he was so scared of what she might say that he backed off every time. If it was as serious as he thought, then it would be a complete confrontation, and he just didn't feel able for that. In the back of his mind he started formulating a plan. He would try to watch her, get some clues, follow her when she took a break from the shop, and see if he could find out who this person was without having that all-out confrontation.

There was a Chamber of Commerce meeting on that evening. Ben felt totally distracted by the photo, which kept playing over and over in his mind, but he had a plan for the evening's meeting, and he was determined to follow it through. Things were becoming intolerable in the house, in the shop, between himself and Deborah, and between himself and the kids. Jack had started staring at him during mealtimes like he was trying to figure out if there was something wrong with him. He found it impossible to sleep at night, and he felt his nerves were really starting to fray. His plan for the meeting was going to be a long shot, a desperate attempt to try to get some definitive proof. He had to go ahead with it.

Ben sat through the meeting, making the odd conciliatory comment so he at least looked like he was taking part. Before he left, he slipped a notebook he was carrying under his chair and then went downstairs to the bar. He hung around the fringes of a group Dave Breen was in. He didn't want to get too involved but, instead, spent his time watching the stairs that led up to the meeting room. Hennigan came down with Pat Doyle about ten minutes later. Ben could feel himself tense up with the expectation of what he was about to do, but he took deep breaths and tried to look relaxed, smiling inanely at anyone who caught his eye from the group.

A few minutes later the conversation in the group got very animated. One of them was telling a long story with lots of detail, and his audience listened with rapt attention. Ben knew he had to take his chance. He took a deep breath and walked quickly up the stairs, conscious of the creaking of the wooden steps under him. He reached the top, looked quickly left and right to make sure nobody was there. The coast was clear, so he went further in, making a beeline for the filing cabinet. As quietly as he could, he pulled the first drawer open. Inside were just the reams of notes from the minutes of the meetings that Dave Breen had taken.

Under that again was a drawer with tax returns and receipts. He rifled through it quickly but saw nothing of interest.

Finally he stooped down to look through the bottom drawer. This one was filled with little bits and pieces, a couple of photos, and what looked like medals. He took one of the photos out. In it he saw what looked like a very young Hennigan in boxing gear, facing the camera, arms in the air. Then a couple of shots of him crouched in a fighting position. Beside those there was a little velvet presentation box. Ben flipped the lid of it open. There was a gold medal inside. Ben took it carefully out, holding it by its gold-coloured ribbon. It was a boxing medal with a pair of golden gloves on the front. He turned it over and read the inscription on the back. It said, 'Golden gloves awarded to Thomas O'Sullivan', and it gave a date some thirty years back underneath.

'Thomas O'Sullivan,' Ben said to himself, and he felt his breath start to come in sharp, staccato bursts. 'Thomas O'Sullivan,' he said again, shaking his head in disbelief, but even as he did, he heard footsteps on the wooden stairs. They were coming quickly up. Ben fumbled with the box, but he didn't manage to get all the ribbon inside. He threw it into the drawer and closed it as quickly and as quietly as he could, but when he looked down, he saw a long piece of the ribbon hanging over the edge of the drawer. He didn't have time to open and close it again. The footsteps were now right at the top. He turned to make for the chair under which his notebook was. At that moment Hennigan appeared, red-faced, at the top of the stairs. He stopped in his tracks when he saw Ben.

'I had just popped back up to get my notebook. Left it under the chair.' Ben could feel the tremor in his voice as he spoke.

Hennigan said nothing. He surveyed the room; then his eyes fell on the bottom drawer of the cabinet with the piece of medal ribbon hanging out. He looked back at Ben, and there was a sudden darkness clouding his eyes. Ben felt himself stiffen with tension, waiting for Hennigan to do something. Glowering, he walked from the top of the stairs over to the filing cabinet. He opened the bottom drawer and stuffed the medal ribbon inside. Hennigan said nothing, just went to the table he normally sat at and picked up a calculator he had left behind.

'Right then,' Ben said and walked stiffly to the top of the stairs. He could feel Hennigan's eyes follow him, but continued on and went quickly down the stairs and out the door. Once outside, he let the air wash over his face and felt himself start to breathe evenly again. He walked up the street towards his car, forcing himself not to look behind, because he could feel a pair of watchful eyes track him as he went.

It was only when he had driven up the road and around the corner that he stopped and took a series of deep breaths, preparing himself for the journey home. He tried to compute the information he'd just gleaned. Mossy Hennigan and Thomas O'Sullivan were one and the same person. That meant he had serious criminal involvement in the past, and he had made a good job of hiding it. Ben had gleaned that information but at a cost. Hennigan had seen what he was doing. He had seen the bit of medal ribbon sticking out of the drawer. He was obviously a shrewd individual, so he would put two and two together. Ben wondered what he might do as a result.

24

The kids had gone to their rooms, and Deborah was still sitting up when Ben got home. He felt a mixture of nerves and excitement as he walked into the kitchen, where she was sitting near the stove, reading. Ben put the kettle on to try to steady his nerves.

'I discovered something at the meeting tonight,' he announced as he put a tea bag in a mug and poured the steaming water in.

'Oh, yeah?' Deborah didn't look up from her book.

'Something significant,' he said, putting milk in, watching it swirl around, turning the mixture a reddy-brown.

'Like what?' Deborah looked up, but her gaze was weary, like something viscous had caught in her eyelashes and was forcing them closed.

Ben sat in a chair opposite her. 'Okay, I went to the meeting, but I had an agenda. To be honest, the meetings are a load of crap where they just air their personal gripes.'

'Yeah, you've said that before.' Deborah still looked weary.

'I'd seen these big filing cabinets in the meeting room, though, and I noticed that Hennigan puts things in and out of them, so I thought they just might be worth a look.'

Deborah was sitting up now, but she was frowning, like she was expecting Ben to come out with another disaster story.

'I sneaked back upstairs after the meeting and had a quick root through them, and guess what I found?'

'What?' Deborah was looking interested.

'I found a photo of Hennigan when he was younger and some boxing medals.'

'Oh,' Deborah had reverted to looking weary.

'Yeah, but the clincher to all this is that the name on the medals was none other than Thomas O'Sullivan.' Ben paused to let that piece of information sink in.

Deborah sat bolt upright and gripped the two arms of her chair. 'Oh, my God.'

'Yes, so it must be the very same Thomas O'Sullivan who was keeping watch the day that consignment of cocaine was intercepted.'

'And the same Thomas O'Sullivan who was involved with David Mertens, the Belgian guy who disappeared from here.'

'Yes,' Ben said, leaning closer to her so he could talk in a low voice. 'Mossy is short for Thomas, and he must have taken his mother's maiden name or something, changed the surname by deed poll so he could start his life afresh.'

'But Mertens came looking for help or maybe a favour to be returned or whatever, and Hennigan decided he had to get rid of him.'

'It's possible, and for some reason he's afraid we

might come across something up here that will expose him.'

'Maybe there's more evidence on our land, and we are literally going to dig it up,' Deborah said, looking out the window as if she were checking the land.

'I'm not sure where that leaves us with Hennigan. He's obviously a man with connections and could be dangerous.'

'I could get my contacts to look more into this Mertens guy and see if they can find out what happened to him or where he went.'

'If he went anywhere. Maybe he never got off this property.'

'So the things of his that we found are only the beginning. What a horrible thought.'

'It seems a bit far-fetched in such a small community, but he must be somewhere. As you say, see what your contacts can come up with.'

There was a lull as they both thought it through. Ben had been keeping the last bit of information back, but he knew he would have to tell Deborah after the incident with Sophie. 'There's one other thing. While I was looking through the filing cabinets, I heard someone come up the stairs, so I closed them quickly and put everything away. I had deliberately left a notebook there after the meeting as an excuse to be there, but the ribbon from one of the medals was still sticking out of the drawer. Hennigan saw it.'

'So he knew you were looking through them and that you saw the medals.'

'Yes, but he doesn't know what that means to us, that we know about his past.'

'But he's obviously a shrewd character. He won't want to take any chances.'

Ben could see Deborah was thinking it through. He

wanted to say that he hadn't messed up again and put the family in even more danger, but he felt to say that would serve to highlight it. He still had his own questions, like who was the dark-haired young man Deborah had been talking to, but felt this was not the time to ask. For the first time since the Sophie incident, it seemed like Deborah was at least partly back on board, and he didn't want to jeopardize that.

'Think I'll check the hens. We've a lot to consider. You get in touch with your people, and we'll see if that gets us anywhere.'

Ben's mind was racing as he checked the hens and then peered out into the darkness, checking that there was no unusual activity. All was quiet, so he set to thinking what the next step might be. Jeremiah was due the next day to help dig the rest of the field. He could use that opportunity to sound him out, not that he had got very far with questioning him before, but maybe if he brought Hennigan's name into it, Jeremiah might just react.

Deborah was going to be doing the shop in the morning while he was in the field, and he was going to take over then for the afternoon. If he left it a little while and then shut the shop, he could have a little mosey around down by the riverbank and see if she was meeting the same guy again. He didn't feel good about snooping around, but he didn't want to confront her directly in case there was some perfectly innocent explanation. If she was meeting someone without telling him, maybe there was a perfectly good reason for it. There had been enough bad feeling between them. He didn't want to make it worse.

Deborah took the car next morning. The kids were hanging around the house, and Ben felt extra guilty that they didn't even have Sophie and the pet farm to look forward to. He'd been scratching his head in terms of things to do for them.

'We'll fly into town once I've finished this bit of work with Jeremiah and get you that fishing gear,' he said to Jack.

Jack shrugged and smiled. 'I'll help with the digging,' he said.

'Great, that'll speed things up,' Ben replied. Molly just stared at her phone screen as if she was waiting for some vital nugget of information to appear.

'We need to start getting you guys ready for school soon,' he said to both of them. That was something he felt might normalize things for them.

'That's ages away,' Molly said, eyes still fixed on the screen.

'It's a few weeks, but you'll see it'll fly by.'

'Nothing flies by around here except for the flies, and there's plenty of them,' Molly replied acerbically.

Ben heard the rattle of the Jeep coming up the drive. It sent a shiver down his back. He knew he had to find a way to stop Jeremiah coming round the house, but he had to do it subtly. They needed to be careful with someone so volatile.

Ben went out to greet him. Jeremiah was striding towards the field, shovel and pitchfork over his shoulder.

Jack and Ben followed him down. He was already digging by the time they got there. Ben watched him to see if there was any caution or reticence in the way he worked, like he was afraid he'd uncover something, but he worked steadily, without apparent caution.

'Our scarecrow is doing a good job,' Jack said to him after a while. He pointed at the lettuce and broccoli that was sprouting up.

Jeremiah laughed. 'I think it's more the rabbits ye'd want to watch out for with them.'

'And you don't think the scarecrow works for rabbits?'

'I don't know, but if you say it does, then it does. You're the boss,' he said, still laughing. He had kind of a gravelly laugh that rattled from inside his lungs. Ben found it scary, but Jack didn't seem to notice.

Ben brought down some tea and brown bread at eleven. Jeremiah slurped at his mug of tea and took huge bites of the bread so it all swirled down his gaping mouth.

'I'm taking Jack in to get his new fishing gear later on,' Ben said by way of opening conversation.

'That's right. Them bad lads caused him to lose the last.'

So he remembered that, Ben thought. *Must have been playing on his mind. So it could easily have been him who attacked Gavin.*

'That's right. But sure you'll meet bad types anywhere, wouldn't you?' Ben said. 'Even a quiet place like this must attract them.'

'Bad types everywhere,' Jeremiah echoed, looking far off out to the fields beyond.

'That was a strange case with the Belgian guy. David Mertens I think his name was.' Ben let that sentence hang in the air.

Jeremiah paused his drinking and eating, then continued again, but he said nothing.

'He was a friend of yours, wasn't he?'

'David? He didn't know if he was coming or going.'

'He left though, didn't he?'

'Well, he's gone now some time and that's for certain sure.'

'And you don't know what happened to him?'

Jeremiah threw the remnants of his tea out and picked his shovel back up again. 'I have to get off to work soon.'

'I don't think Mossy Hennigan was any fan of Mertens,' Ben said in a last desperate attempt to get a response.

'You might not be wrong there,' Jeremiah said before he started digging again.

25

Ben brought Jack in to get the fishing gear, dropped him back home after making him promise he'd wait until evening, and then Ben would go fishing with him. He had to go to the shop and didn't like leaving the kids even in daylight. He dreaded something else happening, but he didn't want them living on edge at the same time. When he arrived at the shop, Deborah was a little perkier than she had been recently.

'Did you get anything out of Jeremiah?'

'Nothing really. He more or less said he knew Mertens and that Hennigan was not a fan of his, but we knew all that already.'

'Not exactly the most loquacious of individuals, Jeremiah. I'm not surprised he doesn't really go to the pub or mix at all.'

'But he carries a good air of menace with him. Jack was down with us, and Jeremiah hadn't forgotten about the young guys leaving him stranded. He seems like someone who would keep a grudge once he has his mind made up.'

'And you think he has a grudge against us?'

'For sure, but to what extent I don't know.'

'We're not really getting anywhere with all this, are we?' Deborah said, almost as if to herself.

'Well, we discovered that Hennigan was the lookout guy, and he is definitely tied to Mertens.'

'Yeah, but where does that get us? We still don't know for sure who is targeting us and why. We're just kind of sitting around waiting for the next thing to happen. I haven't wanted to bring it up, but do you think it could be the gang from Dublin? They're not the types to forget.'

'I've thought about that as well, and I don't think they have anything to do with it. Whoever is behind this has a lot of local knowledge; the thing with Sophie convinced me of that. So that narrows the field to Hennigan or Jeremiah. It seems like whoever it is is trying to scare us off, but from what? From the house? The shop? The town? And why? Maybe they'll feel they've done all they can and leave us alone now.'

'Maybe, or maybe something worse will happen.' Deborah picked up her bag. 'I'm going to pick up a few things in town and then head home. We need to keep an eye on the kids.'

Ben watched her go, waited a short while, then wrote 'back in a few minutes' on a piece of paper and taped it to the door. He left, looking up and down the street as he did. He turned right and then left onto the main street, checking all the time as he went. From the main street he crossed the small square with the fountain and walked down towards the riverbank. He pulled up short behind a cluster of trees and looked around the trunk of one. There was a series of benches dotted along beside the river. From his vantage point he could just see two. One was empty, and two older men sat on the next one. He moved out from behind the trees and walked stealthily towards a low wall that separated him from the riverbank. He was almost at a crouch, head down, so he wouldn't be seen. When he raised his head, he saw what he'd seen in the photograph: Deborah sitting close to a younger man with dark, curly hair, and the two of them deep in conversation.

Ben instinctively dropped lower again to get completely out of sight. He backed up until he found the cover of the trees again. His heart was pounding, and his mouth was dry. What should he do? Confront the two of them? Ask her what the hell she was doing? No, that didn't seem like a smart move given all that was going on. He'd bide his time, then present her with the photograph and just say that someone had shoved it through the door, and could she explain herself.

He texted Deborah before he left the shop that evening to say he'd bring back some Chinese, and then they'd go out for a family walk. He'd wanted to do something with the kids, thinking they were probably going stir-crazy. Ben had told Jack he'd bring him fishing next evening, but he wanted to get Molly involved in something as well.

He brought back chicken in black bean sauce, wonton noodles, pork ribs, rice, and prawn crackers, which he laid out on the table and let the smells and steam suffuse the room. The kids were soon wolfing it down. Molly, who had been threatening to go vegetarian, seemed to have temporarily shoved such notions aside.

Feeling contented, if somewhat bloated, the family set out for the walk, which was to the right of the beach where Jack had got stranded. Ben drove to a small car park just off the beach, and they set off up a grassy path that rose steadily to look down on the beach to the left, and straight in front it faced right on to the rising swells of the Atlantic Ocean. Ben leaned into the strong wind that sent mouthfuls of salty sea air rushing down his throat. The air felt thick and healthy and vibrant. The path continued to rise, and as they got higher, gusts of sea air buffeted them, at times strong enough to push them back inland. Jack and Molly played around with leaning into the wind to see if it could hold them up. Ben and Deborah watched carefully over them to make sure they never went anywhere near the edge. In places the grass went right up to the edge.

At one point Ben saw them wander too close to the edge, and he grabbed both their jackets. They tried to pull away from him, laughing, but he held on for dear life, determined that nothing bad was going to happen. When they settled down a bit, he kept a grip on their jackets but let them get close enough to the edge so they could see the sea swirling around jutting, dark brown rocks below. Ben could see seagulls that wheeled out from nesting spots dotted along the rocky outcrops. They hung like floating paper in the wind, then wheeled back, mewling, into the safety of their nests.

Ben enjoyed the walk as much as he could, the tension of wondering when and how he was going to bring up Deborah's secret meetings playing on his mind. There had been so many negatives that had affected them, he wanted to dwell in this positive moment for as long as possible. The other thing on his mind was that they were walking on an exposed clifftop if anyone wanted to try anything, but to date the bad stuff that happened had been clandestine. He thought it was unlikely that their tormentor would take them on out in the open like this.

The grass track skirted the edge of the cliffs for a couple of hundred yards, then began to run back in again, so it formed a loop that took them back to the car park. They climbed into their car with hair that was sticking out at all angles from the constant wind.

'I look like a wannabe punk rocker,' Molly said, looking into her phone to adjust her hair again.

'That's the Atlantic winds for you. Not for the fainthearted,' Ben said.

'I've been reading about Grace O'Malley,' Jack piped up as they set off. 'She was this really cool pirate queen who used to capture ships around here and get them to pay a ransom before she let them go again.'

'Don't you go getting any ideas,' Deborah said with a laugh.

Ben felt the mood was lighter than it had been in a long time as they approached the house. When they arrived, he could see the hens were still out scratching around in their run, heads and legs making sudden, stiff movements, like clockwork toys. *Jesus, we're not so far from having a proper country house with a nice, natural life if only all this shit would stop happening*, he thought.

Ben opened the front door, and Jack was the first one through and down the hall to the kitchen. Ben heard a little exclamation of surprise.

'Oh, somebody seems to have left us a present.'

Ben immediately felt that familiar sinking feeling in his stomach. He knew instinctively that something was wrong as he approached the kitchen. There, on the table, was a large well-wrapped package in a dusty blue wrapping paper, with a little cardboard present tag sellotaped on.

'Stay back,' Ben said to Jack, who was lunging towards it. 'I'd better check it first. I wasn't expecting anything, and I'm not sure how this got in here.' His mind was racing. *Who could have left it? Jeremiah? Did he still have keys to the house?*

Ben flipped the present tag open. 'Best wishes to all. Woof, woof,' it said, with a little smiley face drawn in.

'Open it, Dad,' Jack said excitedly. Ben looked over at Deborah. She and Molly were standing side by side. Both watched him with features that were tensed up. Ben picked the package up and tried it for weight or hard objects. It felt soft and light. He felt around the edges and came across nothing sharp or unusual. The parcel was long, narrow at one end and broadening out at the other. He began to open it slowly at the narrow end, tearing off the first piece of wrapping paper.

What he saw first was a plastic nose, followed by two still, round brown eyes, then ears, until he had uncovered the full face of a stuffed toy springer spaniel, just like their Harry. Jack was watching intently, but a crease of worry had created a crevice on his forehead. Ben turned again to look at Deborah, but she said nothing. He knew he had no choice but to keep going. As he pulled the wrapper down, he could see the body of the dog, but something was wrong. Looking closer, he saw that the legs on the side he was unwrapping weren't attached to the dog. They hung loosely by its side. Ben stopped unwrapping.

'I'm not going to go any further. This is some sort of sick joke. I'll finish it on my own later, but I think I know what I'm going to see.'

'It looks like Harry,' Jack said, coming closer.

Ben pulled the wrapping paper back up to hide it.

'As I said, it's some sort of sick joke. Listen, we had a good night, so maybe it's best you guys go to bed.' He looked from Jack to Molly. Molly shrugged and walked off towards her room. Jack stayed for a few seconds, peering at the package. He left slowly, looking back at it.

'Goodnight, kids,' Ben said, but his voice sounded hollow.

He sat in the chair by the stove and put his head in his hands. 'What sort of sick bastard would do that?'

'The same sort of sick bastard who would kill our dog, and the same sort of sick bastard who would play his death throes back to us over a Bluetooth speaker, not to mention all the other shit they've done. And we are no closer to finding out who this sick bastard is and what they are planning to do next.'

'How did they leave it here?' Ben said, as if to himself.

'Either somebody still has keys, or they found some other way of getting in. I don't want to spook the kids, but Molly usually leaves her top window open for air. I'm going to have to tell her to stop, which I don't like having to do, but seeing as our house is turning slowly into Fort Knox, I don't have a choice.'

'I'm going to take this thing to the Gardai tomorrow.'

'They haven't done anything for us yet. In fact, all they did was let you know you're a suspect for beating up the publican's son.'

'Exactly, so the more proof I bring them, the better.'

'That sounds like you're defending yourself now. I don't know. I think we need to talk to the estate agents we bought this house from and see if there is anything dodgy from the past.'

Ben looked suddenly up. 'You're right. Maybe they can tell us something about the history of the house. We did pay for it, after all, so we deserve to know.'

'Maybe, maybe not. It's all getting very tiresome. It's not fair to the kids, living like prisoners. We need to set a time limit on this. If it doesn't stop, then we need to get out.'

'But that means whoever it is has won,' Ben said desperately.

'And you don't think they've won already. Look at

us. What's happened to our dream move? When was the last time we actually had a good laugh together? We used to get on, Ben, remember?'

With that, Deborah walked off to their room and left Ben sitting in the chair, staring at the floor.

26

Ben took the stuffed dog to the Gardai next day. Despite what Deborah said, he felt he had to.

Garda Byrne and his red-haired understudy were both behind the counter. Ben heaved the still-wrapped dog up. Its face was sticking out of the front of the wrapping. Ben had wanted to keep it just the way it had been left for him.

'Is this a gift?' Garda Byrne asked with a smile. The other Garda moved closer to get a look, a giddy smirk playing around the corners of his mouth.

'This was left inside our house last night while we were out walking,' Ben said, ignoring the giddiness.

'Does it have a name?' the younger Garda asked.

Ben started tearing more of the wrapper to reveal the legs that had been cut off. 'Remember what I told you about our dog when it was killed? The legs had been cut off.' He held one of the cut-off legs in his hand.

'That looks malicious all right,' Garda Byrne said. 'But it is a stuffed toy. As far as I know, there is no law to say you cannot cut the legs off a stuffed toy.'

That brought a stream of giggles from the younger Garda.

'It's not the toy I am here about. It is the fact that someone killed our dog and is now rubbing our noses in it by leaving this in the house. Not to mention they may have broken in to leave it there.' Ben could feel his temper rising. He knew he had to keep it in check.

'Was there any sign of forced entry?'

'No, but the kids sometimes leave the windows open for air.'

'Oh, they do?' He raised an eyebrow in surprise.

'Which you would think was safe enough in a country area like this.' Ben looked from one to the other to emphasize his point but also to check if there was any reaction. Maybe they did know something about the house that they were holding back on.

'You would, but there some's strange characters about. We still haven't got to the bottom of that assault on the young Hennigan lad.' The Garda looked directly at Ben.

He realized they were still viewing him as either a suspect or a fantasist. He was a blow-in in their eyes, and they hadn't got the measure of him. They'd probably heard about him looking into the car up at the viewing point, and they were deciding if he was off his head or a pervert, but definitely one to be treated with caution. Deborah had been right. They weren't going to do anything. Maybe they would if something really serious happened. Maybe it would be too late by then.

He shook his head and turned to leave.

'Hang on a second,' Garda Byrne said.

Ben turned to face him.

'Are you not going to leave it as evidence?' He nodded at the dog. The younger Garda had to stifle another fit of giggles.

Ben left with the stuffed dog dangling from his arms. He didn't have the heart to tell Deborah about the reception he got. He just said they'd be looking into it. Ben didn't say anything either about her meetings down by the river. He'd leave it until a better time. Besides, they had a few customers coming into the shop. There was a German walking tour in town, and they liked shopping around for local produce, so they sold lots of the heather honey and seaweed supplements and creams, which helped to lift the mood.

'Okay, Jack, we're ready to hit the seas or whatever the expression is,' he said after dinner. It was time for Jack to try out his new fishing gear.

'You could just say, like, are you ready to go fishing?' Molly said, darting him a dirty look.

'So I take it you won't be joining us, then?' Ben said, trying to keep the cheery tone going.

'Nope, we're having a girls' night in, isn't that right?' Deborah said with a conspiratorial wink in Molly's direction.

'Yeah, whatever,' Molly replied half-heartedly.

They walked first on a narrow path by the road but were soon into a sandy laneway that led down to the beach. It was a nice evening with the sun dropping slowly through a sky that was dotted with puffy clouds. Swallows darted and dived through the late summer air. There was a sense of abundance about the country, in full bloom before the onset of autumn, hedgerows dripping with flowers, whitethorn bushes bursting with small white petals. Bees hummed as they drifted from honeysuckle flower to flower.

Ben was keeping a covert eye out for Gavin or any of the young lads, but the coast was clear. The tide was coming in, but the rocks were still jutting clearly out of the water. They made for the nearest of these, and Jack seemed to know where was best for casting off. Ben watched him expertly fix the bait on, draw back and pitch the line with weight and bait far out. He left it a few seconds before starting to reel back slowly in again.

The sea was calm, and the draw of the tide pulled slowly in, then washed back out again, the clusters of seaweed on the rocks flopping back and forth with the movement. Gulls tipped against the fresh sea breeze. Ben relaxed into the rhythm of the tide and the gentle undulation of the water around them.

'Think I got something,' he heard suddenly from Jack. Ben saw the rod was straining. Jack gave it a tug, then started reeling slowly in. Ben was half-expecting to see a clump of seaweed come flying out of the water, but Jack stayed focused and kept reeling slowly, every now and then giving it a slight tug.

'Oh, wow,' Ben said when he saw a swivelling, pirouetting fish break out of the water at the end of the line. Once free of the water, it sailed towards them as Jack pulled it firmly in.

'Mackerel,' Jack said triumphantly as he pulled the fish right in so he could get a grip on it. The fish wriggled and slid in his hand, but he managed to grip it tight enough so he could get the hook back out again. The fish was small, silver in colour with a green tint on the upper half of its body that shimmered in the evening sun.

'What'll I do, Dad? Keep it or throw it back in again?'

'Throw it back in, I guess,' Ben said quickly. After all that had been going on, his instinct was to show compassion.

'Good man yerself,' he heard from behind him, and he nearly slipped off the rock. Ben turned to see Jeremiah standing on some rocks behind them, his fishing gear in his hands.

'That's a nice little mackerel ye have there. Fair play to ye. I'd keep him and stick him under the grill, but each to his own.'

Jack launched the fish back into the water. Ben saw the briefest of flashes before it darted out of sight.

'Down here by these rocks is the best spot for the mackerel,' Jeremiah said. He was addressing Jack only, as if Ben weren't there.

'I've got a mackerel lure, a spinner,' Jack said, holding up the lure he had just used.

'So ye have. That'll be a Dexter's wedge. Great for the mackerel all right. I might set up here nearby myself.'

He picked a spot a few yards away, where there was a rock flat enough to stand on, and set up his own rod before casting out. Ben felt uncomfortable having him so close. It felt like he was intruding on their time together, and he didn't address Ben at all. He focused only on Jack. Ben found that unsettling, almost creepy.

Jack cast out again, and the two of them stood there like they had been fishing together forever. Ben watched as they cast and reeled, cast and reeled. Jeremiah caught a couple of mackerel, which he threw into a bucket at his feet. Ben could hear them flop around, banging against the side of the bucket for a couple of minutes, and then they stopped.

Jack brought in another, bigger mackerel, and Jeremiah shouted encouragement as he reeled it in and then released it back into the sea.

Ben decided he had to say something about the stuffed dog. This was an opportunity to see how Jeremiah would react.

'Somebody dropped something at our house last night,' Ben said, turning to look straight at Jeremiah.

Jeremiah gave him the briefest of glances but turned his attention straight back to fishing. He said nothing.

'You didn't call by, did you?' Ben asked.

'Not at all. I was busy doing the hedging down by ours,' Jeremiah said brusquely.

'I'm just not sure how the person got in. They left something on the kitchen table.' Ben had decided to tease it out, but Jeremiah didn't respond either way. He cast again and started to reel in slowly. He kept his eyes fixed firmly on the fishing line. Ben could see he wasn't going to get anywhere with him, so for Jack's sake he decided to drop it. He wanted him to enjoy his first bit of fishing in a while.

Ben felt on edge for the rest of the time there. Jeremiah said nothing, just cast and reeled. He fumbled in his jacket pockets and pulled out some biscuits every now and then, which he stuffed hungrily into his mouth. The sun was beginning its slow descent behind some clouds on the horizon when Ben decided he'd had enough.

'I think we need to be heading back now,' he said to Jack.

'Just a bit longer,' Jack replied.

'Well, the mackerel is a fish that likes the light, so it does,' Jeremiah said as if to himself.

Jack cast out twice more and caught nothing, so he packed up.

Jeremiah cast a furtive look in their direction as they left, but he said nothing.

'He's strange, but he's nice,' Jack said as they walked home.

'I suppose we need to be careful with everyone before we get to know them,' Ben replied. He didn't want to scare him completely, but Jeremiah sent alarm bells ringing for him. He was like an overgrown child trapped in a man's body, full of confusion and secrets. Ben had seen the flashes of ferocity in his eyes, like an animal that feels it's being cornered.

27

'Client confidentiality restricts what I can divulge.' The estate agent was a short, round man with dark, thinning hair. He spoke with sudden, sharp movements of the head, looking down at the file on his desk and then back up at Ben and Deborah. It was a small premises with just the one large desk, behind which he sat.

'Well, we have been having a lot of difficulty since we arrived, and we wanted to know if there was anything unusual about the property. As the current owners, I think we are entitled to that,' Deborah said succinctly.

'Of course,' the agent said, but he just rifled through some of the pages in the file as if he were waiting for something to jump out at him.

'We have already been to the Gardai on several occasions, but they have been unable to find any positive leads,' Ben said. *Unable or unwilling*, he thought to himself.

'I see,' the agent said. He stared down at the paper and rubbed his forehead.

God knows what he's heard about me, Ben thought. *It's a small town, so he's probably heard about the assault on Gavin and the episode up at the viewing point.*

'We are living in fear in that house and concerned for the safety of our children,' Deborah said, looking the agent straight in the eye.

'Well, all I can tell you is whose name the house was in when you bought it, and that was Jeremiah Dunphy's older brother, Roger. The mother was the previous name on the deeds, but as is still the tradition in many rural households, she left it to the older brother.'

'So Jeremiah might have been unhappy that he didn't get left a share,' Ben said.

'That would be in the realm of speculation,' the agent replied.

'Was there any sort of falling-out?' Deborah asked. Ben figured she must be probing for information about the Belgian and any trouble he might have caused by staying there.

'I run a professional estate agent's business. I have to respect client confidentiality, as I said earlier. Now, I sincerely hope whatever issues you have had to date are over and that you can settle into what is an excellent property with plenty of development potential.'

He tapped a pen on the sheaf of paper like a magician who was casting a spell. He looked from Ben to Deborah and nodded to emphasize the sincerity of his good wishes, but also to signal that their discussion had come to an end.

Ben and Deborah walked the short distance back to their shop. As they did, Ben had the feeling they were being watched, an unsubstantiated feeling because he could see nothing to make him believe it. *Am I starting to unravel?* he asked himself. It certainly felt like that. He was losing faith in his own judgement, in his own perception of the world, this world, this new territory that he had never been in before, and now he had to have that discussion with Deborah. It had been playing on his mind, and he couldn't justify putting it off any longer.

'So, do you think that adds fuel to the fire in terms of Jeremiah having a major grudge against us?' Deborah asked once they were back inside the shop.

'It's quite possible. He really doesn't seem like the most stable of characters anyway. That other evening when we met him out fishing, you know, he would hardly look at me at all, like he was really hiding something.'

'It's time we told him that he shouldn't be up at the house for any reason, then,' Deborah said as she fixed up the baskets of fruit and veg, took some of the older stock out and replaced it.

'Yeah, you're right. I was worried that he might turn completely against us if we did that, but it could hardly be any worse than it is. I'll tell him the next time I see him.'

Ben waited until they had the shop set up for the day and he had made a mug of tea for Deborah before broaching the subject that he had been putting off. He felt his body stiffen with tension in anticipation of Deborah's response. Going through it in his mind, he couldn't think of any positive reason she could give. What possible explanation could there be for sneaking off and meeting someone without telling him?

'Emm, there was something that I wanted to bring up, and it's kind of awkward.'

Deborah looked suddenly up at him, like she had been waiting for him to say that.

'I'm not going to bullshit or beat around the bush,

but I got a photograph from our anonymous stalker, and it was a picture of you and some younger guy with dark curly hair down by the riverbank.'

Ben could feel his pulse racing. Deborah was looking at him with a face that was hardening by the second.

'I didn't want to bring it up at the time because we were going through so much anyway, so I left it a couple of days, and then I noticed that you were taking breaks, and I wasn't sure where you were going, so I went down to the river one of those times myself.'

'So you were following me?' Deborah's face had hardened even more.

'I wanted to find out if this was just some other hoax, another ruse to get me into some horrible situation. I've started to doubt myself. I don't know what's real anymore.'

'And, as you know, I have started to doubt this whole project. I can't live like this, Ben.'

'So who were you meeting, then?' Ben felt he had to come straight out with it.

Deborah looked down at her mug of tea. 'It was an ex-colleague of mine. He works in TV in the west of Ireland now. I wanted to let him know that I might be looking for work soon, so he could put the word out.'

Ben felt initial relief that it wasn't something a whole lot worse, but then the relief turned to anger. 'What do you mean that you might be looking for work? Where? With whom? Moving to where? Taking the kids? Just bailing out without telling me?'

'No, of course not, and I don't know where, just not here. I wanted to see what was out there and then make some decisions.'

'And me? Where do I come into it?'

'That's for you to decide, Ben. Where exactly is all

this leading? We've hardly had a single night of peace since we came here. This isn't the life that we signed up for. You seem to be just taking it day by day. I can't do that anymore. I need other options, a safety net. I'm reaching the end of the line, Ben. Otherwise it might just be too late.'

28

Jeremiah was due to come up and finish digging the last bit of the field. Ben spent a restless night thinking about his conversation with Deborah and figuring out how he was going to tell Jeremiah he wasn't to come to the house any more without offending him. If he did see it as still essentially his house and the Higgins were intruders, then he could react very badly to the news. Ben was going to have to be diplomatic but firm. He was used to making decisions and being a figure of authority in his past life when he worked as a financial advisor, but then he had the expertise and the track record. Here he was out of his natural environment, lacking authority, and needing as many allies as he could get. Still, a line had to be drawn in the sand, and he had to step up to the plate.

'So you're going to tell him and be clear about it. I meant what I said yesterday, Ben,' Deborah had said over breakfast. She was going to open the shop and leave Ben to deal with Jeremiah. She had looked tired. Ben felt terrible about the way things had slipped so badly between them in what should have been a move to a peaceful, natural new life. That feeling galvanized him for what he had to do.

Jack came out with Ben to help in the field. Ben felt he had to let him know what was going on as well.

'I wonder if Jeremiah caught anything after we left?' Jack looked up at Ben as they walked to the field. Jack was the only one in the family who seemed to view Jeremiah with anything approaching affection.

Ben looked down at his broad, innocent face. He was due to start secondary school in a few weeks, but he still had a childish sense of wonder about the world. Jack lived half his life in the realm of the superheroes, and Ben felt at times completely inadequate. Jack was a kid who wanted to be able to transfer those superhero powers to his own dad. Ben had always tried to be a steady, reliable dad, but when he worked in finance, the hours had been very long, and when he finally got home in the evenings, he was fit for nothing. Still, he had managed to read stories even though sometimes the two of them would be asleep before the story was over.

The move to the country was supposed to resolve all that. They would have family time together, even if Molly sometimes voiced her protest. They would have shorter days and could mix the farm work with shop work so one of them would be around the house as much as possible. Now, it felt like the house was the problem, that there was no sense of security there, that they were just hanging in by a thread, and all the dreams of a new life of togetherness were evaporating before their eyes.

Just after they reached the field, Ben heard the crunch of Jeremiah's Jeep rattling the gravel at the front of their house. He had to tell Jack quickly.

Jack was over fixing a button on the rough jacket that they had stuck on the scarecrow. Ben went over to him.

'Jack, you know the way Jeremiah has been helping us out with a few things around the place; well, today I have to tell him that we won't be needing him anymore. He's done all that needs to be done.'

'But we'll still see him fishing sometimes?'

'Absolutely yes. It looks like the two of you are the best fishermen in the town.' Ben was relieved that Jack had taken it well; now came the hard part.

Jeremiah arrived with his layers of jackets flapping around him. He had his tools over his shoulder. He nodded in Ben's direction but said nothing to him. He went over to Jack, who was still at the scarecrow.

'Well, how's the little man? I seen them mackerel you caught the other night come back looking for you.' He accompanied the comment with a rough, throaty chuckle.

Ben wondered about Jeremiah's living circumstances. He lived in some sort of small cottage on his brother's property. From what Ben had heard, the brother was a well-known architect and had set up quite a successful business doing state-of-the-art extensions, all decked out with the latest in solar power and underfloor heating. The estate agent had even mentioned his name if Ben was thinking of doing a renovation. Looking at Jeremiah now, he could see how the bitterness at being cut out of the will on the house combined with his own sense of inadequacy and then the guilt over the father's accident made for a combustible combination.

Ben waited until they were taking a break. He brought mugs of tea down from the house. Jeremiah fiddled with a packet of tobacco until he had rolled himself a rough-looking smoke.

'Once this field is done, then that'll be it, Jeremiah,' Ben said, looking appreciatively across the field at the freshly turned soil.

'I look after the fields,' Jack said, looking across it. 'Molly takes care of the hens, but I come out here to make sure those pesky rabbits don't eat anything. We're putting down netting, aren't we, Dad?'

'That's right. Jack's going to help me with the netting. That's all the help I need for the moment.'

Jeremiah nodded and took a long pull from his cigarette. He released a cloud of blue smoke that dissipated quickly into thin, spiralling wisps as it met with the gusts of fresh air. Ben watched him for a reaction and saw there was none. *He doesn't understand what I'm saying to him*, Ben thought.

'So you won't need to come up here to help anymore,' Ben said clearly.

'Maybe later on when all these little lads are ready.' Jeremiah nodded at the sprouting plants all over the other part of the field that were springing lively, green heads above the soil.

'We'll be able to manage them ourselves,' Ben said. 'There's not too much in it.'

He could feel Jack looking from him to Jeremiah, but he tried to keep as neutral and calm a face as he could.

'But we'll be planting more in this field, won't we?' Jack asked.

'I think it's getting a bit late in the season, but we'll see. There won't be much anyway, maybe some herbs.'

Jeremiah dragged on his cigarette and surveyed the freshly dug field, but he said nothing, and Ben was still left with the impression that he might not have fully grasped the message.

'So if you have keys or whatever, you could leave them with us today,' Ben said after a pause.

'Keys? What would I be doing with keys?' Jeremiah replied. This time he made eye contact with Ben, and there was that still, unmoving cold in them. Ben felt an involuntary shudder run up and down his spine. He had to check himself to stop from getting up and moving just to break the contact.

'I was saying, just in case. You know yourself, you don't want to have spare keys to your house just lying around. We need to keep track of them.'

'No keys,' Jeremiah repeated. He threw his cigarette butt into the soil and ground it into the ground with his big brown boot. Standing up, he cleared his throat and launched a thick phlegmy spit in the direction of the butt. Adjusting his jackets, he grabbed the handle of his spade and went back to slice deep into the ground.

Jack grabbed his own shovel and started digging as well. Ben had no choice but to follow suit. Jeremiah attacked the ground with what seemed to Ben like more than customary ferocity. Ben had observed that he was a strong and steady worker, but there seemed to be something extra thrown into his digging as he turned up great sods of dry, brown earth and sliced at them with the tip of his spade until they had crumbled and looked soft and brown again.

There's nothing else I can say to him, Ben thought, *apart from telling him straight out that he's not to come up to the house again. If I do that, he might fly off the handle altogether. Besides, Jack is looking a bit upset by the whole thing. He's been through enough already with all that's been going on.*

'Looks good,' he said to Jeremiah. 'Thanks for all your help.' Jeremiah didn't respond, but gathered his tools and started walking back to his Jeep. Ben and Jack followed in his wake. They could hear the rustle and flap of his jackets in the breeze.

Jeremiah packed his tools into the back of the Jeep,

then paused and swept a long, slow look over the entire house. He shook his head and went to climb back into the Jeep.

29

How many times do I have to tell you? He is throwing you out of your own house, walking all over the memory of your mother. She will never forgive you. I know you can hear her talking to you, and she must be so angry. It will only get worse with time. You have run out of options—it is time to take a final action, to do something that will stop him once and for all.

30

'I'm going to talk to Maureen, Sophie's mum,' Deborah announced the next morning as they were getting the shop ready.

'About what?' Ben asked.

'About everything that's been going on and about the incident up at the viewing point.'

Ben felt himself cower inwardly as Deborah said that. He still felt like a complete fool for having gone up there.

'What are you going to say though?'

'I'm going to tell the truth.'

She held her head to one side in a way that left Ben in no doubt she was going ahead with her plan no matter what. Head held to one side meant he had an opportunity to voice any objections, but they wouldn't affect the eventual outcome.

'I want to do it for the kids. That thing with Sophie meant a lot to them, and Christ knows they don't have a whole lot else going on.'

'Yeah, I'm sure you're right. I'm just not sure how she'll react.'

'Neither am I, but I'm tired of speculating. I feel I need to do something. It's not like we have a whole lot to lose.' With that, Deborah left.

Ben was left alone in the shop with just the sense that he was more the problem than the solution. If he hadn't gone to the viewing point, if he had been firmer with Jeremiah from early on, maybe he could have saved his family from the torment they had been going through. Then, of course, there was the big 'if'. He had been the most proactive in pushing the whole move, in scoping out the house they were in. He felt like a series of bad judgements on his part had brought them to where they were. Ben wasn't used to feeling out of control and rudderless. He'd been successful and well respected in his past. Now he felt all that was draining away. Soon his own family would have no respect for him. And they were in danger. There was someone out there who was trying to do them real harm. What sort of father was he if he couldn't even provide basic safety for his family?

Deborah arrived back ten minutes later. She shrugged as she walked in the door. Ben wasn't sure what that meant, but she followed it with a smile and a shake of the head.

'Maureen was very happy I dropped by. She had been completely thrown by what happened, and she said Sophie was as well. The boyfriend is a different kettle of fish. Hot-headed, apparently, and not so understanding.'

'I could have told you that,' Ben said and rubbed the place on his jaw where he'd been hit.

Deborah walked over to him and rubbed his shoulder. 'I know you've been through a hard time. We all have, but it was really shit of whoever set you up like that.'

'Really shit and really clever. What better way to blacken someone's name than to make them look like a complete perv?'

Deborah stayed leaning against him, and he could feel her warmth soak like a comforting balm right into him. He wished they could have stayed like that for hours, that they could have all those lovely bits of their old life back. It was like they had been snatched from the garden of Eden once all the harassment from the crime gang started, and they had never found their way back in again. Things would never go back to the way they were until this direct and immediate threat to the family was gone. Ben felt a steely resolve flow through him. He was going to be the man of the house and sort this out. He had to. His life, their lives, depended on it.

Just then Dave Breen walked in. 'Oh, very romantic,' he said, seeing Deborah leaning into Ben, her head on his shoulder. With his usual proprietorial air, he picked up an apple and took a large, noisy bite from it. He held it away from his face and twirled it in his hand, giving it a thorough once-over and nodding his head in approval.

'Who supplied these?' he asked.

Ben hesitated. It was absolutely none of his business.

'All right then. Keep it to yourself. See if I care,' Breen said. He suddenly waltzed across the floor and stood in beside Deborah, putting an arm around her waist so that momentarily the three of them were locked together, looking out towards the shop window.

'Imagine if someone walked past right now and saw the three of us standing here like that. Then they'd be talking.' Deborah pulled away from him and stood on the other side of Ben.

'Not enough going on in these small towns sometimes. You have to spice things up a bit.' Breen cackled at his own remark and took another large bite of the apple. 'Well, better be going. People to see; books to keep. They also serve who only stand and wait or whatever that expression is.'

Once he had gone, Deborah shook her head. 'Jesus Christ, that guy is a pain. Kind of creepy and intrusive.'

'I guess he rules the roost around here. As he said himself, he's got his finger in lots of pies. People treat him with respect and maybe even a bit of deference. Probably goes to his head. Now, fill me in on the rest of what Maureen said.'

'Well, the most important thing is that she was receptive to the message. She was clearly divided between loyalty to Sophie and to the rest of the townspeople.'

'The rest of the townspeople?' Ben asked. He could hear the high-pitched tenor in his voice.

'Yeah, well, naturally something like that is going to spread like wildfire.'

'Well, that's just great. So I really am a pervert in the eyes of the town.'

'It's probably not that hard to reach pervert status in a small town like this,' Deborah said and laughed.

Ben felt his stomach tighten. 'I don't think it's a laughing matter.'

Deborah walked back over to him and rubbed the small of his back. 'No, it's not, but we have to laugh at something.'

Ben still couldn't relax. People passed the shop window, and he was left wondering how many of them thought he was an outright pervert. He took a deep breath. He couldn't let it get to him, as he'd quickly feel overwhelmed. Protecting his own family was the number one priority. What the townspeople thought of him had to take a back seat.

'Anyway, Maureen was pretty up front about what people thought of us. She said the town was divided.

Some thought we were okay, and some thought we were just trouble. Maureen was on the side of us being okay until the thing at the viewing point. Now she's back on our side again.'

Ben rubbed his forehead. 'How could people see us like that? We've brought a business into their community. We're obviously doing our best to contribute. I mean, what have we done to anyone since we got here? I just don't get it.'

'Let's just take the good news while we can. Maureen is back on board, and she's going to talk to Sophie. Little glimmers of light and hope. That's what we need.'

'We didn't come all this way and give up everything for little glimmers of light and hope. I mean, what the hell. This is crazy.' Ben ran his fingers through his hair. He could feel tears welling in the back of his throat, so he turned to face away from Deborah. He felt her stand behind him and put her arms around his waist. They stood locked like that for a few minutes. He felt his breath slow down and his heart start to beat regularly again.

31

Sophie walked into the shop the next day as Ben was arranging the freshly delivered bread and pastries. He had his back to the door, and when he turned, he must have given a slight start back because Sophie smiled.

'Sorry, I didn't mean to give you a fright like that.'

'So we're quits, then.' Ben found the words just spilling out of his mouth. He felt himself start to go red as soon as he had said them, but Sophie let out a laugh that immediately put him at ease. He started laughing too. 'Sorry, I didn't mean to say that. It just came out.'

'You gave us a bit of a fright that night all right, but not to worry. I had a chat with my mum and, listen, for what it's worth, I'm sorry you've had to go through all that you have.'

Ben was taken aback by her frankness, but relieved that she had actually come out and said it as well. 'Yes, we've been through a bit all right, and, I don't mean to put you on the spot, but you were one of the positives that's happened, particularly for the kids. That's why Deborah wanted to talk to your mum so badly.'

'Yeah, well, I was sorry for the kids too. I really didn't like to let them down like that. It was just hard to know what to do.'

Ben could have filled in the rest of the sentence for her: ... *hard to know what to do if you think their dad's a pervert.*

'Well, it's great that you called in. Now, what can I get you?'

'Okay, I'm going to get an Americano with hot milk. It's been a while, and boy, was I starved for good coffee the last while. And I'll get a Danish to go with it.'

Ben put the coffee together, a feeling of lightness descending on him for the first time in ages.

'I'm not one of those coffee snobs,' Sophie continued, 'but when you get a mix of good beans and a good coffee machine, it's kind of unbeatable.'

Sophie started walking out the door with her goods when she paused and turned back towards Ben. 'Tell the kids I'll be back in touch soon, okay?'

Ben was very happy to impart the news over dinner that evening. Molly had been so taciturn and monosyllabic of late that Ben was starting to lose patience. He understood where she was coming from with the sudden misery and deprivation of her good friends, but still, it was hard to keep that in perspective all the time as she glared at him from under her fringe.

'So, we had a visitor in the shop today,' he said as he and Deborah dished out plates of noodles with diced chicken pieces and black bean sauce. The remark was ignored. Jack did look up, but, sensing the volcanic potential in Molly's mood, he obviously decided silence was the better option.

'And who was that?' Deborah asked with a smile. Ben had already related the story to her, and she was glad that her clandestine meeting with Maureen had provoked positive results.

'Oh, it was just Sophie.'

Jack looked sharply up. Molly tossed her fringe back.

'And she said to tell the kids that she was in and she'd be in touch.' Ben knew he should have drip-fed the details, but he couldn't wait.

'So we'll be able to go back to the pet farm?'

'Well, she didn't say exactly that, but she said she'd be in touch, so we'll take it one step at a time,' Deborah said.

'So we got our only friend in this dump back,' Molly said eventually.

'You'll get other friends,' Ben said. 'You'll be amazed by the number of young people out there whom you haven't seen yet. Wait until you go to school. There's something like six hundred kids in the community school.'

'If you think about it,' Deborah said with a smile, 'all those wonderful teens like yourself who are glued to their screens and hardly ever see the light of day. They'll be emerging in September.'

'Like zombies,' Jack said, and Molly laughed at that.

After dinner they sat around together and watched repeats of *Father Ted* and *The Office*. Ben made hot chocolate and basked in the uplift in the house mood. It felt like they were at the beginning of a new phase, maybe where things would start to turn around for them.

That feeling was not to last very long.

THE NEXT DAY was a typical late summer's day in Ireland. The sky started off still and grey with a blanket of cloud pushing warm air down. Swallows soared and dipped, picking off any insects foolish enough to venture out in the welcoming heat. As morning went on, the grey cloud began to thin, and patches of deep blue began to peek through in ever-greater quantity. Soon the grey was on the run, and the swallows now zipped through clear, warm air that was heating steadily. Ben could tell looking out the shop window that it was going to be a long, hot day—those ridges of high pressure that the weather forecaster had promised were going to do that rarest of favours in this part of the world and hold that heat, steady and still, over the country.

'We should try to get to the beach later,' he said to Deborah as lunchtime approached. 'Haven't been in for a proper swim yet. It would do us all good to shake the cobwebs off.' Even as he said it, he felt sorrow begin to rise. The beach had always been a place where Harry could really let rip, dashing up and down right where the water met the sand. He'd bark at the waves and the seabirds, and the kids would run alongside him, sprays of water bursting up from between their toes. He pushed the memories of Harry aside with a deep breath and turned to Deborah.

'Yes, I wouldn't mind a dip. Feels like we haven't really taken advantage of our location slap bang beside the sea.'

'No, I guess we haven't, but that's understandable with all the arranging and setting up we had to do.' Ben deliberately didn't mention all the difficulties they'd been through and the mood of helplessness that had dogged them since they arrived. He felt they were both determined to draw a line in the sand now that he had had his talk with Jeremiah and Deborah had spoken to Maureen.

Mid-afternoon he texted both Molly and Jack to see

if they wanted to go swimming later. Molly got back to say, '*Yeah, maybe, whatever, did Sophie call in again?*' Ben had to reply in the negative to that but assured her that Sophie would and, hopefully before the weekend. He knew that Molly was hoping for another day with Sophie up at the pet farm, but at the same time he knew that couldn't be rushed. Sophie's priority was going to be getting her boyfriend on board and convincing him the whole incident had been an unfortunate mistake.

Jack didn't get back to him, but Ben wasn't concerned. On such a lovely day, he would surely be out looking after the field, making sure the netting was all in place and the scarecrow was doing his job. Jack probably spent as much time dreaming about the superheroes he admired so much as actually doing anything constructive in the field, but that was what Ben felt the whole thing was all about, time and space to just drift off without having to stare at a screen twenty-four seven.

Jack had been to the comic book fair every year for as long as Ben could remember, his outfits changing every time, depending on who was top dog in the superhero world. He'd never been a sporty kid in school and had drifted naturally towards the nerdy element, captivated by worlds beyond their own where possibilities of power and strength lay there waiting to be tapped. Ben had found it sweet that he clung doggedly to the world of fantasy. Now, going into secondary school soon, he'd probably be under pressure to change, to put on a tougher exterior, and Ben thought he'd miss that part of Jack if it happened.

As it came closer to time to shut up the shop and Ben still hadn't heard back from him, he texted Molly again to ask if he was in the field. 'Probably' was the succinct reply. Ben felt a little uneasy that there hadn't been contact for so long, but he tried to play it down.

'You didn't hear from Jack, by any chance, did you?' he asked Deborah.

'No, but I wouldn't expect to on a lovely day like this. He'll just be out pottering around.'

'Yeah, I guess. I texted him about going for a swim ages ago, but he hasn't got back yet.'

Deborah looked at Ben, a hint of worry starting to form in her expression. 'I'm sure he's okay, isn't he?'

'Yes, just it's been a while, but I'm sure you're right. On a day like this, he'll be out there saving the world, or at least the lettuce.' They both laughed at that, but Ben still felt a tug of nagging worry.

They drove home in silence together. Ben didn't want to say anything that might upset Deborah, and he figured she was probably thinking the same. He hoped they would just see him sitting at the kitchen table with one of his superhero comic books or playing one of those kill-everything-that-moves video games. Sometimes Ben had found him standing there, staring into the hen run, watching their mechanical strutting and listening to the sound they made, which he said was like a rusty gate closing over.

But he wasn't there at the henhouse, and he wasn't sitting in the kitchen. Instead, a slightly pale-looking Molly came in from outside with a worried look on her face.

'I just checked the field, and I can't see him there,' she said. 'I knew you guys were coming back, so I thought I'd better find him. His fishing gear is still here. I checked. He hasn't been around the house for a couple of hours, I don't think.'

'You don't think?' Deborah asked, her voice becoming high-pitched.

'I was in my room on my phone. He's always roaming around when the weather's good, so I didn't pay any attention.'

Deborah looked up at Ben. He felt a queasy, roiling sensation in the pit of his stomach, but he took a deep breath to calm himself.

'I'm sure he's fine; probably just wandered further than he normally does. Maybe he got lost off one of the small lanes.' He thought his voice sounded thin and uneven, as if he was trying to convince himself as much as the others.

'Let's split up,' Deborah said. 'I'll look around here, and you head down towards the beach. He absolutely has to be in one or the other.'

'Hang on a second,' Ben said and dashed into the house. They hadn't done the obvious and searched the house properly first. He could be asleep somewhere or just hiding out reading a comic. Ben felt an initial surge of hope. *These are the little things that people forget to do when they get flustered*, he thought as he went methodically through every room, but he found no sign of Jack.

'Just thought I'd give the house a thorough search,' he said by way of explanation to Deborah and Molly.

'I already did that,' Molly said sharply.

Ben bristled at her irritation, but he managed to check himself. They were all stressed, and tempers were going to be frayed until they found Jack.

'Thanks for doing that,' Ben said calmly. 'The best thing you can do now is just wait here while your mum and I go off. If you hear or see anything, get straight onto us.'

With that, they all parted company, Deborah to walk the perimeter of their land, Molly into the house, and Ben, walking on shaky, nervous legs, first down the road that led to the beach, then down the sandy path that led to the beach proper.

He could hear the lonely swish, swish of the tide as he approached, and he felt the wind blowing in from thousands of miles away across the Atlantic, making its way across that desolate, empty space to reach land on this quiet strip of sand. The call of seabirds carried in the wind, and he could hear again the flap of seaweed clinging to the sodden rocks.

'Jack,' he called desperately, but the salty wind just threw his voice back at him. Nothing moved on the beach except the thin, stalking wader birds that searched the shore for shellfish washed in by the sucking tide.

'Jack,' he called again, moving towards the rocks where they had fished that one happy evening that now seemed so distant. The rocks were black and bare except for the earthy brown crusts of molluscs that flecked them here and there. He felt the magnetic pull of the tide, driven by forces way beyond the human scale, and it seemed a place of terrible loneliness where life could be tossed and crushed and never seen again.

Ben peered out towards the horizon, not sure what he might see, just feeling the salty air sting as he strained to keep them wide open. To even see the young lads who had taunted them and left Jack stranded would be a relief at that moment, to see anyone who might be able to give this a human context, whether friend or foe. He started to walk down to the far side of the beach, past the rocks to where the strip of sand narrowed and merged into grassland and then beyond into fields of grazing sheep and cattle. He saw nothing and no one and felt like collapsing and lying right there where he was, but he turned and started back towards Deborah and the house, hoping that Jack might have strolled up, returning from some mad mission that had brought him into town.

BEN HURRIED BACK from the beach, hoping against hope for some news, but he knew in his heart that his phone would have been hopping the second they found him. He walked the perimeter of the house and saw Deborah desperately searching in the thick bushes and vegetation at the end of their field. Down there were copses of tightly packed trees and sodden patches of land where the light-green, moss-covered soil had no foundation. A foot could sink suddenly as if treading on air, places where the rainwater or river water had never seen enough light and sun to dry out, untouched for decades if not centuries, left to trap and deceive those who were foreign to the land.

Ben had warned both kids about straying beyond the boundaries of their own land, explaining that some of it was just wet bog and needed to be treated with utmost caution. The kids had shrugged their shoulders as if to say *why would we bother going into somewhere so wet and uninviting anyway?*

Ben heard Deborah call Jack's name, saw her peering over walls, and he thought how desperate and lonely the land looked. He wondered what had happened on their land or the land around them. Suddenly it felt like the spirit of the place was revealing itself to him with its buried secrets. *Why did we come to such a desolate place?* he asked himself. This land seemed so easy to read on the surface, but once you dug deep, what would you find? He felt a darkness lurked there, one they had only scratched the surface of. It felt like the land had finally bared its teeth and consumed them.

Ben ran over to Deborah. He took a deep breath and tried to look strong for her sake. 'Any sign?' he asked.

Deborah started when she heard his voice. He could see a flitting panic in her eyes. 'No sign here. Do you think he might have gone into town for something? Maybe to do with fishing?'

'It's worth a try.' Ben jumped into the car and tore off towards town. He kept his eyes on both sides of the road as he drove. The late summer sun glinted off the mirrors of passing cars, blinding him suddenly when he careered around a bend, but he kept going, at speed, until he reached the centre of town and parked up near the square. He ran to where the fishing tackle shop was, but the shutters were down. He looked up and down the street. At that moment he saw Dave Breen emerge from the pub, and he dashed over to him.

'Do you know my son, Jack? He's missing. Have you seen him or heard anyone say they saw him?'

Breen paused and looked left up the long street, then turned to Ben and shook his head. 'Can't say I have. What time did he go missing?'

'That's the thing. We don't know. We got home from the shop, and he was gone.'

'Sure he could be anywhere, I suppose,' Breen said with a shrug. 'I'm sure he'll turn up. You know kids at that age, up to all sorts of devilment.'

'But it's not like him,' Ben said insistently.

'Well, they change overnight. That's what I'm told anyway. Sure I'm no expert not having any myself. Pat Doyle, now, he'd be better equipped to discuss such matters.' He then put a conspiratorial hand on Ben's arm to draw him in closer. 'That's if he's ever home between the taxi driving and the pub.' He finished that statement with a wink and a slap of the hand onto Ben's arm.

'I'd better let you go and look for the young fella. If I hear anything, I'll be the first to give you a shout.'

Ben looked hopelessly at him for a second, then turned and ran back towards his car, leaving Breen watching with a bemused expression.

32

'I texted all my friends in Dublin, and I tried the few of Jack's friends I know, but no one's heard anything,' Molly was saying in the kitchen. The three of them had decided to sit down and take a deep breath and see if they could come up with any new angles. 'Like, Jack wasn't really one to go online unless it was for gaming, and seems he hasn't played since this morning. Plus, his phone is here. I know he doesn't use it much anyway, but if he was planning to go off for the day, he'd definitely take it.'

'It's only half seven,' Ben said desperately, checking his watch. 'We can't let ourselves get into too much of a panic yet. He could walk in the door any second with one of those off-the-wall excuses that only Jack could come up with.'

They smiled at that, but nobody laughed, and the silence that followed the comment was uneasy, each of them flicking their eyes here and there as if Jack might magically appear from a corner of the room.

'I think it's time we went to the police,' Deborah

said. 'When you think of all that's happened. We can't wait any longer.'

'Mum's right,' Molly agreed. 'What are we waiting for?' She looked directly at Ben, and he saw real concern in her expression.

'Yeah, I guess you're both right. I was thinking he might just have wandered off and got lost, and then we've been to the Gardai a few times, and would they take us seriously, but yeah, you're right. Let's go.

Ben and Deborah jumped in the car. They left Molly to wait at home, phone by her side.

'Well?' Garda Byrne said as they burst in.

'It's our son, Jack. He's missing,' Deborah blurted.

'Ohhh,' the Garda said and frowned. 'Since when?'

'Well, we went to work in our shop this morning at eight thirty, and we haven't seen him since. His sister was at home with him, but she doesn't know exactly what time he disappeared, but she hasn't seen him since this morning either.'

'So you wish to file a missing persons report?' Garda Byrne looked from one of them to the other. Ben got the distinct feeling he was hoping they might say no.

'He's twelve years old, and he doesn't know the area well. He doesn't know anybody, so there's nowhere he could be,' Deborah said.

'Young lads that age can get up to mischief that they may not want anyone to know about,' the Garda said, looking from Deborah to Ben.

'He's not like that,' Ben replied evenly. 'He's a real kid still even though he's twelve.'

'Right so.' Garda Byrne disappeared into an office behind and emerged with a thick sheaf of papers.

'Now, I'll have to take some particulars. Could I have the name of the child, age, height, rough description of appearance, clothes he was last wearing.' He said all this with one breath.

'Jack Higgins, twelve years old, fair hair, slight build, khaki shorts, a T-shirt, and he had a navy hoody on this morning.'

'Underwear?' the Garda asked. Ben looked at Deborah, and he saw her take a breath before answering. Ben could feel a sudden ratcheting up of worry, and he thought Deborah was feeling the same. There was something so personal and intimate about giving that last detail. *It's almost like they expect to find a body*, Ben thought.

'He usually has superhero underwear, but I'm not sure today. He's twelve, so he dresses himself.'

The Garda scratched that down on the paper; then he looked from Ben to Deborah again. 'Do you have any reason to believe that he felt unsafe or in danger from anyone in the house?'

'You mean from a family member?' Ben asked. 'No, definitely not.'

The Garda wrote that down too. 'Or from anyone outside of the family?'

'Well, that's it. We don't know what's going on, but, as you know, our dog was killed, and I was shot at, so there is somebody who is trying to harm us.'

'But no specific threat to—' here the Garda had to scan the sheet of paper to find the name '—to Jack.'

'No. Not a specific threat to him, but as I say, our family is under threat. We just don't know from whom.'

The Garda didn't write that down. Instead he looked through the sheafs of paper. 'It's been a while since I filed a missing persons report,' he said as if to himself. 'Now, social media. Do you have access to his accounts?'

'No, but he wasn't really active on social media. He's into games.'

'As far as you know,' the Garda said, going back to writing. 'Medication, any special condition we should know about?'

'No,' Deborah said flatly. Ben could see the endless questions were wearing her out.

'Okay, then, we'll pop over to your house shortly, as that's the last place he was seen. I'll pass this report to my supervisor, and we'll launch a missing persons investigation.' He handed Ben a card. 'Here's my mobile number if he shows up or you have anything further to report.'

DEBORAH HELD her head in her hands once they were back in the car. Ben leaned over and held her. 'I know,' he said. 'It makes it seems so serious when they're firing all those questions at us, but it's just procedure.'

'I don't like procedure,' Deborah said through her hands. 'I've seen enough of it in my time, and I do *not* like to see it so close to home.'

They arrived back at the house to a silence that was broken only by the clucking of their hens and the melancholy braying of a donkey in a distant field.

They waited restlessly, pacing the kitchen, going to the front door and looking across the fields, down the driveway, but no sign of Jack.

The Garda car arrived about an hour later. Garda Byrne stepped quickly out, followed by his red-haired understudy. They walked around the premises as if they were prospective buyers, checking over walls, looking at the henhouse, tapping pipes.

'Do you mind?' Garda Byrne asked at one stage, indicating he wanted to go into the house.

'Sure,' Ben said, and he led the Garda up to Jack's

room. He took in the superhero duvet cover, the posters on the wall, then homed in on the fishing rods in a corner.

'He liked fishing,' he said matter-of-factly.

'Yes,' Ben said. 'But I wouldn't allow him down on his own, not after the incident when he got stranded.'

'But it's an avenue we need to look at,' the Garda said. 'We'll be alerting the Coast Guard anyway as part of the investigation.'

They prowled around for a few minutes more. 'Okay, I think we've seen enough,' Garda Byrne said. 'A full investigation is now under way, and we'll be in touch with any developments.'

When the Garda car left, they stood there for a while watching the empty spaces around them. The light was starting to fade. The sun had become a stark red ball slipping under the horizon. To Ben it felt like the window of opportunity to find Jack was slipping as the sun dipped below the horizon. The feeling of panic that had dogged him all day was starting to turn into something more hopeless. He felt so ineffectual. The world out there seemed so huge and full of infinite possibility where a kid like Jack could just be swallowed up.

They moved into the kitchen. Molly went to her room.

'I'm going to lie on my bed. I'll keep an eye on my phone in case any of my friends or Jack's get in touch.' She walked off stony-faced, but Ben could hear the brittleness in her voice. She was at times the sarcastic sister from hell to Jack, but Ben knew that deep down she loved him and felt very protective of that innocence he carried everywhere he went. Ben often wondered if she was in a way jealous of the bubble he managed to wrap himself in. She was such a part of the lippy, ironic teenage world.

'At least they took it seriously,' Ben said to Deborah after a prolonged silence. He got up and made them both mugs of tea, then realized that none of them had eaten since early on.

'Of course they did. That's what worried me.'

'They'll do their best. He can't have gone far.'

'Does it occur to you that he mightn't have *gone* anywhere?'

'Meaning?'

'He might have been taken.'

'By whom?' Ben asked the question, but that horrible thought had already wormed its way into his consciousness as well.

'By whoever the hell has given us such a hard time since we arrived.'

'But why would they do that? Why take a child? If anything, I seem to be the target of whoever this malevolent force is. They shot at me; they set me up. They've been sending me photos and texts.'

'Well, what better way to get at someone than to target their child?'

Ben rubbed unconsciously at the arm of the chair he was sitting in. He felt the hand that held his mug of tea start to shake. 'Nobody would do that. Only the worst, the very worst. A child, for Christ's sake.'

'They've shown themselves to be pretty bad so far. I'm not trying to jinx it, but I think we need to be ready for anything.'

Ben jumped up and went to their front door. He paced around outside, searching again through all the space around their property. He was looking for something, anything that would yield a clue, but he saw nothing. When he went back in the house, he checked in on Molly to see if she had heard anything, but she was sound asleep on her bed, her phone still in her hand.

There was an electronic clock that they had put up in the kitchen, an old-style one that would have had chains and chimes, but this one just had a steady electronic tick, housed in an old-style wooden exterior. The ticking was usually inaudible, but as they sat and watched the minutes drag by, it began to take over the whole room. Neither Ben nor Deborah could do anything but wring their hands and stare hopelessly at their phones, praying they would explode suddenly into life and draw a clear line between the horror they were experiencing now and what might be a final release from the gnawing passivity of waiting.

After one full hour Ben could take no more.

'I'm going to drive to the beach and see if I can see anything. I know it's hopeless, but I have to do something.'

'I'll stay here,' Deborah said wearily.

33

The beach was a grey-blue in the dusk. The tide was in, and the black tops of the rocks were jutting shadows on the dark water.

Ben walked hopelessly from one end of the beach to the other. At one stage he saw what looked like a searchlight arcing across the sea, and he heard a boat's motor, but it was too dark to see anything. He felt shells crunch underfoot as he continued pacing. He knew he was wasting time down there, all alone, but at least it gave him space to think.

If Jack didn't have some terrible accident that sent him into the sea, then the only logical explanation was what Deborah had said—someone must have taken him. But why? Ben didn't want to think that someone would actually want to harm Jack. He was such an innocent and harmless child. Who could possibly have a grudge against him?

That led Ben down a couple of avenues of thought. First one was the group of young guys who had taunted him. Maybe they got in trouble for what they did and held it against Jack. Gavin, their leader, had got assaulted by a person unknown, so maybe they thought that was something to do with the way they had treated Jack. Gavin was obviously the ringleader, so he could have convinced the others that they needed revenge.

Ben thought briefly of the gang from Dublin. But why would they want to get involved with something as messy as kidnapping a child? If they wanted to get at Ben and Deborah, they could find much easier ways to do it.

A third scenario was that whoever it was that was stalking him and his family was going to hold Jack as some sort of hostage to get whatever it was they wanted. Whatever it was they demanded, Ben would make sure they got it straight away. No doubt this person was disturbed, but if they were fixated on one thing, then he and Deborah could focus on that one thing and negotiate with them.

Jeremiah was the person who came to mind most for Ben. He had the grudge, and he was obviously disturbed, but Ben knew that he had to be careful. If it was Jeremiah and if he was as disturbed as he thought, he could be very volatile and capable of anything. What Ben needed was evidence.

Tortured by all the possibilities and with darkness now blanketing the beach completely, Ben walked back up to the car and drove home.

'No sign?' Deborah asked as soon as he appeared.

'Afraid not. Anything from the Gardai?'

'Nothing.' Deborah sat back in her armchair, and they looked at each other. Ben felt weak with worry and exhaustion. His mind was jumping all over the place, but he knew he had to try to stay calm and focused.

Thirty minutes later the Garda car pulled up their drive. They both ran out, hoping to see Jack's bob of fair hair in the back, but it was just the two Gardai. They looked grave as they stepped from the car.

'The Coast Guard has been stood down. They will resume their search in the morning,' Garda Byrne said. 'We have spoken to all people we felt may be relevant to the investigation in town, and as yet we have no positive leads on the whereabouts of your son.'

'So you spoke to Gavin? Jeremiah?' Ben asked.

'To all people we believed could be of assistance. I am sorry, but for the moment we will be returning to the station, but we have all units on alert and will report to you immediately on finding anything we believe may help the investigation. Should you receive any information yourselves, please inform us immediately.' The Garda nodded at them in conclusion, and the two of them got back into their patrol car.

Ben and Deborah watched the lights of the car disappear down the drive and off into the enveloping darkness all around them.

'It's two o'clock,' Ben said. 'You go to try to rest a bit. I know you won't sleep, but you'll need your energy. I'll wait up.' He held Deborah close and could feel her tremble against him. Without saying anything else, she went back into the house and turned towards the bedroom. Ben went in and sat in the armchair, watching the occasional flicker of a passing headlight far out on the road. Every light, every noise gave him hope that was quickly followed by a crushing despair, a feeling of helplessness, leaving his only son out there, frightened and alone. He tried desperately to stay awake, but eventually the flickering lights that grazed their windows sent him into a fitful sleep, one where he was falling all the time, grabbing at something to stop himself but finding nothing. The speed he fell at made it hard to breathe, so he felt this gasping, choking sensation as he plummeted. Around him were violent sounds of rushing and a grey-black darkness through which he could see nothing.

Ben woke suddenly with a start. He was gripping both arms of the chair, his fingers white with the pressure. It took him seconds to come through and see the dawn lighten the kitchen shadows. At first he felt relief that the falling sensation had stopped, that he could breathe again. Then he remembered. Jack. Gone and now dawn was breaking and still no Jack.

He stood up sharply and ran his fingers through his hair. It wasn't making sense to him. What was he doing here in this house, on this land, a strange place that had taken his son. What sort of stupidity had led him here? How would he ever forgive himself?

He went outside and felt the cool air against his face. Birds had begun to chirp high in the trees. Otherwise there was no sound. He checked his watch. Five thirty, Deborah must have fallen asleep too. He'd leave her to sleep as long as she could. Hopefully she wasn't having the same nightmares. With no other idea what to do, Ben began to walk their land again. His mind was racing as he looked desperately over walls and behind hedges. In his heart he knew there was nothing to see, but he had to keep moving. To stop would bring him back into that dark place of questions that had no answers.

It took him a full thirty minutes to walk all of their land, to look everywhere he could think of looking. Back, standing outside their house again, he stopped to listen. The hens were beginning to stir in the henhouse. The chirping of the birds was turning into birdsong. He heard a clatter of hooves as a bigger beast moved in a field nearby. Then he heard a motor, an engine that sounded bigger than a car, smaller than a truck, and it was somehow familiar to him. He held his breath and listened carefully. It was heading back towards town. There was a rattle off it that he recognized, so he went to the side of the house, and as he did, he was just in time to see Jeremiah's Jeep flash by. His heart skipped a beat as he watched its dirty, green, metallic body rattle past.

Ben felt a choking sensation as it passed. *What's he doing out at this hour of the morning?* Ben's instinct was to jump in his own car and fly down the road after him, but where would that lead?

He ran into the house and woke Deborah. It took her a few seconds to come around and to remember what was going on.

'Did they find him?' she asked breathlessly.

'No, but I just saw Jeremiah's Jeep going past. It was heading back into town.'

Deborah looked at him, like she didn't compute what he was trying to tell her.

'It's only six a.m.,' Ben said emphatically, 'and he was going back towards town, towards his own house.'

Deborah shook her head to speed the waking process. 'Okay, but maybe he's just out working. He works all over the place, and he has to get stuff done before he starts the work with the council.'

'Yes, but six is very early, and where would he be coming from? He can't have finished whatever work he was doing already.'

Deborah nodded. 'I see what you mean, but we need to be very careful.'

'I know. That's why I woke you. I wanted to jump straight in the car and go after him.'

'You need to let the Gardai know what you saw. They'll check it out.'

Ben dialled the mobile number he'd been given.

There was a long series of rings before a groggy voice appeared at the other end. 'Hello?'

'It's Ben Higgins. I just saw something unusual, and I wanted to tell you straight away. Jeremiah just passed in his Jeep, and he was heading towards town.'

This was greeted initially by a lengthy silence. 'Right so. We'll look into that, but I have to advise you that we spoke to Jeremiah yesterday, and he assured us he had no idea where the boy was.'

'I know, but what was he doing so early? Also, he knows Jack. They had a kind of a bond. Jack might trust him.' Ben let the implications of that sentence hang in the air.

'We will look into it in due course. Emotions are understandably high, Mr Higgins, but we don't want to rush into anything.'

The Garda hung up after that, and Ben was left wondering at the lack of urgency in his tone. He shook his head at Deborah, who was looking expectantly at him.

'Sounds like they're just going through routine procedure. He didn't make much of me seeing Jeremiah.'

'I suppose that's exactly what they would be doing, not getting our hopes up unnecessarily and not pointing the finger at any one person until they have evidence.'

'Yes, I know,' Ben said, 'but time is ticking by. Every second counts. Routine enquiries are not going to be enough.'

'I had another idea. We can contact the local radio station and maybe the local press and see if there's a Facebook group. We'll plaster pictures of Jack all over the place. Something is bound to come out of that.'

'Good idea. I'd say Maureen will know a hell of a lot about all of that. Why don't you go down to her as soon as the shops open, and we'll get the message out there, loud and clear.'

They had a bit of tea and toast and checked that Deborah had up-to-date pictures of Jack on her phone. They even had a couple of hard copies from Jack's primary school graduation ceremony. Deborah left at eight o'clock, as the shops opened then, and they wanted to get to Maureen before she got too busy.

'I'll take the car,' Deborah said. 'You sit tight and let me know straight away if you hear anything. I'll let you know how I get on with Maureen.'

'Okay, good luck.'

Ben watched Deborah take off down the driveway, then went inside for his jacket and the poker that was still there beside the stove. He'd had enough of waiting around. It was time for action.

34

Ben walked the road into town. Jeremiah lived in a small house on his brother's property about half a mile away. Ben had only ever seen it from the road, and it was a kind of typical country set-up, a sprawling affair that had the couple of houses, a big barn, and a couple of outbuildings. It was surrounded by high hedging and had a row of tall pine trees running parallel to the road, so it wasn't visible to passing traffic. From the start of the driveway it climbed slowly up to a slight incline, so it was just the tops of the buildings that Ben would have seen as he drove past before.

The morning was calm and quiet, a clear day with just a hint of cold waiting to be banished once the sun rose higher. Cars swished past, but there was a narrow footpath that led all the way into town, so Ben could ignore the traffic, keep his head down, and stay focused on the task at hand. His story was that he was just out checking everywhere for Jack, and he felt it was worth doing house-to-house calls. Everyone in town would know by now what had happened, so he was prepared for someone to stop and ask if he was okay or if they had got any closer to finding Jack.

Jeremiah's driveway was flanked on either side by two rusting, metallic silver gates, which were tied open. The driveway was rough, sandy ground pockmarked with divots and potholes. Ben stopped at the entrance and looked up the length of the drive. Nothing stirred. He could see the outline of the two houses at the top: one clean, neatly presented with wide, wood-framed windows; the other small, shabby, with plaster peeling off grubby whitewashed walls. Ben listened for the sound of a dog as he began to walk tentatively up the drive. He heard nothing, so he continued walking, taking care not to slip on the rough ground. He could hear his own breath, and his heartbeat thumped all the way from his chest to his head.

As he got to the top of the drive, he could clearly see the two houses, so he stopped again and checked for movement. He heard and saw nothing, so he kept walking. Then to the side of the smaller house he saw the dirty green outline of Jeremiah's Jeep. He was home. That caused Ben to stop in his tracks. His instinct was to dive for cover, to stop himself being seen, but he had come too far now. There was no turning back. He felt the weight of the poker in his jacket pocket and took another few steps towards the smaller house. Just then he heard a noise, a creaking sound, like that of an old, rusty door being pulled over. He heard it again, and this time it was followed by a sharp bang. He walked slowly around the side of the Jeep and could see the rough brickwork of an outbuilding. To the right was a dark-red wooden door, and right beside that door he could see the bulky jackets of Jeremiah as he fiddled with something. Looking closer, Ben could see that he was closing over a padlock.

Ben felt his legs go weak as the blood drained from his body. What did Jeremiah have in that outbuilding that he needed to padlock in? Ben knew he had no choice now. He walked out from behind the Jeep.

'Jeremiah,' he said, 'I wanted to have a word.'

Jeremiah looked suddenly up at him. A look of panic scorched across his face. He finished snapping the padlock into place.

'You might have heard Jack is gone missing. We haven't seen him since yesterday. I was wondering if you had seen anything.'

Jeremiah's look of panic had gone now, but it was slowly being replaced with something else. He was holding a bag in his right hand, made of a woven sack-like material. He pulled the bag in closer to his chest. The look on his face was now challenging, defiant.

'What would I know about that?'

'I'm not saying you would know anything. I'm just asking if you saw something that may help us.' Ben took a couple of steps closer to Jeremiah. He felt his hand tremble as he held the poker in his pocket.

'I saw nothing. What are you doing on my property?'

Ben moved closer again. He was listening to see if he could hear any noise coming from inside the shed, but he heard nothing, just his own heart thumping in his head.

'I'm checking everywhere for my son. I saw your Jeep driving this morning at six o'clock. Where were you coming from at that time?'

'That's none of your business what I do with my day.'

'I think anything that helps me find my son is my business. Maybe you saw something at that time. Maybe you know something that can help me.'

'I know nothing. I told you. Now, get out of my way.'

Ben had moved in close to Jeremiah, so he was blocking his way to the Jeep. Jeremiah stepped forward and pushed him aside, but as he did, he lost his grip on the hessian bag, and it tumbled to the ground. As it did, a pile of food cans, chocolate bars, small cereal boxes, and a carton of milk tumbled from it. Jeremiah reached quickly down to shove them all back in, but Ben stuck a foot in front of his hand to stop him. Jeremiah looked up, then grabbed Ben's foot, lifted it and shoved at the same time, sending him flying back to crash onto the hard ground behind him.

'What are you doing?' Ben shouted. 'What are you doing with all that food? Where is he?'

'I'm after telling you. I know nothing,' Jeremiah shouted and started to clamber into the Jeep with the bag. Ben leapt up and lunged for him, grabbing onto his jackets and pulling him back from the Jeep.

'Get the fuck off,' Jeremiah roared. The bag fell from his hands again, the food rolling both inside the Jeep and all over the ground outside.

'What are you doing with all that food? Where have you taken him?' He pulled at Jeremiah again, and this time he tumbled right out of the Jeep on top of Ben. Ben tried to push him off, but he was too heavy. He tried to reach inside his jacket pocket for the poker, but his arms were trapped under the weight. Jeremiah sat up slowly, keeping Ben pinned down, inching up his chest so he could hardly breathe. Jeremiah looked around beside him, grabbed a large stone, and held it above Ben's head.

'I told you to leave me alone,' he said. 'You have no business coming here. You have no business up above in that house and all the things you've done to the memory of my poor mother. She'll never forgive me, never.' He lifted the stone higher. 'I had to save the boy before something terrible happened to ye all.'

Ben wanted to scream, but the weight on his chest had pushed all the air from his lungs. He was struggling to breathe. There was no sound other than Jeremiah's heavy breathing. Ben looked at the stone clutched in his hand. If he brought it down hard, that would be the end. He had to think of something.

'He likes you,' Ben whispered. The words just slid out of his mouth.

Jeremiah lifted the stone higher again, but a flicker of doubt ran across his face. 'What did you say?'

'He likes you,' Ben whispered again. That was all he could say, his lungs empty and burning.

Jeremiah lowered the hand with the stone, but he still kept it poised over Ben's head. 'What are you saying to me?' Jeremiah asked, his brow creased in consternation.

'I can't breathe,' Ben said and nodded towards his chest. Jeremiah shunted down a bit so he could suck some air into his lungs. 'I said that Jack likes you. He looks up to you. He sees you as his friend. You'd look after him, wouldn't you?'

'Of course I would. Sure he's safe and sound where he is.'

Ben felt a surge of relief when he heard that. 'That's what we all want to do. We want to keep him safe. It's so good that you realize that.'

'He's a great boy. I knew from the way he liked the mother's stuff in the house and then the superheroes. He loves them, so he does.'

'Boys that age all need heroes. You could be his hero too.'

Jeremiah pulled his head back in surprise. 'Me? A hero?'

'Yes, you could. If you bring me to him and show me that he's safe.'

Jeremiah frowned and shook his head. 'No, but then the Gardai and everything. I'd be in trouble. I can't do that. Something terrible was to happen. Something terrible. I had to protect the boy.'

Ben felt a chill run through him when he heard the words 'something terrible', but he took a breath and looked Jeremiah in the eye. He had to take a gamble. 'Think about your mother. She'd want you to be a hero.

'No, she'd want ye out of the house for good is what she'd want.' Jeremiah's face was getting flushed. His lips were beginning to tremble. He raised the stone again.

'No, but she'd want you to be a hero more than anything. She'd want you to save someone if you could. She'd forgive everything.'

Ben saw Jeremiah's eyes darken, like he was being drawn back to some terrible place. His lips were trembling fully now. Emotions flashed like lightning across his face, distorting his flushed features. He lifted the stone higher. Ben shut his eyes and waited. The blow never came. Instead he heard a quiet sobbing that turned slowly into a messy, blubbery crying that convulsed Jeremiah's body so Ben could feel him start to shake uncontrollably. Ben opened his eyes. The hand with the stone was down by his side. Jeremiah's face was creased with little streams of tears that coursed from both eyes.

'She would want me to be a hero. You're right. I never meant to do that to my dad,' he blubbered.

'It's okay,' Ben said. 'It's okay, Jeremiah. Everything's going to be okay.'

Jeremiah stood very slowly, and Ben could feel the air rushing back into his lungs. Sharp pains darted from his ribs, and he could feel rough stones jabbing into his back, pains that had all been suspended in the initial struggle.

Ben stood and put an arm on Jeremiah's shoulder. He was crying still, the tears streaking dirt down the rough skin of his face.

'It's okay. You just show me where he is, and you'll be a hero.'

'The Gardai will come,' he said suddenly.

'There'll be no Gardai for now,' Ben said. 'You just show me where he is.'

Jeremiah stared at Ben; then he nodded his head, walked towards the Jeep and climbed into the driver's side. Ben stood on one of the steel rungs and pulled himself into the passenger seat. They took off down the rough driveway, the Jeep making a clanging, metallic sound with every bump it hit.

35

From Jeremiah's house they took the road towards the coast. Ben prayed that they wouldn't meet anyone they knew or the Gardai as they drove. He felt the situation with Jeremiah was too delicate, and anything could throw him. If he felt cornered or if someone told him he had done something wrong, then the whole thing could change in an instant. Ben felt the urge to talk, but at the same time he was terrified of saying the wrong thing, so he just kept quiet. He could hear Jeremiah muttering to himself.

They drove down the sandy lane that led to the beach. Jeremiah pulled up just short of the actual beach, climbed out and starting walking over to the right. He kept going, further than Ben had gone before, to a small, sandy area between two big sets of rocks. There was a small, wooden rowing boat with an outboard motor tied up just above the tideline.

Jeremiah untied it, dragged it down to the water. Once it was in the water, he turned it to the side and pointed to the front, indicating to Ben that he should get in. Ben climbed cautiously in, feeling the boat rock perilously under him as he did. Jeremiah pushed the boat out a little more, then followed him in and turned the motor so its propellers dropped into the water. He gave the starter rope a couple of quick pulls, and the engine sputtered into a low droning sound, and the boat started moving out to sea.

Ben felt like shouting at Jeremiah to stop, to grab him and ask where the hell they were going. *Am I mad going out to sea in a small boat with someone who is so unstable?* he thought, but he knew he had no choice. To question anything now might derail the whole thing and lose any hope of getting to Jack.

The boat sputtered out past the rocks and into open sea before Jeremiah turned it off to the right, away from the beach towards the cliffs where they had gone walking a few days before. Waves slapped against the side of the boat, sending it pitching and rocking so much that Ben gripped the seat underneath tight, turning his fingers white.

They passed some bobbing buoys that scraped against the side of the boat.

'They're to mark the lobster pots,' Jeremiah said, seeing Ben look down at them. 'I catch the lobsters out here sometimes. That's how I know the place; every rock I know. The boy is safe. Safe and sound.'

Ben said nothing, but he wondered how anyone could be safe out here.

After a few more minutes Jeremiah steered the boat in between two rocky outlets that created a cove with a tiny beach. He drove the boat straight for the beach, and Ben felt the hull jar suddenly against the sand. Jeremiah climbed out and threw the length of rope around a rock on the beach.

'You get out now,' he said to Ben, who had no choice but to jump into the water, so it sloshed around his knees. Jeremiah flipped the engine up so the propellers were out of the water; then he pulled the boat fully up on the beach. He turned and started walking in towards the base of the cliffs. Ben followed, and soon he was able to make out the gaping mouth of a cave in front of them. Jeremiah walked straight into the cave and flicked on the torch on his phone. Ben followed him in, peering into the gloom. It was damp and cold inside.

Ben stopped suddenly. He heard what sounded like a voice.

'Hello?' it said. 'Who's there? Is that you, Jeremiah?'

'Jack,' Ben said. *'It's you.* Are you okay?' The relief he felt at the sound of Jack's small voice in the middle of this huge cave was overwhelming. He felt like dropping to his knees in gratitude, but at the same time he saw how delicate, how perilous their situation was with Jeremiah, exposed, in this isolated place. Nobody knew they were there. Anything could still happen.

Jeremiah led him in further. Ben could see the glow of some kind of light coming from the side of the cave. Jeremiah shone his torch to reveal what looked like a big wooden crate. The light emanated from that. Ben rushed over. The crate was open at the front, and looking inside, Ben saw Jack huddled in some blankets, his feet tied together with big plastic cable ties.

'Jack,' Ben shouted. 'Jesus, are you okay?' He grabbed him and held him close to his chest. He could feel Jack starting to sob, his breath coming in short, sharp bursts.

'I'm okay, Dad,' he said eventually. 'I was just scared. I didn't know what was happening.'

Jeremiah pulled a bone-handled switchblade from his jacket pocket. Ben pulled Jack away from him. 'What are you doing?' he said, but Jeremiah leaned over to cut the cable ties around Jack's feet with the blade.

'I'm setting the young lad free is all,' he said. He stood back after he'd cut the ties. 'I'm sorry. I am. This is one super young lad here. I shouldn't have took him like that. Like I said, I only wanted to protect him.'

'It's okay,' Ben said. 'We can talk about it later.' He was thinking they still had to get back out of there, and without Jeremiah, that wasn't going to be possible.

'This is my place,' Jeremiah said, sweeping a hand around the huge crate. 'I made it from pallets and bits of wood that got washed up. Sometimes I come here to be on my own and think about Mam.'

Ben could see that he had used pallets and plywood to put it all together. It was at least dry and gave some shelter, and it was far enough away from everyone so you would never be disturbed. Ben thought about the Coast Guard out searching. They would never have found Jack here.

'Right so,' Jeremiah said and walked back to the boat. Ben held Jack's hand and led him down the spit of sand.

'Just try to act normal,' he whispered to him.

Jeremiah pulled the boat into the water and dropped the propellers. Ben and Jack climbed in. They pushed through the choppy waters without saying a word. Ben just willed the boat on and prayed that Jeremiah wouldn't have a sudden change of heart.

He didn't, and a few minutes later they were landing on the sand at the far end of the beach. Ben felt surges of relief flood through him as he led Jack onto the sand and watched Jeremiah pull the boat in.

He hugged Jack and felt him tremble in his arms. 'We're safe now,' he said. 'Everything's going to be okay.'

'Dad, I was really scared, but I kept thinking I had to be brave for you and Mum.'

'You did fantastic, Jack. You poor kid.' He held him close and felt his small body shiver, and his fluttering heart beat quickly.

'Right so,' Jeremiah said. 'I'll give ye a lift home. Ye'll want to call the Gardai, I suppose. I don't mind. I brought you to the boy. Maybe Mam will forgive me now. She won't think I'm a useless pup. Maybe she'll think I'm a hero.'

They took the lift home, and Ben let Jeremiah take off before he called the Gardai. He didn't want a big scene at the house. Jack needed to get inside and get warm.

Ben called Deborah, who came rushing back and clung, crying, to Jack, repeating over and over, 'Oh, thank Christ you're okay. Thank Christ you're okay.' Ben got Jack a change of clothes. He took a short, hot shower, and then, with the stove lit for extra heat, they sat around the kitchen.

Jack told them how he had been looking after the hens when Jeremiah came up and told him there was a great fishing spot he wanted to show him. Jack thought he shouldn't go, but, as he knew Jeremiah and they both loved fishing, he went with him. Jeremiah told him they needed to take the boat to see it properly, and even though Jack was a bit scared, he thought taking the boat would be a real adventure.

Jeremiah brought him to the cave then and kept apologizing, but he tied up his feet with the cable ties so he couldn't go anywhere. He told Jack that something terrible was going to happen at the house, and he just needed to keep him safe. He had a little stove there to heat food, and he made sure Jack was warm inside the wooden crate.

'I was really worried about what was going to happen at the house,' Jack said. 'Jeremiah kept coming and going, and I was waiting for him to tell me that the terrible thing had already happened.'

Ben felt so bad listening to his little voice recounting what must have been a terrifying experience. Even as he listened, he wished he could project himself back in time so he would be there beside him, holding him, making him feel safe again.

'You were so brave,' Deborah said. 'We were so worried about you.'

'God, must have been creepy out there at night, waiting for crabs or something to come into the cave,' Molly said.

'It wasn't too creepy. Jeremiah left me a light, and the night-time was so short anyway. I was scared, but mostly I was just worried for all of you.'

'Okay,' Deborah said to Ben, 'we need to let the Gardai know that Jack is safe and tell them what happened. The faster we do it, the better. Jeremiah is still out there, and Christ knows how he's going to react now. He could do anything.'

Ben called the mobile number, and the Gardai were up at the house twenty minutes later.

'So you'll be pressing charges,' Garda Byrne said when he heard the whole story.

Ben hesitated. They hadn't discussed that, but Deborah nodded her head. 'Yes, we will. We want to put all this behind us, and we want to make sure nothing else happens.'

'Okay, we have interviewed Jeremiah Dunphy and will be formally charging him with kidnap. It will go before the district court in the morning, and I would be pretty confident that he will be remanded in custody until his case is brought forward. You can rest easy from this point on.'

36

It took days for Jack to recover. Deborah had to sleep in with him at night. He kept waking suddenly, covered in sweat. He developed a bad cough that had him sitting propped up, his chest heaving. He sweated so much they had to keep changing the sheets at night. Finally, after four days the cough softened and the sweating eased off.

During that time, it was just Ben at the shop. He had customers drop in and say they were so glad that Jack had been found. Maureen and Sophie were amongst those customers, and Ben felt a surge of goodwill from the local community that he hadn't felt before. Even though he was worried about Jack, he felt like it might be the start of a great new beginning.

He and Deborah made sure they spent as much time as they could around the house with the kids. The hens got more attention than they ever had before. They looked at adding a couple more animals to their collection, arguing the merits of goats versus sheep, and the kids were pushing for a new dog.

Ben was delighted to see Sophie drop in the next

week with the news that the kids were welcome to come to the pet farm the following weekend. That really lifted the mood in the house. Molly and Jack took a trip to see the school that they would be starting in a couple of weeks. Deborah took them around the town, looking for new clothes. She told Ben that Molly wasn't too impressed with the fashion ranges on offer locally, having described it as 'hickey', so Deborah took them to the nearest big town that had shops that stocked all the well-known brands.

Garda Byrne called Ben to tell him that Jeremiah's defence lawyer had entered a plea of temporary insanity. He was undergoing various psychiatric evaluations but was being remanded in custody with no imminent sign of a release date, so the family could 'breathe easy', as the Garda said. Jeremiah had been forthright about kidnapping Jack, saying it was for his own safety, and he also recounted how he had killed the dog and was very, very sorry for that.

Ben decided he'd had enough of the Chamber of Commerce meetings, so he stopped going. He met Dave Breen in the street one of the days, and Breen was quick to commiserate with him over the trouble they had been through.

'You came down the country for a bit of peace and quiet, and look what was thrown at you,' he said, shaking his head.

'Well, they're looking into his mental state. It can't have been easy for him with the death of the father and all the guilt,' Ben replied.

'No, but there's no reason why you should have gone through that, a respectable family like yourselves with so much to offer a little town like ours.'

'Listen, it's onwards and upwards from now on, and we'll put it all behind us.'

'Onwards and upwards is right,' Breen said with an emphatic nod, 'onwards and upwards.'

Business picked up in the shop. They got more orders for delivery. Ben was confident that as the colder weather kicked in, the deliveries would pick up even more as people didn't want to make the trip into town. They even talked about taking someone on to help out.

'That would probably be the final step in our integration around here if we started actually employing people,' Ben said to Deborah.

That night they went for a drink in Hennigan's pub. They felt it was time to finally relax and start enjoying their new environment. It gave them a chance as well to go back over what had just happened. They found a secluded table where they wouldn't be overheard.

'How do you think Jack's doing?' Deborah asked.

'He's a resilient kid, but we'll have to keep an eye on him. He doesn't seem traumatized, but maybe a little counselling will be needed down the road. Funnily enough, it's bringing Molly's maternal side out.'

'Yeah, she's up there now playing board games with him. Said she wouldn't be letting him out of her sight.'

'Ah, it's nice to see the two of you getting out again.' Dave Breen was standing beside their table, pint in hand. 'Hope they keep that loon locked up and throw away the key. If you ask me, there's none of us safe with the likes of him strolling around.'

'As I said on the street, they're looking into his mental state.' Ben was curt with him. This was their night out, and he didn't want to engage in small talk.

'Absolutely. There's a lot to look into, I'd say. That whole family. They had their troubles all right.'

'We all have our troubles. It's just trying not to let them get on top of us,' Deborah said.

'Now you're talking,' Breen said. 'There's the experience of the crime reporter coming through.'

Pat Doyle spotted Breen and came over as well. Ben shuffled uneasily in his seat. He really didn't want it to turn into any sort of general gathering.

'Glad to see they caught that madman,' Doyle said and raised his glass to Ben and Deborah. 'Now you can settle in and go about your plan to turn that old shop of mine into a thriving business.'

'Thanks,' Ben said and raised his glass in turn. There was a brief pause, so Ben decided to take the opportunity. 'Listen, thanks to both of you for coming over and showing your support, but myself and Deborah really wanted to have some time together after all we've been through.'

Breen looked at Doyle. 'You know what I think, somebody's telling us we're surplus to requirements.'

'I think you're right there, Dave. Sure they want quality time after what they've been through.'

'Of course they do.'

Breen and Doyle headed back into the throng at the bar.

'Jesus, what a double act,' Deborah said once they were out of earshot.

'Yeah, they're not the worst,' Ben said.

'So, do you think that stuff with Mertens and finding his stuff on our property was all just a coincidence?'

'Looks that way. He was a friend of Jeremiah's, or was at least using him as a person he could stay with while he was here, so no surprise, I guess, that some of his stuff would be on the property.'

'I suppose. He sounds like he was a drifter, so he must have just taken off after whatever that row was in the pub that night.'

'Hennigan is just gruff and unfriendly by nature, I

reckon. I think he probably just wants his past to be left exactly where it was. He didn't want Mertens around, and he probably made that quite clear, but I don't think anything more sinister happened.'

Ben and Deborah stayed for just two drinks. They wanted to get back home before dark. The walk home was balmy, but the evening was noticeably darker than even a week before.

'Oh, God, I get the heebie-jeebies when the days start getting shorter,' Deborah said. 'Must be some subconscious trigger left over from childhood. You know the freedom of summer's over, and it's back to sitting still for six hours at a time.'

'Or race memory, seeing as we're in the countryside. Your ancestors would have been bringing in the harvest and preparing for the long, gruelling winter.'

'Don't get carried away there.' Deborah laughed. 'We're hardly here a wet week. I don't think the ancestral memories will be stirring quite yet.'

'No, anything else stirring?' Ben pulled her close to him, and they kissed for a long time there on the edge of town, ignoring the odd car that slid past.

'God, that felt nice. We haven't done that for a while,' Deborah said.

'We haven't done very much at all for a while. Too much crap going on, but that's all over now. By the way, that kiss was only an entrée for the main course once our little kiddies go to bed.'

'Oh, look, smoke,' Deborah said as they got nearer the house.

Ben felt his heart jump. He could see a steady cloud of smoke rising from near the house. There were sparks flying up in the smoke. The air smelt acrid. The two of them started hurrying towards the house. Getting closer to the house, the smoke was almost choking in intensity.

Ben felt his face that had been flushed with joy just minutes ago go pale as the blood drained away.

Shit, he thought, *not this, not when we were just getting back to normal.*

Turning up their driveway, the two of them were panting with the effort, but they almost ran up the rest of the way to the house. They saw Jack and Molly standing at the front door, looking out over the fields. Ben felt a surge of relief that at least they were okay. Hurrying up, he looked over to the west from where the smoke was coming. The source of the fire seemed to be a couple of open fields that were on a hill. He held his hand over his mouth to block the smoke and looked around the fields. The fire was about a hundred yards from their house, not right on top of them, but not at a comfortable distance either. Looking closely, he could just make out the figure of a farmer at the back of the blaze with a rake in his hand.

'It's okay,' Ben said finally. 'It's just someone burning the gorse off their land. It's a thing the farmers do every year.' *Still a bit bloody close to our house,* he thought, but at least he knew what it was.

They kept the windows and doors closed until they went to bed, but the smell of smoke still managed to seep in.

'Glad it's just once a year,' Deborah said.

'It might save us on heating bills if it were more,' Ben said with a laugh.

37

Ben walked into the shop next morning. The weather was sunny but crisp, and he felt like taking in the country views. Deborah was staying back at the house to have a long breakfast with Jack and Molly. They were spending as much time as they could around Jack and making sure there were no after-effects from his ordeal. He seemed cheerful enough and was sleeping at night. They'd brought him to the doctor, who said he checked out as perfectly healthy and didn't see anything to worry about, but yes, he had said it would be a good idea to keep a close eye on Jack.

Ben had to pass Jeremiah's house on the way into town. Looking up the driveway, he could see the top of the battered Jeep, but no sign of life. Jeremiah was still undergoing psychiatric evaluations, and it would be some time before he came to trial. 'If at all,' Deborah had said. 'He might be transferred to a psychiatric unit.'

Ben couldn't disagree with that analysis. Jeremiah seemed quite disturbed. He was attached to Jack in a childish way, as if he had never grown out of his own childhood. Ben had heard theories around personality growth and development where people got stuck at a certain stage in life because of a traumatic event that happened at that stage. Ben thought that the death of Jeremiah's father and the guilt that he had picked up from that would certainly be classed as traumatic.

Despite what Jeremiah had done to them as a family, Ben couldn't help but feel sympathy for him. He was a tortured soul who felt alone in the world. *No wonder the likes of that guy David Mertens homed in on him,* Ben thought.

Opening the shop door, he took in the smells of the fresh herbs, including lavender and thyme, that really added to the atmosphere in their shop. Deborah was great for finding subtle, yet interesting essential oils for the oil dispenser that she always had on the go. It made for a pleasant work environment and, he hoped, a pleasant place for shoppers to come into. Ben and Deborah both had an interest in health foods, but they didn't have the religious zeal that some health food shop owners had. It was something they enjoyed, and they just wanted to pass that enjoyment on and hopefully make enough money to get by.

Ben picked up the post that had already been slipped through their letterbox. He sifted through lots of promo letters and a couple of bills, but there at the end of the pile he saw a brown envelope, one that was the same as those he had got with the photographs before. He felt suddenly dizzy, like he was going to faint, so he sat down behind the counter. He didn't want to open the envelope but knew he had no choice.

Slowly he pulled the top open and reached two fingers inside. He could see the top of an A4 photograph. As he eased it out, he felt his heart thump rapidly. His fingers trembled. Inching it further out, he saw first the top of his head, then Deborah's. Pulling it further out, he could see it was a photo, taken from a distance, of the two of them as they'd kissed on the way home the night before. Underneath was scrawled in black felt pen, 'The happy couple'. Looking closer, he could see red marks had been drawn across his face, like he had been slashed with something. Ben found it hard to breathe. He reached to the countertop and leaned on it for support. *This can't be happening,* he thought.

He picked up his phone and dialled the mobile number the Garda had given him.

'Something terrible happened this morning,' he said once he got an answer. 'I got a photo in the post. The same type I'd got before. There's somebody still out there who wants to get us, no, who wants to get *me*.'

There was a long silence on the other end of the line. 'You have just received a photograph in the post. Is that correct?' The tone coming from the Garda was weary.

'That's right. It's exactly the same pattern as the ones before.'

'The person who abducted your son and who may have committed other acts against your family and property is now in custody.' He spoke like he was explaining something to a child.

'Yes, but this picture is only from last night. Whoever took it is still out there.'

'Mr Higgins. The Gardai have put considerable work and resources into protecting you and your family. Should there be another malicious act, we will most certainly be following up on it, as is our duty. Please inform us immediately if it does.'

Ben put the phone down. His hands were still trembling. He would have to tell Deborah. Their very short dream of peace and tranquillity had been shattered.

Sophie came in early for her coffee.

'The kids will be busy on the pet farm Saturday if

they're up for it. My friend's expecting a couple of tour buses down.'

Ben prepared the coffee as if he were in a dream. The sudden gush of steam for heating the milk made him jump back. He turned to smile at Sophie, but he could see she was looking curiously at him.

'That's great, Sophie. They'll be so happy to hear that.' He could feel his facial expressions weren't matching up with his words. His skin felt taut and strained as he tried to smile. He could see Sophie still looking at him. *She's probably wondering if the guy up at the viewing point is really a pervert after all and that inviting the kids again is a bad idea*, he thought, but he managed a forced smile as he handed her the coffee. He tried to pass the coffee over too quickly, though, as he felt his hands were still trembling. Coffee sloshed around the top, and some spilt over the edge.

'Oh, sorry,' he said. 'Early morning doesn't suit me. Here, let me get you a new one.'

'No, not at all. This is absolutely fine.' Sophie took the coffee and left quickly, looking back once at him as she went.

Oh, Jesus, I can't handle this, Ben thought, holding his head in his hands. *I can't take any more.*

Dave Breen walked into the shop and stopped when he saw Ben with his head in his hands. 'Oh,' he said. 'Have I come at a bad time? I'm just in for morning coffee, but I can come back.'

'No, not at all, 'Ben said. 'It's just we've been through a lot, and I thought it was all over, but I got a photograph this morning that makes me think maybe it's not.'

Breen frowned. 'That doesn't sound good. Any specific ideas on it?'

'Not as such, but it feels like someone is letting me know they are still out there.'

Breen ran his fingers through his hair and sucked in a lungful of air. 'Ben, when you were telling me about Jeremiah the other day and what a relief it was, well, I didn't want to spoil the party and, I'm not completely sure about something, or should I say somebody, but I have my suspicions.'

Ben looked hopefully up at him. Breen turned to see another customer was about to come into the shop. 'Listen,' he whispered, 'meet me around the car park at the end of the beach, and we'll take a walk. Bring the photo with you. Say about seven.' He winked at Ben as the customer came in. 'Yes, please, I'll have a latte, Ben, something to put a bit of zip in my step.'

After Breen had gone, Ben was left puzzling over whom he might be talking about. It sounded as if he had a strong hunch. Ben hoped it was going to be something solid. He was done with speculating, but Breen, for all his faults, seemed like someone who dealt in facts and knew a lot about what went on in town.

Deborah floated in about twelve. She was all smiles as she made herself a coffee. 'Nice to have a slow start to the day,' she said. 'I saw those gorse fires died down and left a lot of blackened stumps behind. Is that really good for the land?'

'Apparently. It freshens it up for new growth.' He could feel the same plastic smile on his face as he had with Sophie. Jesus, *I really don't want to tell her this*, he thought as he watched her make the coffee. She looked over at him and smiled. He tried to smile back, but he saw hers fade slowly.

'Is there something wrong?'

Ben rubbed his forehead. 'Yes. I think so. There was something in the post this morning.'

'What, an eviction order? It can't be that bad,' Deborah said with a laugh.

'It's worse than that.' Ben got the A4 envelope, slid the photo out, and passed it across to Deborah.

'Us last night,' Deborah said slowly. She looked at the angle of the shot. 'That was someone with a lens who was standing no more than fifty yards away. Jesus, that's creepy.'

'We're back to square one. Whoever it is, is still out there.'

'Or it's someone who knows what Jeremiah had got up to, and they want to keep us scared. It could be someone who was working with him. Say, if they did the groundwork, but he did all the nasty stuff, like kill Harry, shoot at you. So maybe this person has no teeth, or no balls more like, and they just want to put the wind up us again.'

'I don't know,' Ben said, 'but Dave Breen was in for coffee, and he saw the distressed state I was in, so he asked what was up, and I told him. He said he hadn't wanted to tell me before, but he has a hunch he knows who that someone else is. I'm meeting him after work to talk in private.'

'Dave Breen?' Deborah asked, as if to herself.

'Yeah, if he has a hunch, I want to hear it. We can make our own minds up then what we want to do with the information.'

38

Ben was on edge for the day. In the back of his mind, he was just hoping that it was, as Deborah said, someone out to play mind games with them. There were a few customers in, and he put on as cheery a front as he could, but he couldn't help looking at them and wondering if they were the stalker. It could literally be anybody in the whole town. Thinking like that made him even more agitated. He was glad when Deborah went back home because at least he didn't feel he needed to put up a front for her.

He arrived a little early for the meeting with Breen, so he took the opportunity to walk up towards the cliffs and mull over what had happened earlier. It was definitely a setback, but Deborah might well be right, and this was something that would just peter out over time. Whoever it was might be disappointed that Jeremiah was in custody. Maybe they enjoyed watching what they were doing to the family—some background perversion. Ben resolved to find out who it was eventually, but that might take time. He would have to be more integrated into the day-to-day workings of the town.

Meeting and developing a relationship with Dave Breen might be a step in the right direction. He wasn't somebody Ben would naturally gravitate towards, but he was obviously somebody with influence in the community.

Ben heard the crunch of a car's wheels across the stony ground below and turned to see a silver saloon car pull up beside his own. Breen stepped out, and the wind immediately caught his straight, brown hair to blow it up perpendicular to his face, exposing his pale forehead. Ben thought of him as someone who spent a lot of time indoors. Out here in the Atlantic breeze, he looked out of place. Nevertheless he smiled and waved up at Ben, then climbed the few hundred feet until he reached him.

'You decided to get a bit of air in, I see,' he said with a thin smile.

'Ah, yes, trying to clear the head and make sense of everything. I had a chat with Deborah earlier though, and she settled my mind a bit.'

'Good to hear. She has that magic touch, I'd say. Not many women like her in the world these days.' Breen gestured on up the path. 'We might as well walk a bit, seeing as we're here. Now, tell me what you were thinking when you got that photo this morning.'

'Well, as I said, it made me think that our troubles weren't over just because Jeremiah was behind bars. The first inkling that I had that anything was wrong was when we had a photo stuck on our front door with "welcome" written underneath. Funny thing about the photo, though, was that I was barely to be seen in it.'

Breen shook his head in disbelief. 'Like someone wanted you out of the way. You know, that brings me closer to my hunch as to who is behind it, but tell me a little more so I can be sure.'

'Well, our chicken run was broken into, and some of the chickens were killed. Then, worst of all, our dog

Harry was killed and not just killed. He had his legs cut off, and he was eviscerated.'

'Oh, Jesus. That's twisted. Nasty. I'd heard he was killed, but that. The kids—how have they coped through it all? Your family must be torn apart.'

'It's been very stressful, but not torn apart.' He turned to look at Breen and saw he was looking around as if he thought someone might be following them. *He must be nervous*, Ben thought.

Ben started to turn around, thinking they should start going back towards their cars. Breen acting nervous like that was putting him on edge. He took a few steps to go ahead of Breen, then felt a thunderous impact on the side of his head. A white light flashed in front of his eyes, then turned pitch black as suddenly. He didn't even feel himself fall.

HE CAME AROUND SLOWLY with a deep, painful throbbing at the side of his head and a buzzing, electric noise in his ears. He went to touch the throbbing on the side of his head but found his hands couldn't move. They were tied with something that felt like cloth behind his back. As his vision began to clear, he could make out that he was lying on the ground, the sky directly above him, and to the right the leering face of Dave Breen looking down at him.

'Sorry about that, Ben. It was all starting to bore me. I know the story already, didn't want to hear it twice.' Breen was smiling now. He looked relaxed. Ben felt a warm trickle of blood seep from where he had been hit. Breen held what looked like a tyre iron in his hand. He wasn't looking at Ben, just gazing out towards the pounding ocean.

Ben felt nauseous. He wanted to say something to Breen, but he couldn't speak. Finally Breen looked down at him, the smile still playing around his lips.

'Are you surprised, Ben? A guy like me, regular, responsible man about town. There's a lot you don't know about me, Ben. One thing in particular, which I would say was really the driving force behind everything else. I love Deborah. I have always loved her. We were in college together, believe it or not. She was doing her fancy media thing, and I was slogging away at the spreadsheets. She was always in the middle of the crowd, guys hanging off her arm. Ooops, maybe I shouldn't be saying that. Don't want to release the green-eyed monster, do we? Anyway, we ended up working on one of the college balls together, me on the boring money end, and she was doing all the promotion. She paid attention to me then. I really felt there was a connection when we worked together, so I asked her out. She said sure, but she was busy, so it'd have to wait. I waited, Ben, and I saw her disappear back into the popular crowd, and then she didn't seem to see me anymore. But I saw *her*. I never gave up hope. I remembered that connection we had, and I know we can have it again.'

He went on. 'After college I tracked her all the way to her crime reporting job, and from the time she first appeared on the TV screen, that was my life. That was what I lived for. I have recorded and documented every move she made, because, in a funny way I knew we would be together one day.'

He flipped the tyre iron in his hand and went back to dreamily looking out to sea.

'You're crazy,' Ben managed to say. His voice was weak and low.

'That's a matter of opinion. It looks like I'm going to

get what I want, so I wouldn't call that crazy. Would you? I've always been ambitious in my own quiet way. My plans worked out. Except I could never find Mrs Right, and I think that's because I always just had the one person on my mind. There are women, of course, but I pay for them. It's a transaction, no strings attached. You can find them in every town in the country now. We've really come on as a society, haven't we? I drive, though, Ben. I don't shit in my own backyard, so to speak. Keep it nice and anonymous. You've got Eastern Europeans, Brazilians, whatever you want. Lovely women, but you know what I think of when I'm with them ? Yes, I think you can guess. That's why I like to do it from behind. I can imagine the face. Well, pretty soon, I won't have to imagine at all. A vacancy is about to be declared, and I think I am the top candidate for the job.'

Ben's head began to clear. He could feel the blood seeping from the side, and the throbbing was still there, but the fuzz was slowly starting to go. He felt the material that bound his hands. It was some type of cloth, and it was tight. He could feel stones digging into his back. He shifted ever so slightly so his wrists were directly over one of the stones; then he started to rub the cloth against it. The material was strong, but, he thought, *If I can keep Breen talking, then I might just get through it.*

'What's your plan, Breen? You know you'll never get away with this.'

'I got away with everything else, didn't I? I'm clever, Ben. That's a quality Deborah will come to appreciate. I used Jeremiah to do all my dirty work. He wasn't happy that you were up there in his darling mother's house, so I slowly turned him on you. It didn't take much persuading. Poor little doggy, woof, woof. Oh, yes, did you like the stuffed dog and the little joke? I thought that was a nice touch. It was me came up with all the ideas like the Bluetooth speaker and poor Jeremiah with all his jackets and all that guilt. It was so easy to talk him into doing the dirty work. I told him you were the enemy, in to destroy the memory of his mother. That really got him going, poor oaf, all messed up over what he thinks he did to his dad. Guilt, that's a real Irish specialty, isn't it? I used to meet him up by the viewing point. I put myself in a kind of father-figure role, you know, helping him to get rid of his troubles. God, he was like a lost child, just lapping it up.'

Breen paused and swept the hair from his face again. 'Well, we won't be seeing him for a while, will we? Kidnapping your son, Jack, that was never supposed to happen. I told him something terrible had to happen, and I guess he took that the wrong way. Very fond of your son, he was. I think he saw himself in your Jack or some deep shit like that. He wanted to save him before the "terrible thing" happened, I suppose. Who knows? The guy's a mess. I should have known I'd have to do all the serious work myself. Well, Ben, you know what that terrible thing is? I think you can guess, because it's just about to happen.'

Breen looked off into the horizon and smiled.

'I managed to turn the townspeople against you. They were all suspicious from the start. Crime reporter and some financial hotshot. Not your typical local residents. I had them well primed and then the couple of little incidents like the viewing point and young Gavin Hennigan. I had it all thought out. Once you're out of the way, Ben, I'll smooth it all back over again, and Deborah will be so grateful, won't she? You can get a woman to do all sorts of things when she's grateful, don't you think?' Breen cackled sharply into the wind.

Ben kept rubbing at the cloth material. He felt a

couple of threads come loose, but it was going to take time. 'You still haven't told me your plan.'

Breen shook his head disapprovingly. He pulled a small, brown, medicinal-looking bottle from his pocket and held it out so Ben could see it. 'Now you are getting impatient, aren't you? I would have thought you'd be begging me for mercy, but maybe you realize that would be a waste of time. I've come too far, haven't I?' Well, the plan, as such, involves this little bottle and then, eh, the cliff edge, if you know what I mean.'

Ben rubbed at the cloth material again. He felt another couple of threads come loose. The material was much tougher than he thought. He had to keep Breen talking. 'What's in the bottle?'

Breen smiled warmly as he held the bottle up higher. 'It's good old-fashioned chloroform. I managed to get it online from some dodgy crowd in the Far East. So, just to explain the plan, so you'll know how clever I am and you'll feel Deborah is in safe hands with me—I'm going to knock you out, untie your hands and let you have a little swim down below. They'll find that photo in the car and think it tipped you over the edge. Literally. I'll have to step in then and offer some comfort, won't I?'

Breen laughed at this last piece. The wind caught his hair and blew it off his pale maniacal face. Ben rubbed desperately against the stone underneath. He could feel more threads come loose, but when he tried to pull the cloth apart, he couldn't, so he set to rubbing it again. His only other hope was that a walker might arrive and disturb Breen, but even then he would be able to see them far in the distance, so he could carry out his plan before they arrived.

'What about the kids?' Ben said desperately. 'I've only heard you talk about Deborah. What if they don't want you around?'

'They'll like me, don't you worry. First thing I'll do is buy them a nice little doggy. That'll give me a special place in their hearts. I didn't notice you getting any little bow-wow after whatever his name was got carved up. Very remiss, Ben. That's what makes me think I'll be so much better as a father than you ever were. You know, I always felt there was something magical linking me and Deborah. First, she got the job on the telly, so I was able to see her nearly every day of the week. Then they announce that she's leaving the job, and I'm like, who can tear us apart like that? But then, lo and behold, I hear she is moving west and not only west but right into my own little town. Now, is that not a whole lot more than coincidence? I'm not a superstitious man, but when the signs are all there, Ben, you can't just ignore them. Now, I think we've chatted enough. We wouldn't like anyone to disturb us, would we?'

Breen gave the brown bottle a shake; then he took a piece of cloth from his pocket. He doused the cloth heavily with the chloroform, put the cap back on the bottle, and leaned down towards Ben.

Ben gave a last, hurried rub against the stone and felt the cloth snap beneath him. Grabbing the stone with his right hand, he pivoted his body as Breen leaned in close, and brought the stone whistling through the air to crash against the side of his head. Breen stopped in mid motion, and a shocked, glassy look flooded his eyes. He stared vacantly down at Ben before sliding slowly to the side to lie motionless on the grass.

39

Ben sat still and stared at the motionless form beside him. He couldn't process what had just happened. Survival instinct had flooded his body with adrenaline. Now he could feel utter exhaustion seep slowly through his limbs. The pain on the side of his head came back with a relentless throbbing, but he knew he had to act fast. Breen was unconscious but breathing normally. He could wake at any moment. Ben got the cloth that had bound his hands and used what remained of it to tie Breen's hands tightly behind his back. He dragged him over so he was further from the cliff edge. Ben didn't want him waking suddenly that close to the edge. He needed Breen alive and well so he could get the full story out and let people see the torture that he and his family had gone through.

He pulled his phone out and called the Gardai on the mobile number. It was answered after multiple rings.

'Yes?' Ben heard wearily from the other end.

'It's Ben Higgins.'

'I know who it is.' The tone was laboured.

'I'm up at the cliff walk, and I have David Breen beside me. He's unconscious. He tried to kill me.'

There was a long pause from the other end, followed by a sharp, '*What?*'

'I said I am on the cliff walk about four hundred yards up, and I have the man who tried to kill me unconscious beside me.'

THE DAYS after felt like a recurring nightmare to Ben. Exhausted from the ordeal and still dazed from the blow, he slept long hours and woke fitfully, sweating, sometimes crying out. Deborah was beside him as much as she could be, with cooled water, cloths to soothe his face and the throbbing pain. He started when he heard noises outside, listened intently for movement, watched the doors and windows.

Jack came in at one point, and it took Ben a few seconds to compute who he was. Then he felt a rush of guilt at not recognizing his own son.

'Are you okay, Dad?' Jack asked quietly. He looked warily over, and Ben wondered what sort of freakish creature he looked like with the lump sticking out from under his hair, his face unshaven, and with the small amounts of food he had taken in, he thought he must look gaunt and frightening.

'I'm okay now, Jack. Thanks.' He reached a hand out toward Jack, but his son didn't come forward to take it.

'What happened?' Jack asked.

Ben had to think about that. *What did happen?* he wondered. *What's been happening to us since we arrived here?* He tried to piece the bits together. All he could see was Breen's pale, maniacal face on the cliff, and he felt a cold sweat break out on his forehead.

'I don't know, Jack. I just know it's over.' He tried to project as much conviction as he could into his voice, but it felt hollow. Jack lingered a little longer, then sidled back out the door.

It took another few days before he felt strong enough to walk, and when he did, it felt like a marathon just to get down to the kitchen. Deborah linked his arm and led him to the front door.

'I think you need some proper fresh air. I have some news for you anyway.'

Outside, he was grateful to feel the soft autumn air soothe his face. He saw the hens fuss around inside their run, and it lifted his spirits to know that normal life had been going on all the time. It somehow lessened the darkness that he felt he and the family had been going through.

'Breen is in custody,' Deborah said. 'They searched his house and found all sorts of weird shit about us. He had photographs of everything, including Harry with his legs cut off. He was there with Jeremiah when Harry was killed. They found a bottle of poison, something he'd picked up on the dark web, and his computer revealed searches on how to administer it. So I guess that was his backup plan if he didn't persuade you to go up on the cliff. The Gardai still need a statement from you, though, once you have recovered.'

'That'll be my pleasure,' Ben said, and even as he did, he felt the first pulses of his old strength start to return.

'I can't believe it,' Deborah said. 'I had met Breen in passing at college. Apparently he had photos of me from back then all over his house. He was just this innocuous background sort of character, but I do remember he asked me out once. I don't recall seeing him after that, but, obviously, he thought differently. I wouldn't have recognized him in a million years, but now I think of it, he's put on a bit of weight, lost a bit of hair, but he's still got the same bland, steady-eddy appearance he had back then. Jesus, so much for the *regular guys*.'

EPILOGUE

It took Ben weeks to recover fully. He had dizzy spells, was in and out of the doctor's, but ultimately it was time that fixed him. By the time he felt truly well, the rhythm of life had changed completely for their family. Jack and Molly were in school, and after initial wariness, they had settled in. Jack had some gamer friends and was already showing signs of pre-teen defiance. Ben felt the way he looked at him sometimes had a sense of a creeping distance that was never there before. At first Ben worried that it was the scars of what they had been through, Jack in particular, but when he saw Jack come back to the house with a couple of friends and they all had the clothes, the language, the beginnings of what looked to Ben like a pimp roll when they walked, then he started to breathe easy again.

'Funny how the onset of the troubled teens can actually seem like a blessing,' he had said to Deborah when he was voicing his various concerns.

'Who would have thought?' she replied. 'Clouds and silver linings, I guess.'

'Jesus, hope the cloud isn't quite as dense as the elder sibling's.'

'Molly is finding her feet now. Wait and you'll see. She's got a good group of friends, and she'll find her own groove.'

Ben had been wary going back into town and back to the shop. He felt people were watching him. That sense that Breen had instilled was so hard to shake off. He wondered if there were people in town sympathetic to Breen who would see Ben rather than Breen as the real troublemaker.

Breen's case took time to go to court, but the evidence against him was overwhelming. He had left so much on his computer, had photographs of their house at all times of day and night, had documented Ben's movements, and highlighted key times when action could be taken against him. There were notes on what he would advise Jeremiah to do and how he should do it. Not all the plans had come to fruition. He had searches for how to cut the brakes in Ben's type of car. He had even gone online to research the possibility of hiring a hitman if Jeremiah failed to kill Ben.

Ben felt huge relief when Breen got sentenced to ten years, but at the same time it left him feeling jumpy and unsafe to know that someone would actually go so far as to kill him for their own warped reasons. Jeremiah was still being detained indefinitely on mental health grounds.

Sophie's mum, Maureen, provided reassurance when she came to the shop. 'Dave Breen had worked his way into everyone's business in town, but that didn't mean he was popular. People had their misgivings about him. He liked to throw his weight around, and he acted like we owed him something. He had a reputation for being a bit sleazy as well. My Sophie couldn't stand to be near him.'

Hearing that made Ben feel better. If Maureen thought that, then plenty of other people in town probably thought the same. He felt himself slowly start to relax and get into a routine where he and Deborah made sure to spend time with each other outside of work and the kids. He was able to fulfill that promise to himself to be around more for the kids. Whether they wanted him there or not was becoming a moot point as they branched out into their own worlds, but Ben at least felt at peace with himself that he was there for them if they needed him. Business in the shop stayed steady, which helped to steady things on the financial front.

'It'll keep us ticking over,' Deborah had said.

'Well, that's what we signed up to,' Ben had replied. 'We were never in this to make fortunes, just to give ourselves a nice lifestyle and a complete change of scene.'

'Looks like we got there finally,' Deborah said.

'Well, we won't count our chickens, or our hens for that matter, but yep, looks like we may have finally arrived.'

ABOUT THE AUTHOR

Kevin is a Guidance Counselor by day and a psychological thriller author during his off hours. He puts an original slant on some common experiences and creates engaging stories with a personal twist. Kevin lives in Dublin, Ireland with three great kids, a frenetic Westie, Alfie, and a wife who makes him laugh, which is really all he could ask for.

Want to connect with Kevin? He'd love to hear from you via email - kevinmflynch@gmail.com.

Did you enjoy Somebody Out There? Please consider leaving a review to help other readers discover the book.

Leave a Review

Published by Inkubator Books
www.inkubatorbooks.com

Copyright © 2021 by Kevin Lynch

SOMEBODY OUT THERE is a work of fiction. People, places, events, and situations are the product of the author's imagination. Any resemblance to actual persons, living or dead is entirely coincidental.

No part of this book may be reproduced, stored in any retrieval system, or transmitted by any means without the prior written permission of the publisher.

Printed in Great Britain
by Amazon